Edge of
Tomorrow

A Novel by
Clifton LaBree

FORT LEWIS SERIES

Fort Lewis is a fictional Cree Indian village in the vast Canadian boreal forest on the shores of the beautiful Lake Diamante. It has a Hudson Bay Store, a Catholic Church, a Royal Canadian Mounted Police barracks, and a newly-built infirmary. The Crees are in a transition period trying to adapt to modern civilization. The infirmary was established by Bright Cloud, a beautiful Cree nurse who saw the need for a medical facility to care for her people. For centuries they have survived the brutal winters with plunging temperatures and deep snows. They had traditionally followed the reindeer herds which provided them with sustenance and shelter. Survival has been their greatest achievement. It's a tribute to their woodland skills, undaunted courage, and a triumph of the human spirit.

The four books that make up this series portray a Cree family in cataclysmic events during World Wars I and II, the Korean War, and the Vietnam War. The series pays tribute to the brave men and women who served to defend our right to live as a free people. The beauty and tranquility of Fort Lewis helps to heal their troubled souls. The families return every summer for renewal and spiritual growth.

Book 1 – Edge of Tomorrow

Book 2 – Starlight Starbright

Book 3 – Give Me Tomorrow

Book 4 – Beyond the Horizon

Dedicated to my wife Pauline, and my family, with thanks for all their support and encouragement

Chapter One

The clicking sound of solid steel wheels against ribbons of steel rails had momentarily lulled him to sleep. Upon waking, Mark found the coach shrouded in darkness and was thankful for the veil of blackness. Once again he was surprised how vivid his dreams could be. They embraced his being with an almost uncontrollable sadness. It always seemed to happen the same way. First the promise of rest, then the horror of nightmares, and finally, awakening to reality with a moist brow and shortness of breath. He was not ashamed that tears could still come so easily. What he feared most of all was that the memories would never set him free.

The train pulled into a small town in the coal mining region of central Pennsylvania. Lights from the station illuminated the interior of the darkened coach car. It was half full with most of the occupants sleeping or resting quietly. When the lights were turned on to allow several people to get off the train, Mark looked out the window and studied his own reflection looking back at himself. He was shocked at how taut and drained the face appeared. It was the face of a stranger.

Mark was a small-framed young man of slender stature dressed in a well-pressed forest green uniform that made him look even thinner. His angular gaunt facial features reflected his serious demeanor. He wore the twin bars of a captain in the Marine Corps and several rows of campaign ribbons on his left chest. However, his days in uniform were fast coming to an end, and he would soon be returning to his home in Maine. Mark had just returned from the Marine Corps base at Quantico, Va. where he was ordered to proceed to the Marine Barracks at Portsmouth Navy Yard for additional orders. A stranger would see him as a trim young officer with an easy smile, sad eyes, and a haunting air of detachment. Like most young Americans of his generation, he had gone off to war with an eager anticipation to do his duty without any thought of the price some men would have to pay. He was returning from the horrors of war a weary, disillusioned warrior who had seen more than he bargained for.

The war seemed far away, yet, he could not escape its shadow, and carried its memories with him wherever he went. How could anyone who has never been there imagine the pain, the excitement, or the futility of war? His most unshakable image of combat in France concerned an incident near a small town called Bouresches, where a close friend was killed in a gas attack. He could still see the deadly greenish-yellow mist that enveloped the trenches, and feel the terror of knowing that you may be too late to put your mask on. The natural urge to rise above the gas was countered by the steady hammering of German machine guns spraying bullets overhead. A feeling of helplessness had drained his energy as he watched those unlucky comrades that had not been fast enough. Mark watched his friend, Flying Eagle, drop to his knees, clutching his throat as he gasped for breath. His eyes opened wide in terror when he realized that he was too late, and cried out in disbelief, falling to the filth of the trench floor, twitching convulsively in the mud. Inhuman sounds erupted from his crumpled body.

Seconds later, the ultimate degradation took place. A heavy mortar round arrived overhead and plummeted to the ground, creating a large crater where his friend had once been! Watching a comrade succumb to such a grotesque death was the last conscious act Mark witnessed before the war ended. He had also been badly burned around the stomach, arms and neck by the same mustard gas attack because he was sweating heavily. When the gas makes contact with moist skin, it burns deeply. Two days later, he awoke in a hospital ward at a monastery.

* * *

The "all aboard" call of the conductor brought him back to the present. The train slowly started forward. He felt strangely detached. That had been one of his main problems ever since the gas attack. Nothing was the same anymore. Mark lacked specific goals in regard to where he wanted to go or what he wanted to do with his life. He had some apprehension about what the future held for him. Do all warriors experience the same homecoming jitters, he wondered? How could he answer those questions he knew were bound to be asked? "How was the war...?" There was never a good answer. If anyone has to ask, then they can never know the truth, and maybe, he thought, that was just as well left unsaid. He was very self-conscious of his stay in the hospital and the fact that his most serious wounds were emotional. It still made him feel inadequate. After his discharge from the hospital, Mark served in the occupational army for a year and a half. It helped him recover from the relapse, and was instrumental in getting him back with the Marines where he belonged. He chuckled to himself over that. He was a marine, but he had served as an officer in an Army regiment during his tour of combat in France. The Army lacked officers and the Marines had too many; it was that simple.

He had landed at St. Nazaire with his original regiment, the Sixth Marines. It was a part of the 4th Marine Brigade, which in turn, was a part of the U. S. Army's Second Division. He was serving as a replacement at that time, so he was assigned to the Army as a platoon leader. Within a few months of combat, he was promoted to captain and given an Army company to command. Throughout all of this he had maintained his identity as a marine. His original second platoon was one of three infantry platoons that made up his company.

The men were younger than Mark. His uniqueness as a marine was a distinction that the men also shared. He became closely attached to them, looking after their needs like a mother hen. In turn, they swiftly carried out his orders. Loyalty within the company started at the top with Mark. As soon as the men realized that fact, they reciprocated with their own special kind of loyalty and pride. Behind his back they called him "Our Marine Captain".

Within this group of men there was one soldier which stood out from all the others, Lieutenant Joseph "Flying Eagle" Mann, a Canadian Cree Indian. The lieutenant was the bravest man Mark had ever met. The strong young Native American was still in France, entombed in an unmarked grave. Flying Eagle would always be a part of him, because he owed his life to the courageous Cree. He had relived the same events over and over, hoping to draw some direction for the future.

3

When Flying Eagle, a fresh second lieutenant, visited company headquarters to take over the platoon, they took a liking to each other. The young Cree radiated dignity and confidence. He was a little taller than Mark, with broad shoulders that tapered to a small waist. Flying Eagle was a man of great physical strength and had a way of walking that was effortless and relaxed. His dark eyes were always searching, never missing anything around him. There was a trace of sadness in them that vanished when he smiled, which was often. Flying Eagle wore the responsibility of command as if it was his natural station in life. There was never any doubt who was in charge when Flying Eagle was around. His men soon responded to his solicitous care of them. He demanded and received instant obedience to his orders. When there was a question he would calmly and patiently go over the problem. If he saw hesitation, he gave counsel and encouragement in that full deep voice which never failed to get positive results. Most of the men treated him with the respect usually reserved for much older officers. He was intelligent and kind, and he commanded by example, not by authority.

Flying Eagle was an ROTC graduate from the University of Syracuse with a degree in civil engineering. When the war was over he said that he wanted to go back to his people in northern Quebec and work for their welfare.

"Lieutenant, the platoon you're taking over, was mine. They're a great bunch of guys. No longer boys, but men in every sense of the word. Every officer has a special spot in his heart for his first command, so you and I'll always have that in common."

"Thank you, Captain Leroux," he said. "I'll do my best to care for them. This profession of ours takes the best we have to offer, and gives very little in return. The young grow old very quickly."

"I've been going over your folder and frankly, you interest me. Don't get me wrong, your record is superb, but what's a Canadian citizen of the Cree Nation doing as an officer in the United States Army?"

Flying Eagle smiled as he often did. "Sir, it really is the story of my life — no pun intended."

"We're both oddballs in this outfit and we're Reserve Officer Training Corps graduates. When I graduated from the University of New Hampshire with a degree in forestry, I had a reserve commission in the Army. A close friend made it possible for me to obtain a commission in the Marine Corps. Then I find the Marines can't use me here in France, but the Army can!" Mark chuckled over the absurdity of the situation.

"If you have time for my story, I'd be glad to tell you, Captain."

"I'm not going anywhere until I hear it all," Mark smiled.

"It really has to start in the frozen boreal forests of northern Quebec Province, some still call it New France." Flying Eagle's tone was steady, choosing each word with precision and clarity. Mark silently observed the young Indian with the bronze complexion and high cheek bones. He was a handsome man with all the pride and bearing of the noble warrior that he represented. Looking carefully, trying not to be obvious, Mark noticed a slight nervous twitch in the vein under Flying Eagle's left eye.

"My people, the Crees, are brothers to many of your New England Indian tribes such as the Abenaki. We're all Algonquins, primarily hunters and trappers, taking what we need from the land as we need it. In the past, we were nomadic, building shelters out of caribou hides for easy erection and takedown. It was my legacy and obligation to continue the traditions as my father had done before me. Then, my mother died." Flying Eagle paused a moment, as if to honor her memory and continued.

"She was buried at the mission cemetery when I was eight years old. The kind Catholic Priest at the mission suggested that my little sister of six years and myself be sent to Quebec City for school. My father approved of the arrangement because he had no means of caring for us both, and at the same time continue with the constant struggle of survival that is a way of life in those latitudes. He was very poor and very proud, and I love him with every fiber of my body. My sister and I were educated and went on to college, compliments of a grant from some rich families in Quebec. I chose engineering and took the ROTC course because it helped pay some of my expenses. The military life seems to suit me. I'm one of your original American warriors, Captain Leroux.

"I didn't turn my back on Canada as much as you might think. We Indians aren't full fledged citizens in Canada. We're considered as minors even though we're adults. Besides, the fight in France is all about people being free. I thought it should be my fight, too. So there you have it, Captain. I'm very proud of this uniform, and I'll do my best to not disgrace it. When the war is over, I plan to go back to the northern forest to help my people improve their living conditions."

"That sounds like a noble plan for the future, Lieutenant. When we finally get this war over with, maybe then we can get our lives back on track," Mark added. "Welcome aboard."

"Thank you, Sir, I'm glad to be aboard." They saluted each other and heartily shook hands.

* * *

The rhythmic clicking of the train's wheels still hummed through the car as it sped through the coal region in the vicinity of Scranton. It would be mid-day before he arrived in Portsmouth, New Hampshire. He didn't know what was being asked of him upon his arrival. He had not thought very much about it other than it was a little irregular. The pattern of being different would follow him right to the end of his military career, he mused.

In many ways this trip home was the perfect opportunity for him to plot a course for the future. The extensive gas burns he had suffered, along with his emotional upheaval were the main reasons that Mark questioned his fitness for a career in the Marine Corps, so he reluctantly resigned his commission. He would surely miss the security and excitement of the service, and the loss of that very special camaraderie of being with other marines.

Ever since the war ended, everything seemed anticlimactic. He was waiting for something to happen. Mark was certain about his desire to get on with a forestry career, but he was unsure just what would be available for him. A part of his anxiety was always the vivid vision of Flying Eagle's death and the guilt that accompanied it. He was coming home, Flying Eagle was not. Acceptance of that fact was his biggest mountain to climb.

Whenever Mark thought of Flying Eagle, the incident of March, 1918, at the southwestern section of the bloody Verdun killing fields always came to mind. Mark's company had sent out a patrol to gather intelligence on their segment of the front. He chose to lead it himself.

The patrol was routine and uneventful until they started to return to the Allied perimeter when they were ambushed by a large German patrol. All hell broke loose about them. Mark had anticipated such an encounter and prepared a contingency plan before leaving for the patrol. The men were to fall back on their original positions keeping wild shots and confusion in the darkness to a minimum.

The Germans fired first at Mark's patrol of ten men. He was crawling beside his men when he was hit on the helmet with a bullet, knocking him out. He regained consciousness about fifteen minutes later, disoriented and alone in the dark. It was comparatively quiet on the front. His first thought was for the safety of the men. Had they all made it back? Then he heard the metallic sound of a canteen scraping against a rock and his adrenaline started pumping. Suddenly, a German soldier charged him with a bayonet at the ready. Mark clasped his .45 automatic and fired once. He hit his assailant but several other figures loomed into view through the heavy evening fog. Without thinking, Mark started to squeeze off the last few rounds remaining in the magazine of his pistol. Then, without warning, a blur came between Mark and the Germans.

It was Flying Eagle with his rifle and bayonet. He was a fighting machine. He met two Germans with the rifle, bayoneting one and knocking the other in the head with a wild swing of the butt. A third and last enemy soldier caught Flying Eagle in the lower calf of his leg with a bayonet. The German was desperately trying to operate the bolt of his rifle when Flying Eagle caught him by the rim of the helmet throwing him to the ground. The German barely touched the ground when Flying Eagle fired his Enfield rifle at arms length directly at the enemy soldier.

"Come on, Captain, this way back to the company," Flying Eagle whispered in his ear.

Later in the safety of their own trench line, Mark was still shook up and disoriented. They didn't talk about it until the next day when Mark called for Flying Eagle. "Thanks, friend. Why did you come out there for me?"

"Well, Sir, I didn't think about it. The patrol came in and said you were hit. I couldn't just leave you there and not know what was going on, so I came out to find you."

"I'm thankful you did; my pistol was empty."

"I knew that because I was right beside you counting your shots."

"I owe you my life, Flying Eagle, and I'll always be grateful. You defended me at great risk to your own life. I'm going to recommend you for a medal"

Flying Eagle, blushing with natural modesty, replied, "If the situation had been reversed, you would have done the same thing, Captain. It was spontaneous and I think we should drop it. In the short time I've known you, we've shared the most traumatic events of our lives. Comrades do things like that for each other as a normal part of our profession of arms." Flying Eagle reverted to the traditionally stoic Indian and looked penetratingly at Mark saying, "Remember me if something happens. Like everyone else in this war, I've been obsessed by the closeness of death. It would be some comfort for me to know that a friend was available when needed…"

* * *

The train slowed for a short stop at a small town in New York State. Mark wanted a cup of coffee and went forward through two cars to the attached dining car. The coffee and its rich aroma were most welcome, for he was addicted to the stuff.

Taking a seat beside a window in the dining car, he watched the birth of a new day. A bright sun rose out of the east with bright red rays reaching out in every direction of the sky. Mark could already feel the evening-time depression lifting from his shoulders. Soft shadows, tinged with rose red colors played across the landscape as the train sped northeastward.

The warm rays of the sun reached higher and higher, casting shorter and fewer shadows on the ground. Mark drank his coffee and watched the rolling countryside pass by. In the distance he caught sight of a small sawmill, which made his heart beat a little faster. His father's small mill, he remembered, was solidly draped across a small brook near the house. When the mill was not being used, its wooden gears would be at rest while the water rushed through the by-pass chute on its way to the sea. He pictured his father at the controls of the mill, with his floppy hat on his balding head, a gentle, small man, much like

Mark, with the energy of a much younger person. The corn cob pipe seemed to be a permanent fixture in his mouth. Half of the time it was unlit. He had missed his father these past years. They'd been the best of friends. Whenever he discussed difficult problems with him, they were put on the block and systematically split into workable solutions. He had been a good father and Mark loved him dearly. While Mark was in France, his father died. Mark never realized just how much he had depended on his father until he was gone.

There was less for Mark to come home to than most soldiers. His mother, whom he vaguely recalled, died when he was four years old, a victim of the vicious flu epidemic which took thousands of lives at the turn of the century. His father had kept her memory alive for his remaining years by telling him what she would think or desire at important stages of his childhood. It was the finest tribute of love and fidelity that Mark had ever experienced. He was looking forward to seeing his Aunt "Maddie" again. She was like a mother to him. Life had been simple and uncomplicated on the coast of Maine. Those precious memories of childhood had helped to sustain him during his ordeal in France.

The train stopped at another station with milk cans and packages piled on high-wheeled wagons. He could see the sign, Town of Newburgh, painted on the station wall. He remembered attending a summer training session as a green ROTC recruit at West Point, the United States Military Academy just south of Newburgh, on the Hudson River, peacefully nestled among large granite hills.

The presence of more familiar surroundings made him feel more relaxed. It was a part of the past he had set aside for too long. The summer he went to West Point was a happy one. He had done well at school and he particularly enjoyed the Army field exercises at the Point. The field problems were easy for him mainly because of his forest engineering background. His group had to prepare the area south of the Military Academy for defense, then plan its assault and capture. It was an innocent and idealistic period in his life, and he mourned its demise.

The turbulent Hudson River was a thrilling sight to see. Every time he passed over it he hoped the engineers that built the long bridge span had done it right! People were waiting for a seat at the diner car so

Mark took his leave and slowly made his way back to his coach seat. He was surprised to see that a young lady was sharing the seat against the window. He picked up the hat he had left on the seat and sat down.

"Pardon me!" she exclaimed. "I didn't mean to take the whole seat."

"No, you're fine," Mark answered.

"I would've taken another seat if one was empty." Her voice was soft and apologetic. She was about his age and very attractive. She seemed slightly nervous. Mark had not been around many young ladies for a long time, so he welcomed the opportunity to share some time with a fellow passenger.

"Are you traveling far?" the young lady asked, glancing sideways from the window.

"I've been on the train since Washington, and I'm going as far as Portsmouth, New Hampshire."

"I'm getting off at Boston," she replied smartly. Several minutes of silence gave her a chance to observe Mark. 'He looks young,' she thought to herself, 'except for his eyes, which are a little frightening... they betray some of his vulnerability. This young man looks more alone than anyone I've ever met.' She had a tendency to reach out and engage people, and she was drawn towards the young soldier beside her.

"You're obviously a soldier, but the insignia on your uniform is different from others I've seen."

"That's because I'm not a soldier, but a marine. Many people don't know very much about our Marine Corps. I was proud to serve with them, though it won't be long before I'll be a civilian again. I'm resigning my commission."

She noticed the way he blushed at the attention she had shown him. He was self-conscious, talking about himself.

"Thank God the war is finally over. My cousin was injured in France. Not too seriously, but enough for him to be sent home after having been in the Army for only a year. Now he's continuing his school work and we're grateful for his safe return to us."

"Your cousin is one of the lucky ones," Mark answered soberly. "I'm sorry I didn't introduce myself to you. My name is Mark Leroux. I'm from Maine." He extended a hand to her with a big smile on his face.

She smiled and took his hand, "I'm Michelle Gurney. I'm from a small town near Lake George called Diamond Point. I'm on my way to my first full time job as a nurse. I graduated from the Albany Hospital School of Nursing, and I'm really excited about it."

"I've heard of Lake George. I've also heard that it's very beautiful there. I've been around West Point. Most people think of New York City whenever you mention the state, but it has a large area of rural beauty."

"Yes. I'm a little apprehensive about leaving, but one can always come back. Right now I'm looking forward to seeing new places and experiencing new things." Michelle's enthusiasm was contagious.

"I know how you must feel about getting out in the working world for the first time. I felt that way myself. The real world is a lot different than I envisioned it to be. The war sort of got in the way, but now that it's over, I hope to begin my career as a forester. I went to the University of New Hampshire, which was not far from my hometown of Wells. I was able to get home most weekends." Surprised at how much he was telling this young lady, he settled back in the seat and relaxed.

"I envy you for that. I had to board at school for the whole year without getting home."

The sun was warm and high in the sky. The soothing rays filtered through the train's windows casting a friendly air of cordiality. The earth was recovering from a long cold winter with the promise of renewed life about to spring forth. As the train sped along its ribbon of steel, the warmth of the sun and the aroma of the newly sprouted vegetation were answering the call for a rebirth of life and hope. The promise of new life always came at the same time, in the same way, and with the same results every year. Yet, it was always a wondrous gift to those who watched for its cycles. Life leaped from a dormant winter with vigor and beauty. Man as well as plants responded to the rejuvenation process. Mark thought of himself as one in desperate need of that renewal and prayed daily for God to answer those prayers.

After a long silence, Mark casually asked Michelle, "There's a good dining car on the train, would you care for a breakfast or a lunch? I'm always ready for a cup of coffee,"

"Okay, that would be nice," answered Michelle.

11

They headed toward the front of the train with the deliberate steps you have to take when it is moving. Michelle had a little trouble and had to steady herself on a chair back as she made her way cautiously down the train's aisle.

"It's just like walking on a moving ship," he said, soliciting a dubious smile from Michelle.

The dining car was warm and full of food aromas, with coffee being the most prominent. Finding a booth empty, they sat opposite each other. Mark ordered coffee for both of them. Both seemed to enjoy the moment, if only for the fact that neither was alone in a strange place. Watching the passing forests through the window gave her an opportunity to observe Mark a little more closely.

Michelle Gurney saw Mark as a person at the closing stages of an emotional crisis. He blinked his eyes often in rapid succession and coiled from loud noises regardless of their origin. Short lapses from reality made him blush and apologetic for his behavior. He was of medium complexion with intense brown eyes and a countenance that reflected his innate gentle nature. He was not handsome by current standards, yet he had an aura of decency that drew people to him. His hair was starting to recede. The furrows that lined his forehead disappeared when he smiled, transforming him into a little boy again. She expected that the smile pointed to his natural disposition. On occasion, his anguish manifested itself with a far away stare. Michelle guessed that he was about twenty-five years old, even though he looked a little older. The right side of his cheek still carried a few scars from the gas burns. Michelle admitted to herself that the young man sitting across from her may be a stranger, yet she felt that she knew him better than most people after such a short introduction. He may have been a warrior, but her keen insight saw a gentle person who was now searching to find himself, and was frightened by the possibility that it might not be within his reach.

The waiter served coffee. Mark asked Michelle, "Do you want breakfast or anything to eat? I'm going to have a late breakfast."

"I'll have some toast and marmalade then," she replied, smiling at his spontaneity. He was not always intense and serious she thought; he could also be warm and enthusiastic.

"I'll combine breakfast with lunch and have scrambled eggs and bacon plus a top up of coffee for both of us, please. Congratulations are in order for your graduation from nursing school. Are you going to Boston to work in one of the hospitals? I understand that there are a lot of good ones in the city."

"No, not to work directly," she said, hesitating for a moment to collect her thoughts. "I've promised to be part of a medical missionary effort. I'm not sure where I'll be sent. The center for the work is in Boston. I'll find that out after a few days of orientation. I'm enthused over the prospects, and I must admit, a little apprehensive. There's so much I don't know."

"Ah, yes, but the most important thing of all is the desire and open-mindedness to make oneself available," Mark commented. "I've found that inexperience is compensated for by positive attitudes and a willingness to tackle the unknown. New challenges are what make us tick. You'll do well no matter what the circumstances, I'm sure."

The waiter served their food, and Mark paid him.

Michelle's eyes registered a protest before she could speak. "I didn't intend for you to pay the bill. I can pay my share…"

"I don't mean to offend you. Please allow me this honor. I just received my travel allowance. Let this be a salute to your graduation, and to my discharge from the Marines." He was in an expansive mood, and Michelle was pleased by his warmth and sincerity.

"Thank you, Captain Leroux." They laughed and enjoyed each other's company during the meal. After Mark finished his breakfast, he leaned back to take a pipe and tobacco pouch from his pockets.

"Do you mind if I smoke?"

"Of course not. My father smokes a pipe. I like the smell of it. His is unlit most of the time. He always said he smoked more matches than tobacco." She laughed again in that infectious way she had about her.

"I seem to do the same thing myself. I took up smoking during the war, and I'm sure it was a calming influence for me," rationalized Mark.

The ritual included filling the pipe with tobacco, tamping it down just right so as to not draw too hard or too easy, and then smelling the rich aroma from the pouch. Finally, it was carefully lit with a match to obtain the proper glow in the pipe bowl. He sat visibly relaxed, thoroughly enjoying himself.

"Nothing tops off a good meal like a pipe. Do you have friends in Boston?"

"No, I don't. I've had correspondence with the director of the mission; we spoke on the phone yesterday. They're expecting me this evening. My parents could not make the trip with me, but then, I wanted to do this on my own. It's my first job since graduation, and they understood."

"I'm sure they're very proud of you. Do you have any brothers or sisters?" Mark was surprised that he was asking so many questions of a virtual stranger.

"Yes, I have my younger brother who's a pest at fifteen years, and an older sister who's married with two children. They're adorable and I enjoy my role as an aunt. My mother and father indulge their every whim."

"I noticed that we passed into Connecticut a while ago. It won't be long now 'til we're in Massachusetts," Mark mentioned on their way back to their seats.

Michelle calmly settled into the seat and listened to the rhythm of the rails as they carried her closer to her destination. She was still in a state of elation and was savoring every moment of her new adventure. The promise of tomorrow was bright with hope and wonder. She had never considered herself especially religious in the formal sense; however, she did have a deep seated trust and faith in a benevolent God. She was not sure at this stage of her life whether she was willing to be a part of a religious order or not, but was pleased to be part of a missionary effort, no matter where it took her. She was not afraid of the future. To the contrary, she embraced the unknown with deep faith. Michelle thought about Mark, sitting quietly beside her, watching the passing landscape. She candidly admitted to herself that if the situation could have been different, and there was more time, she would have liked to have known him better.

It must have been mental telepathy because Mark was thinking similar thoughts about Michelle. He had not been in the company of a lady for a long time and the experience was opening a door to an awareness that had been dormant for a long time. She was pretty, but not showy, and wore her sandy colored hair in a large bun on the back of her head. The hair style and a small black hat on the very top of her head made her appear older. There was an air of invincibility and independence about her. It was comforting for Mark to be in the company of such a lady.

Within a short time, the conductor made his rounds through the cars announcing Boston as the next stop. For Mark, the ride that started too slow had ended sooner than he would have liked. He had found an acquaintance at a time when he needed one. Their lives had crossed for a mere moment, yet he was surprised by the sudden flood of emptiness that came over him at the prospect of her leaving. So far in his life he had had to reconcile the fact that many things he held dear were taken away from him. A simple good-bye to Michelle was a variation of that same predisposition to mourn whatever was important to him.

"I'm sorry the journey has to end so soon," he said. "I've enjoyed our visit, and wish you well in your new endeavor."

"Thank you, Captain Leroux." She tilted her head and looked straight at him. "We've met for such a short time, it's true; yet, I have a feeling that we could become good friends if we had a little longer. But time has a way of being meaningful only when something important has happened to us. I want you to know that I'll always remember this train ride for many reasons, not the least will be meeting you."

Mark blushed at the remark.

"What I'm about to say to you is probably bold and presumptuous on my part," continued Michelle. "Please don't take offense. I've been thinking as I sat here beside you, Captain, that you're a person carrying a heavy burden of sorrow and guilt. That shows in your eyes along with the effort you're making to stabilize your life. You deserve much credit for that. We can never know what soldiers such as yourself have gone through, but you must know that it's appreciated and you're never really alone. If that ugly war is to ever have meaning for you as a man, Captain, you must put it where it belongs. Yesterday belongs only to memory. Tomorrow belongs to whomever finds it."

She reached out to take his hand. He grasped it and held it firmly. "I did not know that my condition was so visible."

"I worked all through nursing school at a veteran's hospital, and I appreciate the high price paid for liberty and freedom. My respect and admiration for your sacrifice is sincere."

"I'm going to give you my mailing address in Maine," Mark mentioned, handing her one of his cards. "Maybe we could correspond in the future."

Michelle nodded in agreement, searching her purse for a note pad, then calmly wrote her address. She handed him the piece of paper and said, "Whatever lies ahead for you, Mark Leroux, may God be with you and guide your footsteps. Thank you for making this trip special for me."

The train came to a lurching stop. Michelle stepped past Mark, who had stood to allow her passage from the seat, offering to assist her with the suitcase.

She gently declined with a smile. "No, thank you, I can carry it myself. It's not heavy. Good-bye and good luck."

"Good-bye. Thanks for your kind thoughts. The French say it better than we do, au revoir, Michelle Gurney."

"Au revoir," she answered, walking down the aisle, disappearing from sight in the crowd on the platform. She reappeared near the station door, where she turned to seek him out, waving one last time.

Mark returned her wave. Her sudden departure had filled him with a strange sense of abandonment. He admonished himself for such fickle emotions over a person he had just met. Then, he read the sheet of paper he held in his hand:

Michelle Gurney c/o Saint Paul Missionary Society
15 Beacon Street, Boston, Massachusetts.

Chapter Two

It was a short ride from Boston to Portsmouth and Mark felt a warm glow in his stomach. He was coming home. Portsmouth was as familiar to him as his own home town of Wells. He had often accompanied his father to Portsmouth where they purchased household provisions and mill supplies. His journey to France began from the same station he was returning to. The circle was complete. How much younger he had been stepping onto the train, almost three years ago. The war had robbed Mark, and every other soldier, of their innocence and youth. They had gone from boyhood to manhood, in a matter of seconds, amid a crescendo of violence. The war had destroyed many things for many different people, but he still thought that the loss of innocence was the harshest legacy of the war.

Mark had been introduced to poetry early, as soon as he could read. Both he and his father had enjoyed all types of verse, especially the classics. A verse that often came to his mind since his departure from Portsmouth a few years ago was an old refrain from a Chippewa Indian chant:

"Fare thee well.

The time is come for our sad parting.

We who take the road to war

Travel on a long journey."

More than ever he understood just how long that journey could be. Once started, it seemed to have no destination; it just continued for a long, long time.

Mark collected his baggage and stepped onto the familiar sidewalk. The station was not very busy. He noticed a young marine corporal approaching him.

"Captain Leroux?" the corporal inquired with a salute.

"Yes, Corporal," Mark returned his salute.

"I have a car waiting out front. May I help you with your bag, Sir?"

"This is an unexpected surprise. Thank you."

They made their way through the terminal to the car parked at the curbing. It was an older Dodge, similar to the ones the Army had used in France. Mark slid in beside the driver, pleased with this turn of events. Normally it could have been a chore to find transportation across the river to the Naval Yard where the Marine Barracks were located. The city of Portsmouth had not changed much. A few more people, a little more hustle and bustle than he remembered, but pretty much as he had left it. When they crossed the bridge between Maine and New Hampshire he had the strange sensation that the person he had become was a stranger to the young man who had departed from the same station, and that they were meeting on this familiar ground for the first time. He was returning to the scenes of his youth, and was angry at himself for not being able to experience more joy. Instead, he was feeling a sense of detachment. It was unsettling.

"Are you from around here, Corporal?"

"No, Sir. I'm from Illinois. This is my first time in New England. I've enjoyed my duty at the Marine Barracks. I served with the Sixth Marines, 96 Company, in France. This is my first duty station since that time."

"I grew up in Wells, Maine, not too far from here. My father ran a small sawmill. I guess I developed sawdust in my veins because I'm going back to see about running it. A few more days and my commission will be resigned. I don't know if I should be glad or sad. Who's the commanding officer of the Marine Barracks now?"

"It's Major Arlo Korsman, Sir."

"I can't believe my luck," Mark was jubilant to hear that his best friend was back at the old Barracks. "I knew him before I received my commission."

It did not take long to travel through the main street of the small town of Kittery where they crossed over the bridge to the Portsmouth Naval Base, coming to a stop in front of the large wooden structure that served as the Marine Barracks.

"Here we are, Captain. I'll give you a hand up the porch with your luggage."

"Thanks, Corporal."

The old barracks had not changed a bit. It was a wooden structure with a large white porch overlooking the well-groomed parade ground extending to the water's edge was just as he remembered it. The commanding officer's quarters were to the left with junior officer quarters on the right side of the building. The three floors between them were the enlisted men's billets. The corporal led the way to the CO's office. Mark was already familiar with the office setup. Opening the office door brought him face to face with a man he knew very well.

"Captain Leroux reporting, Sir." Mark gave his best salute and came to a proper attention.

"Mark Leroux, if you aren't a sight for these old eyes," exclaimed Major Korsman, returning the salute. He quickly stepped around the desk to shake Mark's hand. "I'm awfully glad to see you again, and that you're looking so trim." He was a large man with light blond hair and piercing blue eyes that could see your backbone if he chose to look hard enough. He was known as a fair-minded disciplinarian who tolerated no breaches of conduct.

Mark knew Major Arlo Korsman when he came to Durham to deliver lectures on special military science topics to the college students. Mark first met him on one of those lectures when Arlo was still a lieutenant. As a matter of fact, the major was responsible for the commission Mark received in the Marine Corps. At the time of his graduation, Mark had received a temporary reserve commission in the Army through the ROTC Program, yet he could not get a regular commission, because none were available at that time. Major Korsman knew the Marine Corps had several commissions available and made it possible for Mark to obtain one. That had been in May, 1917. They had not seen each other since that time.

"Corporal Turner, would you take the Captain's luggage to officer's quarters and return the car to motor pool?"

"Yes, Sir." The corporal saluted and hastily left the office.

"Sit down, Mark. We've got a lot of news to catch up on since we last met. It's really good to see you again. It's a little sad for me to learn about your retirement. I'm sure you've examined all of the possibilities, so I won't bother to give you my reenlistment pep talk." Arlo laughed easily, taking a pipe from his desk and started to clean it with a small pocket knife.

"Do you still smoke? Try this cavendish blend tobacco. A Navy Commander here on base gave me some. It's not bad if you like strong tobacco."

Mark filled his pipe with the mixture and lit up with his old friend. "You're right, it's not bad."

Arlo looked inquiringly at Mark, observing his overall condition. Arlo detected some mannerisms that were not characteristic of the Mark he had known before the war, but that was to be expected after all he had been through. Mark's movements were not as sharp or deliberate as the man he had known in years past. He remembered Mark as a bundle of energy with quick precise movements. His heart went out to the young man before him. Fortunately, Arlo had returned from the war relatively unscathed and thanked God for that blessing. He remembered Mark as a lively and cheerful officer with excellent judgment.

"Mark, before you arrived, I went over your records forwarded to this command from Washington Headquarters. They came by special courier yesterday. That's why I knew you were coming."

Mark was uncomfortable with that statement. "What is there about my resignation that makes all of this irregular routine necessary, anyway? I don't understand why I couldn't be discharged at Quantico, like everybody else."

"Your surprise is understandable and I'll get to it in a minute. I was not aware you'd been in the hospital, or that you were still recovering, otherwise I would not have recommended you for one more assignment."

One last assignment! Mark was beginning to be uncomfortable with upper level machinations, confused by its irregularity. Arlo held up his hand to Mark, as if to stop his thoughts, deliberately lighting a match and held the flame to his pipe.

"Now be calm, Mark. Just a little longer and it'll all become clear to you. Back in France, you went on a patrol and was rescued by the actions of a Lieutenant Mann. You recommended him for a medal for that action. Is that correct?" asked Arlo.

"Yes. He was also bayoneted in the right leg during that incident. I assumed that the medal had been refused. I never heard about it afterwards."

"Well, it was approved. He was supposed to be awarded the Distinguished Service Cross (Army) for gallantry. With his death, it got delayed in the rush of the Armistice and a lot of bureaucratic stupidity. To make a long story short, Mark, the Army, the Marine Corps, and the United States Government all want this medal to be awarded posthumously, and personally delivered to his father as soon as possible. I personally talked to the Commandant about this and recommended you as the logical person to take it to Lieutenant Mann's family."

"My God, I don't know what to say." Mark paced from the door to the window twice without realizing he was doing it. The painful expression on his face betrayed his surprise and bewilderment.

"Forgive me, Mark," pleaded Arlo. "I didn't realize that you hadn't been briefed on this decision. I certainly meant you no harm."

"You had no way of knowing all the facts until you saw my file. I don't blame you. Good Lord, Arlo, I never dreamed of such a situation confronting me when I reported to you. I was expecting to be mustered out by the C.O. of the Marine Barracks, Portsmouth. Then I planned to go home to Wells and see what I could put together for a new life. Now Flying Eagle's death has got to be faced all over again…"

"If you feel that this is beyond your ability to carry out, then I'll understand and support your reasons." Arlo left his chair and came around the desk to grasp Mark around the shoulders. "Old friend, sometimes this uniform asks far more of us mortals than we're ever able to give, and it frequently keeps asking for more and more from the same person. I try to not question its rightness. I just do as I'm told in the best way that I can. You've done the same thing. I never knew that you had been through a bad gas attack when Lieutenant Mann was killed. I just found out that you were released from the hospital in France and were with the occupation forces for several months only after reading your file this morning. If I had known about your condition, then I never would have initiated this operation."

"Well, garrison duty was a stabilizing factor in my recovery. I've been slowly improving ever since," explained Mark, avoiding Arlo's keen scrutiny. "Sometimes I slip back, but in general, I'm getting better as time goes by. I hope that I can reclaim the person that I used to be, and that you once knew."

"My prayers are with you, Mark." Arlo was visibly moved by his friend's comments. "It's just fate that placed me back here in Kittery. I received a brevet colonelcy during the war, and reverted back to a major when I decided to stay with it for retirement. I've just barely settled in here again. Like I said, I could easily arrange with Washington for some other means of carrying out this assignment. Maybe through the Canadian Ambassador..."

"I didn't say I wouldn't or couldn't do it, Arlo. It's just so unexpected and so sudden. I've resigned my commission effective today. Was I expected to take this on as an officer, or as a private citizen?"

"I'm sure it's the intention of all the parties involved for you to do this as an officer representing a grateful nation."

"Needless to say, it would all have more meaning for Flying Eagle's family if I was the messenger." Mark thought of the proposal and was beginning to feel excited about this unexpected turn of events.

"I could hold up your resignation until the mission was accomplished. I've got a suggestion for you, Mark. Why don't you go to Wells for a visit and then decide. You can stay at quarters tonight and head out first thing in the morning. If you decide to proceed, we can go over the plans later. I know that this has been a lot to swallow so soon, and I'm sorry to have been the bearer of uncomfortable news."

"Your offer sounds good to me. I'll take you up on it." Mark felt better now that a course of action was unfolding.

"Corporal Turner will show you to your quarters. After you've freshened up, I'll treat you to the best steak dinner you've had in a long time," promised Arlo.

"Consider it done," Mark answered.

The next morning, the crisp spring breeze blowing from the sea awakened in Mark a long-dormant feeling of enthusiasm. He was going home. Not exactly a homecoming, but a visit to the site of his childhood nevertheless. Arlo assigned Mark the same Dodge car that picked him up at the station. He was thankful for the freedom of movement that the automobile gave to him. Of all the people he had been privileged to serve under, none commanded any more respect and affection than the powerful Arlo Korsman. His blond hair and blue eyes reflected his hardy Finnish ancestry. He was a fair man who respected everybody's feelings. Mark had modeled his own leadership skills after him. It was typical of Arlo to treat him as an equal, and to extend all the courtesies possible. Dinner, as promised, had been one of the best meals he had eaten in years.

The road to Wells was fraught with memories. Once, when Mark was a small boy, he accompanied his father to Portsmouth with a wagonload of apples destined for a grocer. It took all day for the round trip. He had just passed the spot where a bump in the road had upset three barrels of apples on that trip. Mark's father had laughed about the mishap while the two of them were busy picking up the spilled fruit. He was a patient man, but his most memorable personality trait was his gentleness. They had been the best of friends.

Mark was glad to be back in familiar surroundings. He had just passed the road leading to the summit of Mount Agamenticus where he and his father had often driven to enjoy the view of the Atlantic Ocean. After the fire tower was erected at the top, they could locate, with a telescope, a small opening on a knoll behind their house at Wells.

The road was improved from what Mark had remembered. His father was the common thread that wove together all the visions and memories that came to him as he traveled along the roadway. Mark saw him everywhere. In France he had been a witness to death on a magnitude so horrifying, that even now, three years later, the memories were still vivid. The manner in which Flying Eagle was killed still haunted him. One other death, which he did not witness, was the reason for his apprehension of what was ahead. He had not faced the death of his father, yet...

The flu epidemic of 1918 had taken twenty million lives; Mark's father was one of them. His mother died at the turn of the century during an earlier epidemic of the same disease. Loved ones at home are a safety link to sanity that helps to make the nightmares of combat tolerable. More lives had been lost at home than in the war. His Aunt Maddie had written the sad news in one of her many letters. She was his father's sister who had cared for him during the illness. She told him that he died gently in his sleep, and Mark wanted to believe that it was true.

The small town of Ogunquit, which translates to "Beautiful Place by the Sea," was almost deserted as Mark drove slowly through, straining his neck to see if he recognized anybody.

The brisk sea air always hit you with a refreshing blast directly from the beach, once you reached the corner of the driveway to the house. The house was a small Cape Cod design with weathered cedar shingles that looked the same as he remembered them as a small child. A barn-like structure housed the sawmill across the driveway from the house. When Mark turned into the long driveway a cold chill gripped him. He dearly loved this place. It had been the source of his existence as well as his refuge from the world around him. Mark could almost hear the sounds from yesterday as they used to echo among the buildings. He could still see the old familiar faces. Time had not dimmed his memory. It was an exciting moment for him. Frequently, during the war, he wondered if he would live to see this place again.

The old house was in need of some repairs, but it was still a refreshing sight to Mark. It was surrounded with large stately white pine trees that extended to the rear of the house, forming a dense stand of beautiful mature timber. To the south there was a bubbling brook running high from the recent spring showers. The old building housing the sawmill was constructed over the stream channel and stood on stout granite slabs. Behind the mill building was the pond for the storage of logs. A few logs still remained in the water.

Mark slowly took in all of the familiar surroundings, and, with his heart pounding, let himself in the front door of the house. The door was still unlocked after all these years. It was just the way he remembered it. The living room was arranged the same way throughout his childhood. The wood box beside the fireplace was piled high with dry hardwood. Mark smiled, the box always seemed to be empty when he was a child. He wandered throughout the house without taking time to dwell on all the stories each room could tell. He wanted to be reassured that they still existed in reality and not in his subconscious mind. In his heart, Mark needed to take inventory of these precious places where much of his life had unfolded. A large part of his life was played out in the spacious kitchen, where he now found himself, with its black stove and heavy framed oak tavern table sitting in front of the window overlooking the pond.

There was a thick book with frayed pages and loose bindings on the table. Mark instantly recognized it as his father's favorite volume of popular poems by an assortment of authors. Mark reverently picked it up and sat in the chair before it, his long fingers caressing its threadbare coverings. He opened it to a page he had frequently turned to, a poem by Thomas Hood that he had enjoyed even as a young boy- *I Remember, I Remember.* The lines about the endearing joys of childhood had fresh meaning to him now that he was an adult.

The old house, his sudden return, and now this simple reminder of days past all had a dream-like quality to it. His emotions were all mixed up. It was at times like this that his anxiety about the future became clouded in reality. Maybe coming back home at this time was not such a good idea. The love and security he had always known in this house was no longer present. He had reached back in time to find peace and direction. If he could not find it here where could it be obtained? Now all he felt was sadness and a deep sense of loss. He was more alone than ever.

Returning the book to the table, Mark slowly left the house through the kitchen side door leading directly to the mill. The smell of pine sawdust instantly filled his nostrils. It had been a long time since he had savored that aroma. The clean scent of pine was as much "home" for him as the house. The sawmill carriage still had a partially sawed log on its frame, which Mark knew was an indication that the mill had been shut down in a hurry. The sluice gate was closed tight to prevent water from coming through the trough to turn the mill gears. The boards from the log neatly piled at the end of the mill were slightly weathered. His father must have been at work on the mill when the flu weakened him to the point where he could not continue to work. It appeared to be exactly as he had left it.

Mark had spent many happy hours in the mill with his father. He could remember how he had felt when the machinery was running. Inside the house one could exist in relaxed harmony, but the mill always fired an alertness and excitement of things happening. The wooden gears whined, the channeled water splashed in the sluice box, and the saw blade chattered its way through the logs with its own distinctive hum. He had been so proud the day his father let him operate the controls of the mill for the first time.

Beside the main arbor shaft that held the saw blade was a small shelf used to hold files and assorted tools needed to maintain the machinery. Mark saw something on the shelf that wrenched his composure, his father's corn cob pipe! Nothing was as much a part of his father as the continuous companionship of a corn cob pipe. It was always in his mouth. Mark picked it up with shaking hands and emptied the cold ashes from the bowl. A flood of tears finally broke through Mark's ability to control them. The simple corn cob pipe was the symbol that triggered all the desperation and sadness that had been welling up inside of him for so long. His slender body writhed with convulsive spasms and soft cries of despair pierced his lips. He dropped to his knees and let the tears flow down his face. Later, Mark carefully put the corn cob pipe back on the shelf, fully aware that his father was no longer waiting for him to come home. It was a hard reality check that he had been dreading.

"You saw more good times with dad than anything else," Mark whispered softly to the worn pipe. "If you could talk, I'd sure like to hear what you had to say."

Mark was so involved with his own feelings that he was unaware of the presence of an elderly woman standing alone at the mill door, a silent witness to his grief. She was a short elderly lady of sixty-five with white hair done up in a large bun at the back of her head. Her forehead was heavily furrowed, and her dark eyes misted at the sight before her. Mark felt her presence before he recognized her.

"Aunt Maddie!" It was a cry of recognition as well as relief. Running to her, he embraced her. Next to his father, this lady was the most precious person in the world. She had been like a mother to him, and he dearly loved her.

"My dear Mark, I thought it was you when I saw the military car in the driveway. Nobody was expecting you. What a lovely surprise." Tears of joy streamed down her heavily lined cheeks. She had prayed so often for his safe return, and now those prayers were answered. He had been like one of her own and she was immensely proud of him. When Mark's father had collapsed at the controls of the mill, Aunt Maddie, who lived beside them, noticed the inactivity, and ran to see what was wrong. She helped him inside before calling the doctor.

"I was going to write you about my coming. Events overtook me until, well, here I am," Mark cried, clinging to her. "Gee, it's good to see you again, Aunt Maddie." He was a little embarrassed to have her see him in his present state of mind. He took a clean handkerchief from his pocket and gently wiped away her tears. "I never dreamed it would hurt so much. Dad's presence is so strong here in the mill. One of the old pipes he used is still there, on the tool shelf."

"Yes, this is where he spent a large part of his days. It's only natural that you should associate it with Ray. He was such a hard worker. This mill was his pride and joy."

This was the first time Aunt Maddie had seen Mark since he graduated from forestry school, and she winced at the sadness she saw in his eyes. She noticed that his eyes were set much deeper in his head, and he seemed to stare through her, which he never had done before. These things frightened her, but she said nothing. He was much thinner than he used to be; but, she thought with pride, acknowledged that he was still a handsome man in his uniform.

"I've seen that look before, Aunt Maddie. Let me explain, if I can. I was unable to deal with some of the events thrust upon me during the war. Others handled it better than I did, but I'm getting better."

Aunt Maddie squeezed his arm. "You were always a very serious and sensitive boy, Mark. You must not apologize for being the way you are. Don't look upon it as a weakness or an inadequacy, not ever! I've received so many acts of thoughtfulness and kindness from you. I see it as strength and a wonderful part of a person's character. That's what always made you special, even as a small boy."

Without another word, Mark led the way out of the mill to the pond behind. It was a small pond created by the dam across the brook. Tall majestic white pine trees, lining the edge of the pond, swayed in the gentle breeze, filling the air with a soothing, melancholic whirring sound. This small piece of God's earth had always filled him with contentment. He yearned to reclaim that illusive state of grace again.

"What are you going to do now, Mark? Have you been released from the Army?"

Mark smiled at her. "I don't know exactly what I'll do. I thought I'd return home and see what happens first. In answer to your question, yes, I'm almost released from my military commitments. Something has come up that I want to do before I leave the service. I'd always planned on coming back to be with Dad. I've had some offers from the U.S. Forest Service, but I'm not sure what direction I want to take right now. I was doing very well in Germany on occupational duty. I relapsed a little when I got your letter about Dad. Since then, I haven't been able to pin my hopes on anything definite, but I can tell you with certainty that before too long, I'll be my old self again."

"One step at a time, Mark. I'm sure that someday you'll find whatever you're searching for. Your father never wanted you to feel obligated to return to this operation, you know. As a matter of fact, he always hoped you would go on to something of more importance. He was so proud of you, and I shared those same expectations." She reached out to put her arm around his waist and squeezed him tight like she had so many times in the past. "Why don't you come over to the house so that I can fix you something to eat and put on a pot of fresh coffee? I haven't fixed a meal for my nephew in ages."

Mark gave in to her suggestion. He knew better than to resist. She was the best cook he had ever known. They walked across the well worn path connecting the two houses. Aunt Maddie's place was larger than his father's. They had needed it too, with six children that were all grown up and away from home. Mark had always been an integral part of that large family. Two of his cousins had served in the Army. They were both married now and living near Portland. Four of his cousins were girls as pretty as their mother. He hadn't thought of them in a long time. The two younger girls were in school with him. They used to attend dances and other affairs together. Aunt Maddie's large immaculate kitchen still had the aroma of fresh baked bread, just as he hoped it would.

"Oh my, I'd almost forgotten what a treat it is, just to be in your kitchen. Smell that bread! It reminds me of being a kid again."

"I wish I had all of you kids back as small children. Life was less complicated then and we seemed happier," she sighed.

"I don't know if we were happier, or just ignorant of what can come our way, but I'd take the innocence if I could return to it," admitted Mark.

Aunt Maddie busied herself with the bread and coffee while Mark watched. He was anxious to ask her about his father's last few days. She cared for him here in her home. Now she was alone since her husband died five years ago. His cousins were all living their own lives away from Wells. Mark thought that she must be lonely at times.

"You know, Mark, your Dad's illness was very sudden. The high fever made him delirious for two days. I did what I could but the good Lord took him anyway." A tear slowly ran down her left cheek. She deftly wiped it away with one of her beautifully crotchet handkerchiefs. "I loved him. He was a good person, and a wonderful brother. If you use him as a model for your own life, you'll be as special as he was."

She set out the coffee cups, then served the hot bread from the oven. "You're in luck, Mark. I just did a batch of boulla rolls and bread. I remember how you used to like them."

"Aunt Maddie, I would've gone AWOL for some of your Swedish boulla rolls." They laughed together. It was then that she saw that special twinkle she had always seen in his eyes. From that moment, she knew that he would be able to find his way back to his former self.

"I'm going to stay for the night. I've got a lot of things running through my head right now. I'm glad to be home. I feel better already just being here in your kitchen, Aunt Maddie. I'll be over for breakfast with you in the morning before I leave."

"I understand completely. You're like your father in that respect. When all is said and done, we're the only ones that can solve our problems. Just remember, though, you're not alone."

"I've never doubted that for a moment, Aunt Maddie."

The Swedish rolls tasted as he remembered; the delicate taste and aroma of cardamom seeds gave them their distinctive flavor. It was almost as if Aunt Maddie had known he was coming, and she prepared them just for him. She always gave of herself, asking nothing in return. Serenity surrounded her. "Thanks, Aunt Maddie. I'm going down to the shore for a while. Don't stay up for me. I'll be fine in my old room. I'll see you in the morning." Mark went over to her chair and kissed her on the cheek without another word.

The sun cast longer shadows across the yard as it settled towards its westward track. You couldn't see the ocean from the yard, but you could hear and smell it. He crossed the Boston Post Road to pick up the old trail that ran beside the rushing brook. The pungent smell of the scrubby pitch pine trees at the bottom of the hill signaled to him that the ocean was close by. The ground flattened out onto the fine sandy soil that supported the pines. It soon gave way to the beach sand that extended easterly along the edge of the shore. The brook formed a small delta where it met the sea. It was at this juncture of fresh water and salt ocean water which he and his father had found most enjoyable. He never tired watching the relentless churning of the water. Its power and its beauty had not diminished as he grew older. In the winter months, especially after a storm, he used to come down here to collect hen clams that were washed up on the shore by the heavy tides. Some of the clams weighed one or two pounds each. They made a deliciously hearty clam chowder which he could almost taste.

Stepping out of the pine grove onto the sand dunes, the familiar roar of the surf filled his ears. He could feel the restless power of the waves as they threw themselves against the rocks. The tide was slightly past its ebb. About two hundred yards to the east, the sandy dunes gave way to rocky outcrops that still had a few thousand years to go before they were ground into minute sand particles. There was a well-worn path leading to the rocks. It felt good to have the wind in his face, smelling the sea air. Mark climbed to the top of the rocks and sat down with his legs hanging over the edge. He had sat at this same spot many times over the years.

The rolling sea inherently becomes a focal point for a person's meditation, much like the flames of a fireplace in a darkened room. Searching for answers in the pounding waves and flickering flames sometimes helps to clarify and define problems. His father told him you had to throw your thoughts into the sea. Then, in order to sort them out, you simply had to view them from a different vantage point. This secluded spot full of memories gave him a melancholic yearning for the past, even though he knew it was impossible. The past is always there to revisit whenever needed, but it can never be repeated.

The big decision Mark had to make right now was an easy one. He could never allow anyone else to take his place on such a delicate assignment as Arlo described. If it was up to him, he would prefer a little more time in Wells, and if he insisted, it could probably be arranged. However, his strong sense of duty interpreted the request from the Army and Marine Corps as an obligation on his part. Rekindling old memories about Flying Eagle would not be easy, yet he owed his friend that one final act of recognition. If the situation was reversed, Flying Eagle would not have hesitated to do what needed to be done. Mark decided to take the mission without any reservations. It just might be the healing experience he had been searching for.

It was dark by the time he made his way back to the house. Aunt Maddie had already come over to turn on the lights for him. It was a typical manifestation of her thoughtfulness. The steps leading to the two bedrooms upstairs seemed smaller than he remembered them. As a kid he took them two at a time and always counted them. Twelve steps — very few homes had the same number!

His bedroom was the same way he left it before going to France. The light coating of dust on the furnishings brought a smile to his lips. His father didn't like household chores. The room was small with his bed tight against the sloping roof to the north. Anytime he had gotten out of bed too fast, he was rewarded with a bump on the head. The single window opened to the west overlooking the pond. On summer nights, when the window was open, he could hear the brook cascading over the dam like a heavy curtain of water. It was like music to his ears. In the distance he could hear the lonely call of the whippoorwills that had sang outside his window for as long as he could remember.

The wall across the room from the sloping roof was a bookshelf full of books of all types. Most of the top two rows were filled with Mark's forestry text books from Durham. Reading had always been one of his passions. Sometimes he thought it was an escape mechanism for his vivid imagination. He had never known a boring moment in his life. He removed his uniform, carefully folding it away in the closet. The soothing flow of the waterfall put him to sleep, the way it used to do.

It was late in the morning when Mark awoke to familiar sounds. The steady song of the waterfall had worked its magic once again...he had overslept. Looking out the window he could see that it was going to be another fine sunny day to start something new in his life, a good omen. He quickly washed, shaved and dressed. His decision to accept the assignment made him feel good.

He could see smoke coming from Aunt Maddie's chimney, which told him that coffee was already percolating. He loaded his bag into the Dodge and went one more time to the mill. Today he felt stronger and much more in control of his emotions. More than anything else, he was motivated by a decision and a goal to be reached. He gently touched the corn cob pipe hoping to be worthy of his father's industrious legacy, and rushed to Aunt Maddie's, where he ate a hearty breakfast under her approving eye. She saw an improvement in Mark.

"Well, Aunt Maddie, I've arrived at a decision. I'll be gone for a while; I'm not sure how long, but I'll return to start fixing up the old house. I've got to get my own life in order first. I feel this assignment is important, and I'm anxious to get on with it."

31

"I was worried when I first saw you yesterday, Mark. This morning my fears are quieted because you're more like the young man I've always known. Thank God for our blessings."

"I'm stuffed with your usual good cooking. I can't eat another mouthful." Mark reached across the table, taking her hands in his and continued, "Aunt Maddie, it would be impossible for me to put into words what you've been for me all these years. Whenever you saw a need, you've always been there for me and Dad. I love you with all my heart. My biggest aim in life is to make you proud of me. I have a good feeling about this assignment. I'd like to bring back the old Mark for you." He went around the table and kissed her on the forehead. "Don't worry about me anymore. I'll write and tell you about my plans. Until I return, you take good care of yourself. Say 'hi' to the rest of the gang when you see them. Thanks, Aunt Maddie, for being you."

Mark knew it was best to not prolong his exit. Tears were coming down her face as she waved from the door. "I'll pray for you, Mark." She waved one last time as the staff car turned from the drive.

Chapter Three

Mark entered Arlo's office at the Marine Barracks with an air of confidence that was lacking the day before.

"Reporting back, Sir."

"Welcome, Mark." Arlo looked up from some papers on his desk with a confident grin and asked: "Did you make a decision, or do you need a little more time?"

"I've thought it over, and I definitely want to take the assignment. It's an obligation that I should fulfill. Besides, it'll be a privilege to help memorialize one of the finest persons I've ever known. It's the least I can do for his family and for his memory."

"I knew you'd come back for the same reasons you just gave for wanting to carry it out," Arlo answered. "I'd have been disappointed with any other response. I'm glad I left it up to you. How's that aunt of yours?"

"Aunt Maddie is ageless and an even better cook than I remembered. She sends her regards to you. She's a remarkable lady."

Mark's fast friendship with Arlo Korsman dated back to his college days at Durham, N.H. Several times the two of them went to Wells for a Sunday dinner with the family. Aunt Maddie put on some of her most memorable feasts for the benefit of the two young men. Arlo never forgot the dining experience.

Arlo confidently leaned back in his chair clasping his hands behind his head. "Sit down, Mark. Make yourself comfortable. We've got several things to talk about, and we might as well start right now. First of all, a Coast Guard launch will be at dockside in two hours to pick you up and ferry you across the river to a Coast Guard Cutter that will transport you to Quebec City." Arlo could not suppress a smirk.

"You old son of a gun," exclaimed Mark. "You knew what my answer would be even before I did myself. Thanks for the vote of confidence. Now, what's in store for me?"

"As you already know, the decision to award a medal to Flying Eagle took much longer than usual. I suggested to the Commandant of the Marine Corps that you, personally, should be the one to present it to his father. The Army agrees with the arrangements that have been made.

"When you arrive at Quebec, you'll be met by a former Canadian Army officer, a Colonel Gerard Clough. He was attached to your battalion for a short period of time as an observer when you were near St. Mihiel. Do you recall the name?" Arlo looked up at Mark with a questioning look on his face.

"I remember the man, even though I didn't spend too much time with him. However, I do recall being favorably impressed with him and most of the Canadians that I met." Mark answered.

"You're right. There was an easy professionalism with the Canadians. This Colonel Clough is now an officer in the Royal Canadian Mounted Police and will be your official Canadian representative and guide. He should be able to answer any questions you may have, and I assume that he'll arrange for your travel and lodging. He's been fully briefed on the assignment. As a matter of fact, I understand that he asked for it in person, once he found out that the award had been approved. Any questions so far?"

"No, I don't see any problem yet. The Colonel will be our point man for the presentation. How far from Quebec City is the reservation?" Mark checked the walls of the office for a map of North America and found one behind him. They both took a closer look at Quebec Province, a large neighbor directly to the north, which extends all the way from the St. Lawrence River in the south to the North Pole. There wasn't much in between except forestland, lakes, and rivers.

"I'm not sure, but I believe it's somewhere north of Lac St. Jean here where the roads are scarce, or nonexistent," Arlo remarked.

"I remember hearing Flying Eagle speak of large wilderness areas south and east of James Bay. Wow, now that I can see the area on a map, it's a long way from civilization. That's a huge stretch of land between Hudson Bay, the Arctic Circle and Newfoundland," exclaimed Mark, impressed with the immensity and remoteness of the area.

"It's a good thing you're starting out in mid-May. The winters must be brutal up there. However, you'll be in Colonel Clough's hands, so things should go smoothly."

Pointing to a leather bag on his desk, Arlo said, "This diplomatic courier pouch contains the U.S. Army's Distinguished Service Cross. It's to be awarded posthumously to Flying Eagle through his father, Running Deer. There's also a scroll enclosed with the citation. It's worded very much the way you wrote it in your initial report. I must say that the Army is very anxious for this ceremony to go well. It's a meaningful symbol of this country's high esteem for our neighbors to the north, and for one of our brave soldiers. You're going to be an official representative of the U.S. Government and will have diplomatic credentials. Your commission in the Marine Corps will be terminated effective the moment I receive your report of mission accomplished. Your diplomatic status and your pay will end at that point. Do you have any questions?"

"I can't think of anything right now. I returned from Wells with the intention of moving rapidly on this project so that you would be impressed with my determination, but your efficiency has stirred my admiration. I'm glad things worked out. I won't let you down, Arlo."

"I know that, Mark. I took a few liberties you might say, but, frankly, if you'd refused, I would probably be up for court-martial within a week's time." Arlo smiled, and shrugged his powerful shoulders. It was typical of him, for he didn't take himself too seriously. He also had a habit of cutting through bureaucratic red tape, or assigning it to the trash can when the situation justified it.

"The quartermaster is in my officer's quarters right now to measure you for some new uniforms and to outfit you properly. Draw anything you need for the trip, Mark."

Mark accepted the brief case with the manila envelope. "Thanks for your trust and support. It means a lot to me."

Arlo replied calmly, "I've known a lot of men during my career in the Marine Corps and I can honestly say, Mark, that you've been one of our best officers. Your character and your judgment have been beyond reproach. You maintained your integrity and inherent decency during the most difficult test of all. I know that you suffered deeply because of that rare quality of heart and charity, which you always brought to your command. You cared, possibly too much, if there's such a thing, for those under your command, and worked tirelessly for their benefit.

"I'm proud to call you my friend, and I'm going to take the liberty of telling you to be bold in putting the past behind you, Mark. Have faith and step out to the edge of tomorrow. Your tomorrows promise to be fulfilling and rewarding; reach for them with a renewed dedication and passion for life. Vaya con Dios, amigo - Go with God, my friend." Arlo extended his hand to Mark who grasped it firmly. There was a bond of trust between the two of them that time and adversity had strengthened.

The quartermaster had been well informed. He was ready with uniforms, additional baggage and personal toiletry items for the trip. Mark left the officer's quarters with a new dress green uniform and several field service sets. He had never been so well supplied.

A Coast Guard launch was waiting for Mark at the dockside as Arlo promised. He jumped into it while two marines held it tight to the wharf. The Maine shore grew further and further away as the motor launch headed across the river. The young coast guardsman at the helm welcomed him aboard and pointed to their destination on the opposite shore, which was the New Hampshire side of the Piscataqua River. The launch aimed towards the site of the old colonial Fort Constitution where the Coast Guard station was located. Mark could see that the cutter he was going to be traveling aboard was one of the new high sea endurance cutters that had been used so successfully as escort vessels for convoys en route to Europe during the war. He also recalled having read somewhere that the Coast Guard had suffered the highest percent of losses of any service during the Great War. He would be in competent hands.

"Permission to come aboard, Sir," requested Mark, saluting the stern and holding it for the young officer of the deck.

"Welcome aboard, Captain Leroux. I hope we can make your trip a pleasant one. The Captain wants to see you as soon as you come aboard. The deck hands will stow your gear in our guest cabin, and I'll take you to see Captain Sturtevant on the bridge."

Captain Sturtevant was a strikingly impressive looking Coast Guard officer old enough to be Mark's father. He was over six feet tall and seemed to tower over Mark. No one ever had to question who was in command when Captain Sturtevant was around. He conversed in a booming voice and ran a tight ship. The cutter was neat and freshly painted, and the crew had that gift of efficiency and competence that is a hallmark of good captains. He greeted Mark with genuine warmth.

"Captain Leroux, you're an honored guest. Welcome to the Coast Guard Cutter, *DEXTER*. Before we spend too much time getting better acquainted, let me say that we now have a high tide, and I'm anxious to weigh anchor as soon as possible. The river is much easier to navigate when it's at high tide. We're going directly to Quebec City without intermediate stops. Washington wants you to have V.I.P. treatment. I don't know anything about your mission, but rest assured, it's our pleasure to provide you with the full run of the ship. Feel free to ask for anything you need. The weather ahead looks good, so we should have smooth sailing, at least as smooth as the North Atlantic ever gets."

"Thank you, Sir. My mission is not a secret. I'm carrying a decoration to be awarded posthumously to a Canadian that served in our Army. He was a very brave man who now lies in France in an unknown grave. The United States wants his family to know how much we appreciate his sacrifice."

"I understand," said Captain Sturtevant, evaluating the young marine. "It's not just the gentle hills of France that holds our dead from the recent war. The sea we travel upon is filled with the bodies of many brave men."

Mark nodded in agreement for he knew it to be true. "I understand that, Sir."

"If you'll pardon me, Captain Leroux, they need me on the bridge. We'll have plenty of time to talk after we chart our course. The next stop will be Quebec City!"

Mark was glad to be alone with his thoughts. The large cutter throbbed under his feet as the powerful engines slowly moved the ship from the dock. It slipped into the main channel of the river with the ease of a speedboat. The movement from shore gave him a feeling of anxious excitement. He was thrilled to be underway, yet, the old feeling of uncertainty had crept back into his mind. For some unexplained reason, a part of his enthusiasm for the mission was suddenly being eroded by feelings which he could not understand and was having trouble trying to overcome. Was his intuition crying out a warning about the trip?

The powerful engines of the streamlined cutter telegraphed a rhythmic pulsation throughout the vessel, a feeling of unlimited power and energy being held in leash. As the cutter came to the end of the river, the turbulence of the sea increased. Turning on a northerly course the revolutions of the engines were increased, and the mighty cutter effortlessly sliced through the waters off the Gulf of Maine. Mark was standing at the port rail on the main deck just forward of the bridge, hoping, desperately, that the trip would be a harbinger of good fortune instead of an omen for disaster. He loved the sea. There was, he thought, a direct parallel between his beloved forests and the ocean. Both had the power to soothe his troubled spirits.

Looking back at the shore, Mark picked up the unique shape of Mount Agamenticus as it rose out of the relatively flat Maine coastal plane. He had a terrible feeling of being alone again. The Coast Guard Cutter easily lengthened the distance between him and the coast of Maine.

"Pardon me, Sir," interrupted a young seaman. "The Captain wanted me to tell you that the officer's wardroom always has coffee and sandwiches available." The coast guardsman pointed out the way to the wardroom, saluted him, and left.

"Thank you," answered Mark, who was used to the rather rigid military courtesies of the Marine Corps. He could see that the Coast Guard was a lot less formal, and he liked it that way.

A black steward had just finished making a fresh pot of coffee when Mark entered the small wardroom. A large table dominated the room with barely enough space to walk around it. Captain Sturtevant was seated at the table opposite from where Mark came in. "Here's our young passenger. I wanted boatswain mate Harding to trace you down and invite you to our sea-going dining room."

"I'm pleased to be part of your mess, Sir," responded Mark.

"I just came from the chart house. We should make Quebec by mid-morning tomorrow. I'm traveling at top speed to get into the calmer waters between Nova Scotia and Prince Edward Island before nightfall. It's easier to sleep at night then. Once we're in the St. Lawrence River, it's like floating in a bathtub, even though the currents can be treacherous. We're scheduled to pick up a Royal Canadian Navy escort east of the Gaspe Peninsula. I don't mind telling you that we enjoy doing V.I.P. duty. It's a welcome break from our routine chores."

Mark selected a roast beef sandwich from the counter and sat opposite Captain Sturtevant. "I've been traveling a lot lately. I was in France a short time ago, and here I am at sea again headed north. I'm not complaining, just surprised at the hectic pace of things since I left Washington. This operation is a little irregular, and sometimes I feel as if I was less suited to carry it out than others." Mark was surprised how easily he could convey his doubts to a stranger.

"Son, I don't have any answers to your problems, but you should consider that you were asked to do this job by someone in authority who felt confident that you could handle it. They don't generally give out captain bars to weak or incompetent men. War we've just been through has left a mark on everybody, call it the mark of the damned if you like, but that doesn't give us the license to get out of the human race. All combat veterans bear some emotional scars that are known to them alone; that's the price of being part of a distinct brotherhood. The rest of the world, who have never experienced such violence, can never know what it's like. That's as it should be, because we get paid for doing our duty. Sometimes it happens to involve fighting. Your thoughts and feelings about the task ahead may be precisely what makes you the best possible person for the job." The Captain had a tendency to speak freely on his own ship.

"I suppose that's true, Sir. I haven't talked to anyone exactly how I feel about what happen to me. Sometimes I don't know myself. However, from the moment I decided to do this job, I've felt better. There's a clear plan of action ahead of me. I find that reassuring. It's the bigger picture beyond the presentation that concerns me," confided Mark, slowly sipping his coffee, a little uncomfortable with the intimacy of the conversation.

"Son, the ones that handle the future the best are the ones that prepare for it and give it their best shot."

A steward came into the room to announce evening mess call in an hour. The Captain, who never allowed himself to get very far away from the bridge of his ship, excused himself again. Mark returned to the deck, finding a spot forward of the gun turret where he would be out of the way of the ship's work routine. The wake from the bow sprinkled the deck lightly with sea spray. Darkness was beginning to settle upon them. It was too early for the moon to be visible, but a few stars were beginning to glimmer. The cutter was like an oasis of light flowing through the darkness. It illuminated for a moment, then its forward passage allowed the darkness to fill the void left behind in its wake.

In the distance off the port bow, another ship was passing in the night. They were like two planets of light sailing on the sea of blackness as they went on their separate destinations, totally out of touch with each other, remaining strangers. After the Canadian mission, Mark mused, where would he go? Now that his father was gone, he should think of continuing the business at home. It seemed a logical thing to do. Forest management and cutting practices on some private lands in the country were, and continued to be exploitive and destructive in nature. He had seen how vast the unchecked harvest measures were, especially during the war. It had always been a dream that he could help establish sound management techniques and harvesting measures to show woodland owners the advantages of such practices. The destructive practices now in vogue had to be turned around for the benefit of the whole country. The forestry profession had a lot of work to do, and most of it centered around the monumental task of educating the landowners that it was in their own best interest to improve upon their harvesting practices.

At school, he became an admirer of the father of forestry in the United States — Gifford Pinchot. In forestry school, he visualized that the simple application of solutions to the problems that existed should be logical as well as easy to apply, and they should be firmly based on scientific principles and silvicultural characteristics of the tree species involved, but the real world was never that easy.

The air had a brisk chill and Mark was glad to be wearing his overcoat. Captain Sturtevant appeared beside him and calmly said, "I gather that you enjoy the sea at night, also. It's usually good for any of us to get away from our regular duties and experience deep water sailing once in a while."

"It helps to put problems in perspective doesn't it?"

"That it does, Captain Leroux. We should be at the St. Lawrence by daybreak. The trip around the Gaspe Peninsula is a beautiful one. We'll pick up our escort, and you could be in Quebec City by eleven o'clock in the morning. As soon as you've departed, we'll be on our way to start our normal iceberg patrol. It's possible that we won't dock at the

40

wharf. They may send a launch for you. I'll know for sure shortly, and notify you."

Mark started to ask him something, but another call from the bridge took the energetic sailor away again. "Duty calls."

Tomorrow loomed as an important time for Mark. It was the beginning of an adventure into the unknown. He was proud to be doing it for Flying Eagle and for himself. In his heart he realized that he needed this assignment. Arlo had been aware of Mark's need and had acted forcefully upon it. Thank God for such friends. He felt that at least symbolically, life was starting anew for him.

Chapter Four

The Coast Guard Cutter *DEXTER* gracefully knifed its way through the deep swells of the North Atlantic, entering the Straits of Cabot between New Brunswick and Newfoundland, when Captain Sturtevant received a radio signal that a Canadian corvette would meet them at the entrance to the Gulf of St. Lawrence. Mark gingerly found his way to the bridge shortly after sunrise. The seas were increasingly rougher, and the small cutter rolled vigorously. It was a beautiful time of the day. A sunrise at sea was a sight never forgotten. Red and orange colors reflected off the water and the scattered cumulus clouds overhead immersed the ship in its expanse of color.

The ship was a strong runner with good sea handling characteristics, but Mark was glad that he did not have much longer to go on the hard-riding vessel. Captain Sturtevant had skillfully used two features of speed and maneuverability to sink two German U-boats during the war. He loved the ship in a way that no landlubber could comprehend. To him, she had a distinct personality.

Off to the starboard bow, Captain Sturtevant could make out a ship approaching. The signal man was busy with incoming messages, so he assumed that it was the Canadian corvette that he had been expecting. He watched it come at full speed. They were ships of great beauty as well as speed and agility, and the Captain's experienced eye admired its trim appearance.

"Good morning, Captain Leroux," said Captain Sturtevant, standing beside Mark. "You look fit and ready this morning. The escort vessel is approaching on an intercepting course. It should be here within the hour."

Mark also watched the ship in the distance and felt a rush of blood to his temple. The events about to unfold were well beyond his control now. The Captain noticed his tenseness and said nothing. A signal man with a pad in his hand hurried to the bridge.

42

"Captain, a message from the HMCN corvette *RELIANCE* requests permission to put a river pilot and a naval officer aboard."

"Thanks, Jameson. Tell them permission granted. We welcome them aboard." He turned towards Mark again and said, "You know son, this is the beginning of a day that promises to be a very busy one for you. Last night I received new orders. I'm to make myself and the ship available to you if you think it's needed in any way. Then we'll resume our iceberg patrol in the north. For now, we're at your service in whatever capacity you ask. You only have to make a request and it'll be our pleasure to accommodate you in your mission."

The possibility of being with some of his own people appealed to Mark, pleased at the last minute offer of assistance. "Thank you, Captain Sturtevant. My immediate reaction is to take it, but I have to do this one alone. I appreciate your willingness to help though."

"As you wish, son. I'd better get below to my quarters and make myself more presentable for our Canadian guests." With a spry step he disappeared below. The sleek Canadian corvette came abreast of the *DEXTER* and started to lower a boat for the transfer of two officers.

Mark was dressed in his new forest green uniform, compliments of Arlo. He could have worn the formal dress blue uniform, but he wanted to maintain a more conservative tone for the presentation proceedings, so the blues were left behind. After a brisk walk around the ship to exercise his legs, Mark headed for the officer's wardroom which seemed to be the reception center for the cutter.

The small motor launch from the corvette was met at the lower ramp by several coast guardsmen and an ensign. The two Canadians came up the stairs first. One Canadian was dressed in the merchant marine uniform of a river pilot. It would be his job to direct the helmsman through the tricky waters of the St. Lawrence Gulf before they entered the River. It was a job requiring great skill and knowledge of the river and its currents. The wide river was a gateway to the interior of Canada. Some of the most dangerous currents in North America are in the St. Lawrence, especially where the fresh water from the Saguenay River empties into the tidal river. The young river pilot went directly to the bridge without any formality.

The next officer up the gangplank was a Lieutenant in the Royal Canadian Navy. He wore a well-trimmed beard, gave the officer of the deck a salute and asked for permission to come aboard.

"You're an honored guest aboard this ship, Lieutenant. I'm Captain Sturtevant of the U.S. Coast Guard."

"I'm Lieutenant James Heaney of the Royal Canadian Navy. We've been expecting you, Captain Sturtevant. You've made excellent time since you left Portsmouth. The river pilot is one of Canada's best."

"Come with me, Lieutenant Heaney. The man you want to see is in the wardroom. He's a young marine, wounded in France, about your age I'd say." Captain Sturtevant noticed the Canadian observing the cutter with strong professional interest.

"If you think our cutter rides a little easier than your shorter corvette in a heavy sea, I can assure you that it doesn't. If a sailor can keep his stomach on this ship, he can handle anything. I still have to use my sea biscuits on occasion." He smiled at the young lieutenant, who understood what he was talking about.

"Captain Leroux," Captain Sturtevant hailed Mark as he entered the ward room. "This is our official escort from the Royal Canadian Navy, Lieutenant James Heaney. Lieutenant Heaney, meet Captain Mark Leroux of the Marines."

The two young officers saluted, then shook hands with each other. Before either could speak, Captain Sturtevant asked for the steward to bring coffee. "Or would you prefer tea, Lieutenant Heaney?"

"Coffee would be fine, Sir."

They all sat down following the Captain's lead. Mark hoped that his nervousness was not too apparent to the Canadian. Lieutenant Heaney had a medium build and a forceful demeanor that translated into a dynamic personality that had a tendency to be on the move most of the time. He came to the point immediately.

"I've been ordered to accompany you to Quebec City and to offer you the full cooperation of the Canadian Government. Your reason for coming is a tribute not only to a gallant soldier, but for your Canadian neighbor to the north, whom I can assure you is honored by the homage. I'm pleased to be at your service, Captain Leroux." The steward served a pot of coffee and a large tray of cinnamon rolls fresh from the oven.

"At this stage of the journey I know little of what is to take place," said Mark. He liked the habit of the Canadian to speak directly what was on his mind. "I'm only sure of my reason for being here. I was led to believe that your government was going to be responsible for setting up the award ceremony. Do you have more specific information, Captain Sturtevant?"

The question caught the Captain with a mouthful of warm roll. He held up his finger beseechingly for a little time before answering. "My orders are to drop anchor at Quebec City as soon as possible. I expect that the American Embassy will be there to sort things out."

"It's my belief that a special envoy is waiting to meet you at the Citadel. I don't know whom, but I would imagine it would be an officer familiar with your situation and knowledgeable of the Indian Tribal Council." Lieutenant Heaney stopped for a moment and looked at Mark and then Captain Sturtevant with a questioning gaze, then continued, "Maybe you'll go inland to the council village, I'm not sure. If you want me to find out the specifics, I can do so."

"I can wait until we dock at Quebec for the specific details," answered Mark. "I'm prepared for an inland trip if necessary. As a matter of fact, I was led to believe that the presentation would take place inland at the Cree village. Unless there's something unexpected, I don't need the escort you so graciously offered, Captain Sturtevant. I was informed that the embassy was working on the project, so things should be fine the way they set it up."

"We're now south of Anticosti Isle," Captain Sturtevant said, standing up to leave. If you two don't need me, gentlemen, I've got a ship to look after, and a river pilot that I haven't checked out yet." There was a gleam in the Captain's eyes and a broad smile on his lips as the two officers followed his broad shoulders through the door.

"He's an original," chuckled Mark.

"Aye, and a second to that. Captain Sturtevant has created quite a reputation among the sailors in these northern waters. Did you serve in France, Captain Leroux?"

"Yes, I was in France. I'm a marine, as you know, but I commanded an Army company. Lieutenant Mann was one of my platoon leaders. He was beside me when the gas attack took place, then the artillery barrage…" Mark was reluctant to elaborate in any more detail. He lit his pipe with a match which made a loud snap when it ignited.

"I understand, Captain. I didn't mean to drag up ghosts of the past. Thank God the bloody thing is over. It's touched everybody in different ways. My brother was lost at Marne. We don't know where his body is located, and my mother has been paralyzed with grief ever since she got the news. We seem to be helpless to comfort her. All that can be done is to call on the Almighty for help and trust in His ability to provide it."

"I agree with you. It's not that easy for some. I didn't mean to let my dark side show. Sometimes I've felt that I was the only one carrying such pain. Now, I realize it's a selfish thought. The war has created a large brotherhood of bereaved people, all over the world." Mark felt at ease with the red-bearded Canadian sailor.

"A very human thought, Captain," said Lieutenant Heaney.

The two young officers spent the rest of the afternoon in friendly banter. Mark was pleased with himself. He was able to talk more openly about Flying Eagle than he had earlier with Captain Sturtevant. The trip up the river took longer than expected. Instead of arriving in the morning, it was late afternoon before they were in Quebec. The sun was already starting to set as Mark and Lieutenant Heaney made their way to the bridge for a better view of Quebec City. The sun was a red dot directly ahead of the cutter. It radiated red and orange hues across a sky full of scattered cumulus clouds hanging above the city, reflecting the flaming pattern against the City's riverfront. It was a beautiful spectacle for his introduction to the city dubbed the *Paris of the North.*

Mark was thrilled to see the looming skyline of the city off the starboard side of the ship. Within a short time, they were docking in front of the most impressive looking building he had ever seen. The Chateau Frontenac was more stunning in real life than any picture could ever convey. It was full of parapets and turrets with flags flying from every cornice. The aged copper roofing gave the massive structure a green tint which blended with the deep blue patches of the sky that shown between the clouds and the fiery red afterglow from the sun. Mark felt a tingle of excitement run through his body as he stood on the bridge, mesmerized by this beautiful place. Before today, Quebec had only existed in books for him. The French influence in North America had reached its zenith in 1759 when French troops were routed by the English on the Plains of Abraham, a short distance south of Quebec City. The defeat ended French military influence in Canada, but the French language and culture had already been firmly established. Yet, today, the tie to France remains as strong as ever.

Mark's vantage point on the bridge was perfect to see all of the river front. People were watching the American Coast Guard cutter dock. They were at the railings on the dockside, above the wharf at the terrace that rose precipitously from the water's edge.

"I can see you've already fallen under its spell," said Captain Sturtevant, standing beside them. "It's a beautiful structure, isn't it? There's an intriguing aura about it. I never cease to be thrilled by it, and I've been here several times."

The Captain was carefully viewing the crowd at dockside with a small set of binoculars. Finally he turned to Mark and said with deliberation, "Your contact man will be on board shortly, son. Before he arrives, I wanted to offer you my heartiest of wishes for this to be a successful venture for you. It was a privilege to be your transport. Good luck, son." He held out a hand to Mark.

Mark met his eyes and was touched by the sincerity of the elderly Captain. "Thank you, Sir. With all the support I've been given, I can't fail. I appreciate all you've done." He released Captain Sturtevant's handshake, saluted and headed towards the stairs for the lower deck where Lieutenant Heaney was motioning for him to come down. Two men had already come across the gangplank. The younger of the two was tall and well dressed in suit and tie. Mark silently bet to himself that he was the diplomat from the embassy. He had an easy smile and a graciousness of movement that conveyed familiarity. Mark was introduced to the young man by Lieutenant Heaney.

"Mark, this is Robert Holden of the American Consulate Office in Quebec City. Mr. Holden, I'm pleased to introduce you to Captain Mark Leroux."

"I'm at your service, Sir," said Robert Holden, extending a hand. "It'll be a pleasure to assist you in any way that I can. We're proud to play a small part in making this mission possible."

Mark shook hands with the diplomat, noticing they were about the same age. "Thank you, Mr. Holden. I'm sure your office will be of great help."

Mark recognized the second man as a Canadian Army officer he had previously met during the war in France. He was dressed not in the uniform of an Army officer, but in the scarlet tunic of the Mounted Police. His broad rimmed hat and colorful uniform emphasized the fact that he was a large powerful man with an authoritative presence. Robert Holden held out an open palm to the policeman.

"This is Inspector Gerard Clough of the Mounted Police. Inspector, meet Captain Leroux." They shook hands like old friends.

"Inspector Clough, I remember you as a Colonel in the Canadian Army. I believe it was outside of Paris on the road to Soissons. You visited my regiment as an observer. It's a pleasure meeting you again." Mark's apprehension was rapidly melting away in the presence of the two men.

"Our first meeting on the Paris road seems a long time ago, Captain. I remember it well. I trust our time together now will be under less trying conditions, and measurably more comfortable." He smiled from ear to ear the same way Mark remembered. A large scar ran from the lower cheek down his neck on the right side of his face. It was not too noticeable, and the Inspector had developed a habit of presenting the other side of his face to people he was talking to, if he had the chance.

"It's a privilege to be your official escort. I've assisted Mr. Holden here in setting up an itinerary and making arrangements for your stay to be as comfortable as possible. I'm proud to know that one of our own fallen heroes is to be memorialized by your country." The Inspector had a captivating smile and an easy going manner that generated trust.

Mark accompanied the Inspector and Mr. Holden down the gangplank. An open car was waiting for them at the dockside, called Place Royale, ready to carry them up the hill to the large terrace in front of the Chateau Frontenac. Mark was happy. Vibrancy of the city was almost physical in its intensity. The warm spring air mixed with the sea mist to produce a delicate aroma seasoned with the scent of balsam fir from the forests that surrounded the City.

Mark was informed that he would be put up in the Chateau for only one evening. The next day they would start the long journey inland to the interior of Quebec Province. Lights were coming on all over the city. In the failing sunlight Mark caught sight of the Coast Guard Cutter on its way back to international waters and its regular patrol duties. The American flag snapped freely at the masthead.

The view from the promenade in front of the building was an intoxicating experience. With the lower city beneath its ramparts, and the upper town to its rear, one had the feeling that it was an impregnable fortress. He knew the story of the siege of the city by British General Wolfe. The honor of France was defended by the young

French General Marquis de Montcalm. Both generals had died in the battle that took place a short distance south of the Chateau.

Mark felt in good company with the Inspector and the American diplomat. The latter was an agreeable young man who handled the luggage and room assignments with an easy relaxed competence. He would be available to act as an aide to Mark for the trip. It would prove to be a good match; they hit it off well from the first moment of introduction. Mark learned that Bob Holden had been a soldier during the war and joined the Foreign Service shortly after his release from the Army. Canada was his first assignment. He had that typical Yankee nothing-was-impossible attitude, which some Canadians disliked.

Inspector Clough was a warm high-spirited person, a true original. Even though he was easy and relaxed in manner, there was still a reserve that was not readily visible to the casual observer. There was a lot about the man that few would ever know. His very personable disposition was not insincere because he did enjoy people for what they were. His natural reserve simply acted as a screen for his more vulnerable inner self. Not many people ever penetrated the thin veneer of effervescence. He was not intentionally trying to hide anything. He was simply a private person that wanted his private thoughts left alone. He selected his friends with care. Inspector Clough had experienced a great deal of tragedy in his military and police career, and rigidly kept it a secret to himself. His facial features were angular, his graying hair made him look older and more mature than his 45 years would indicate. He had been a policeman for most of his adult life and never regretted the career of service; indeed, he found much satisfaction from it. The Inspector was of Scottish descent, but he loved his chosen country as deeply as any native-born resident. The graciousness and sincerity of the man was a manifestation of his iron discipline and inner tranquility. He radiated confidence with no trace of arrogance.

Robert Holden, Inspector Clough, and Mark leisurely strolled on the large stone terrace promenade above the old town on their way to the Chateau Frontenac, where they enjoyed a fine meal. The steak dinner was followed with another walk along the barricade surrounding the Chateau. The evening was cool but comfortable and the promise of warmer days was in the air. They walked three abreast enjoying the bright lights all around them. Mark was favorably impressed with the beauty of the city. The lights glittered as far as the eye could see, and ships traversing the river were awash with even more lights.

"I have a feeling that this V.I.P. treatment could be addictive for a country boy like me," admitted Mark with a smile.

"Enjoy the moment, but don't get too used to it." chuckled Robert Holden.

"Tomorrow, we start the trip to Flying Eagle's ancestral home," the Inspector said, injecting a more serious tone to the mood. "We've a couple of travel options available to us. We could take a train to Lac St. Jean; after that, it would be a lengthy trip by canoe or boat to the northland. The other option is to fly all the way. It all depends on how you feel about flying."

"I've no objections to flying. It would be a new experience for me. What do you think, Bob?"

"Compared to the hassles of canoes, I'd much prefer going in by air. I've flown before and enjoy it." said Bob matter-of-factly. "The final decision is up to you, Mark."

"I'm not sure if you're prepared for such a trip. We could have Flying Eagle's family transported here if you prefer," said the Inspector. "I, personally, thought it would be more appropriate to go to his village. It would add to the solemnity of the occasion. The church at the village is adequate for the ceremony, and the village priest is the tribal Administrator for the Bureau of Indian Affairs. I don't know what they've told you about the details."

"I was told only the basic reasons for coming, and that the details would be given to me upon arrival. I'm very much in favor of us going to Flying Eagle's village. It would be insensitive to have his family disrupted to come here," Mark answered.

"The area we're going into is difficult, wild, and isolated. It's separated from civilization by many miles." The Inspector watched Mark closely for his reaction.

"I don't mind that, Inspector Clough. I'm a forester by training and profession. The forest is my natural element. I've assumed it would take place in the North Woods, and I'm sincerely looking forward to the trip," Mark replied enthusiastically.

"Then it's agreed, we'll go to the village by plane. We can leave tomorrow morning, weather permitting." The Inspector seemed pleased with the decision to go north.

"Too bad you can't stay in Quebec City a little longer," said Bob Holden. "It's full of great sites to see and visit."

"I'm sure you're right, but I'll feel better after I complete the job I came here to do. Maybe then you can be my tour guide, Bob."

"It's easier to get along here in Quebec Province if you speak French. Many of the people speak English too, but they'll try to draw you out in French first. They're fine people and very proud of their traditions and heritage. The English influence has increased some lately, and it's difficult to conduct business without knowledge of both languages. The Inspector here speaks French fluently in addition to several Indian dialects."

Mark was not surprised to hear this about the colorful policeman. Mark also learned over dinner that the Inspector had joined the Mounted Police immediately after high school graduation. When the great war started, he commanded a company of policemen that became a Mounted Police Yeomanry unit in the Canadian Army that went to France. Good officers were scarce, and Clough quickly rose to the rank of Colonel as a liaison officer for his Commonwealth division. It was in his capacity as an observer that he was attached to the same battalion in which Mark's company was serving. Inspector Clough had spent several days with Mark's regiment in the final weeks of the war.

That evening over supper, the Inspector mentioned that he had been one of the many victims of the infamous and poorly designed Ross rifle of the Canadian Army. The scar on the Inspector's neck was still visible.

According to the Inspector, the Ross rifle had a hurried development period and went into production before all of its problems were solved. The most grievous was that the bolt could be readily field-stripped for cleaning and reassembled exactly opposite from the way it should be done. Then, as it was inserted in the breach and closed on a fresh bullet, the bolt failed to lock on the receiver. When fired, the bolt was blown out the rear of the receiver into the face of the unsuspecting shooter. It had killed many Canadian soldiers. The Ross rifle went to France as the only shoulder weapon of the Canadian Army.

The Inspector told them, "When I fired the rifle, I was not trying to hit a target, but was demonstrating the recoil to a green recruit. Consequently, my eye was not behind the bolt the way most men were injured. It only grazed me in the neck. I was lucky. After that, my unit went scrounging for Enfield rifles."

Mark was enjoying the company of this remarkable officer. It seemed as if fate, for whatever reason, had allowed their paths to cross again after the war. In France the Inspector made a reputation for himself by being cool and confident under fire, with a burning hatred for the Germans. Mark had a gut feeling that the Inspector was a lonely man.

"Inspector, are you going to be with us for the duration of my stay in Canada?" asked Mark.

"Yes, I've instructions to be your Canadian host. I'll be with you all the time. My normal duty station is at the village we're going to in the north. I wanted to have a chance to talk with you two before we retire for the evening, to go over things you can expect to find at Flying Eagle's tribal home. I want you to understand what the native people mean to Canada.

"Up until 1905 all native peoples in Canada were the responsibility of the National government and the Bureau of Indian Affairs. After that date, in Quebec anyway, they came under the control of the provincial government. These people are scattered throughout the province in settlements of different sizes, usually about a hundred people to a village. They're semi-autonomous in their ability to govern themselves. They're not full citizens of Canada, and many do not desire to be. Their world centers around the tribe and family.

"Flying Eagle was a member of the Cree nation, which has traditionally been hunters and trappers. As soon as the Hudson Bay Company established stores throughout the area, they traded pelts for food, clothing and other items with the native peoples. When the tribes began to abandon their old customs and adapted to the white man's way of doing things, it started a transition that's still taking place at an accelerated rate.

"Now, we have another factor that has had an eroding influence on traditions. When animals and fur were plentiful, the people prospered and trapped more. They almost depleted these natural resources which were their sole means of making a living. Desperation became a daily part of their lives. They could not turn to farming, because the soil is too thin and they lack those skills. We subsidize their existence with checks to ward off starvation and disease. In this vulnerable situation, illegal liquor venders have become extremely active. Most of our energies are directed at this chronic problem in the North Woods. With the supplemental payments, we've robbed some of the people of their independence and individual initiative. Most of the people have resorted to the ways of the white man. Flying Eagle is a perfect example. He had the opportunity to better himself and he took advantage of it. Education was his road to salvation. Yet, I understand that he intended to return to his people to help improve their situation."

"Yes, I remember, he often talked about his plans to return to his roots when the war ended," Mark told him.

"He had a sister," continued the Inspector, "that went to a nursing school. She has returned to her people and has become an indispensable ray of hope and inspiration. Flying Eagle's mother is dead. His father, Running Deer, is healthy and energetic and is one of the tribal elders on the council board. They live in a small settlement north of Lac St. Jean in northern Quebec Province half way to James Bay. It's a bleak land, especially in wintertime, yet they are proud of their legacy and ancestry, and continue to hunt, fish, and trap under new resource management guidance set up by the Province.

"When Flying Eagle and his sister, Bright Cloud, were young, their father acted as a guide for a wealthy businessman from New York State. Every year he came north for hunting and fishing expeditions successfully handled by Running Deer. When the businessman passed away, he left a generous amount of money for the education of the two children of his faithful guide. Nothing ever made Running Deer happier than giving the gift of knowledge to his children. His loss of Flying Eagle was devastating, because they had planned many things when he completed school. Hopes and dreams for a better future for his people were crushed. He's a Christian of high standards, and I think you'll like him. He speaks perfect English. I've known him for a long time.

"Whether you realize it or not, Captain Leroux, you've been a part of Running Deer's life since you wrote to him about Flying Eagle's death. Evidently he wrote home about you. Now that you're coming in person, it's an honor they're looking forward to. He's a grand old man who's had a difficult life. I value his friendship. The village where they live is a part of my normal patrol. I used to do the same patrols as a Provincial Policeman adviser. Now the same work is done under the auspices of the Royal Canadian Mounted Police instead of the Quebec Provincial Police. Same job, just a different uniform. Alas, we now have a 'royal' in our name instead of the old North West Mounted Police. Now it's R.C.M.P." The Inspector was proud of his organization.

"Unless you have anything you want me to cover, I'll stop talking. We've a very busy day ahead of us tomorrow, and I suggest that we turn in soon."

The three men retired to their rooms. Mark was glad to be alone so that he could review what was taking place at such a rapid pace. He was impressed by the thoroughness of his companions' preparations for the journey. All he had to do was go through the process.

His room on the fourth floor of the Chateau faced south, towards the St. Lawrence River. In the distance, he visualized his home in Maine wondering which separated people more, time or distance. His head was too full of events of the day to sort it all out and the pillow was soft. Sleep came quickly.

Chapter Five

The four-seated float plane was heavily loaded with passengers and luggage as it labored to lift off from the St. Lawrence River. Mark shared the rear seat with the Inspector. Bob Holden sat beside the Mounted Police pilot up front. The plane was equipped with large pontoons that enabled it to land on water. The pontoons also acted as storage compartments for the passengers' luggage. Mark had never flown before and was apprehensive about the flight. His adrenaline was flowing.

The plane gently lifted off the St. Lawrence River. The R.C.M.P. pilot turned towards the fabled northland of New France as soon as they became airborne. Mark was exhilarated by the experience and watched the scenery below with awe. The small farms below formed geometric patterns. He had read of these homes of the French Canadian farmers called habitants — farms with small frontage on the river, an open area of cultivated land around the buildings, and a large area of woodlands furthermost from the river for fuel, logs, and lumber. From the air it looked like small lines drawn on the landscape, all parallel with one another. A road ran close along the river connecting all of the farms together into a community.

Engine noise in the cabin of the plane made it impossible for normal conversation. The view was so breathtaking that Mark's apprehension of flying soon disappeared. The river soon faded from view, replaced with a continuous expanse of spruce-fir forests. Some logging had taken place, but the vast landscape was relatively untouched by the hand of man. As far as the eye could see streams and lakes were interlaced with woodlands. The interdependency of forests and water became more apparent to Mark as he watched the verdant scene below.

The air was chilly in the cabin of the plane, and Mark was glad to be wearing his great coat, as the Inspector had wisely suggested. Mark took this opportunity to study the countenance of the Inspector who was looking out the window beside him. He had a gentle face with penetrating eyes. Most of the time his forehead was furrowed, as if he was worried about something. He tried to say something to Mark, but they both smiled, shrugged their shoulders and gave up. Since his introduction to the Inspector, several things about him came to mind. Mark recalled a school lecture about leadership given by a highly decorated colonel. "No matter what you do with your men in or out of combat, they'll always have your number. They can spot a phony in no time at all. They don't want showmanship, but they do want solid character. Loyalty and respect always starts at the top and flows downward. When it's perceived to be genuine, then it's reciprocated upward from the ranks. Without character you may be able to command, but you can never lead." Inspector Clough had the right kind of character.

Lac St. Jean came into view on the horizon ahead of them, where they would land for a re-supply of fuel. It was a large body of water that stretched for miles. They flew over the Saguenay River and were inspired by the beauty of the precipitous cliffs that lined both banks. The final destination was two more hours due north!

The pilot slowly descended to the water and touched down with a lightness the passengers appreciated. A small crew of uniformed men waited at the wharf as the plane taxied to it. Bob Holden secured the craft with the line thrown to them, and motioned the passengers to get out and stretch their legs. A two-story log cabin at dockside was the local quarters of the R.C.M.P. who had prepared a sumptuous meal for the travelers.

"I never realized a person could get so hungry in a cool airplane," remarked Bob Holden, removing his heavy coat before sitting at the large table prepared for them.

"Eat hearty, my friends, it'll be a long afternoon, and the air gets chillier by the mile," the Inspector said with a smile.

"Thank you, Inspector, and to your men also. This is certainly appreciated," said Mark.

They ate in silence, which was the usual custom in the North Woods. After several helpings of fresh trout and corn bread Mark eased back in his chair to leisurely enjoy the coffee and his faithful pipe. The Inspector did not hurry anybody, but he did not encourage idle chatter either. Time was of the essence, because the weather in the north could change within a very short period of time.

"If everyone is ready, we can start the final leg of our journey. I want to make sure that we have plenty of time before darkness settles in at the village."

The country north of Lac St. Jean was similar to the outskirts of Quebec. Most of the forest was composed of spruce and balsam fir with an occasional pocket of pine, either banksiana or jack pine. The terrain was flat with an absence of large mountains such as the ones that are present south of the St. Lawrence River. The occasional hill appears to be taller than it actually is because of its rarity. The immensity of the area is most noticeable from the air, where you can see in every direction with nothing to break it up except more trees, streams and lakes. The northern forest types of spruce and fir appear dark and forbidding compared to the native white pine type in central New England. There is a marked absence of clearing for farming simply because the soils cannot support agriculture. The forest below was a contradiction. It was fascinating and challenging to Mark, yet it also manifested itself as cold and uninviting. The lengthening shadows of the trees in the waning sun contributed to its onerous atmosphere which definitely held an attraction for him.

Two hours later, a nudge from the Inspector broke Mark's reverie. Inspector Clough pointed downward at a small lake to the east of them as the plane started its gentle glide to the surface of the water. The area surrounding the lake was solid forest except on the western shore where he noticed a cluster of several dwellings. One of them was a church with a white cross plainly visible. The pilot set the plane on the water and taxied to the wharf that extended out into the lake.

There was a single person standing on the pier. He was a short and wiry person with white hair and fine angular features. His clothes did not immediately disclose that he was a catholic priest. He went forward as they climbed onto the dock and cheerfully greeted the passengers, extending his hand. "Welcome to Fort Lewis, my friends."

"Hello, Father," greeted Inspector Clough. "Allow me to introduce you to our new guest, Captain Mark Leroux, of the U.S. Marine Corps. Mark, this is Father Dumont, and this other young man here beside me is Mr. Robert Holden of the American Consulate. Father

Dumont is the administrator for the native tribes in the area and is the father confessor for the poor lost souls that venture into this country."

Mark thought the man had the countenance of a saint as he took his hand. "I'm glad to meet you, Father Dumont."

"It's my pleasure to have you as our guest, Captain. Your arrival is a blessing, Mr. Holden. You're much younger than I imagined you to be. I thought I was corresponding with a gentleman of my own age. Come, my friends, we'll retire to the church hall for some refreshment and prepare for the evening. Nights come rapidly in the North Woods."

It was a short walk from the wharf to the church and hall. The small hamlet was already shrouded in darkness. Dogs barked from the darkened area of the village beyond the church. Mark had the sensation that he was being watched even though the village appeared empty. Large spruce trees towered over the path to the church which was located close to the water's edge. It was a larger structure made from lumber instead of logs, with cedar shingles on the walls and roof. The steeple towered over the roof for two stories, topped with a large white cross. The rectory hall was built out of cedar logs. Lights could be seen coming from the windows in the hall.

Inspector Clough pointed out the substation of the R.C.M.P. which was a small log cabin that served as office and barracks for the men assigned to the patrol. It had a telephone link to the station in Lac St. Jean. A white flag pole stood in front of the trim and functional-looking headquarters.

"This substation acts as a hub for several patrols up to ten men. It was originally a much larger cantonment for the Provincial Police. They previously used the rectory which now serves as an all purpose structure, with the kind priest acting as the genial host to all that come here," said the Inspector with a sweep of his hand.

"Inspector, I noticed a road of sorts leading north. Is it part of any road system?" asked Mark.

"No, only the foot trails and the waterways are used for travel. You can travel to Lac St. Jean by canoe from Lac Diamante with only two portages."

"Welcome to our humble quarters," exclaimed Father Dumont. "We've tried to carve out of the north wilderness a place where man can renew himself. We've prepared a meal for you, and I see that our ever-efficient policemen have already placed your bags in your rooms.

The large room to the right is our dining room. Your rooms are down this hallway. Mr. Holden is on the left, and you, Captain Leroux, are on the right. I hope you'll be comfortable here. When I found out that you were coming, and what you were coming for, my heart rejoiced. I'm looking forward to the opportunity to know you better. We've never met, but I already know much about you, thanks to the Inspector and to Mr. Holden here. I'll admit that my curiosity prompted a lot of questions. One never knows unless one asks." The wiry priest took off the light coat that hid his priestly vestments.

Mark enjoyed the lighthearted candidness of the priest. He also welcomed the opportunity to remove his overcoat. His wool tunic was adequate now that they were on the ground. The hall was warm and inviting.

The evening meal was served in the large dining hall, with a massive fireplace on the east wall. A large spruce log had been split in two with half serving as the mantel above the stone fireplace. Mark liked the informality and warmth of the log cabin. Not only was the room relaxing to his senses, but the meal placed before them was an absolute feast, designed to please the most discriminating palate. The main course was broiled trout in an orange sauce along with thinly sliced venison steaks browned in a raisin sauce. Mashed potatoes, peas and warm fresh rolls rounded out the menu. The scent of fresh coffee could be smelled all over the building.

"I think I'm going to request these kind of assignments from now on," exclaimed Bob Holden with a wide grin on his face.

"You're lucky to be in the care of Father Dumont. His table is renowned in this wilderness region, with just cause." Suddenly, the Inspector became quiet, looking towards the door where Father Dumont was escorting a native young lady dressed in western style clothes toward the table.

"Now my friends, I want you to meet our angel of Fort Lewis and Lac Diamante. I'm pleased to introduce you to Flying Eagle's sister, Danielle Mann. We call her Bright Cloud. Come, my dear, let me present Mr. Robert Holden of the U.S. Consulate."

Bright Cloud gracefully took his hand and said in a voice so melodious, it was almost as if she was singing. "I'm pleased to meet you, Mr. Holden. The good Father here has told me you two corresponded with each other." She stood proud and erect, meeting everyone with a nervous anticipation.

"The pleasure is all mine, Miss Mann, and I must tell you that your beauty surpasses the Inspector's description."

Bright Cloud blushed under Bob Holden's gaze and compliment. She was of average height, but her erect posture created an illusion of being taller. She walked with a smooth fluid motion as if she was gliding across the room. Bright Cloud had the high cheek bones and tanned complexion of her northern Cree heritage. They were enhanced by her clear brown eyes that looked straight at you without deviation. She wore her black hair in two braids that came to the middle of her back, with red ribbons tied at the end of the braids. It was elegant simplicity. She was beautiful by any cultural standards and radiated a gentle graciousness that made those around her feel at ease.

"Our other guest is a person we've been looking forward to meeting for some time. I'm pleased to introduce Captain Mark Leroux. Captain, I proudly present Flying Eagle's sister, Bright Cloud."

Mark was so surprised by her presence that he was momentarily at a loss for words. He saw similarities in her face that reminded him of Flying Eagle. He took her small hand and firmly grasped it in his own. "I must apologize if I stare. You and your brother had a lot in common; the resemblance is uncanny. It's my privilege to make your acquaintance."

"I speak for all my family when I tell you that your visit here means very much to us," she said with sincerity. "Our tribe is honored by the purpose of your visit. Perhaps, now, we can find some release from the sorrow that our loss has created. Thank you for coming, Captain. This day is destined to be one that we will always remember. The words, 'thank you' don't adequately convey our appreciation for your visit."

"This trip is important for me, too," said Mark. "Up until now, I was selfish enough to think that I was the only one to suffer as a result of the war. If my coming to your village helps to alleviate the grief of you and your people it will be worth any effort. I hope that my coming also brings honor and recognition to a very special person. He was my friend and I lost him."

Father Dumont interrupted and gently touched Mark's arm, "The hardest thing that we mortals must learn, my son, is to accept the will of God. We can lighten the load we all carry by making God a partner."

Father gently guided Bright Cloud to an empty chair at the table. "Come, my dear, sit next to me and Captain Leroux."

Conversation flowed freely around the table over several cups of coffee. It was obvious that Father Dumont and the Inspector were held in high esteem by Bright Cloud. The priest was responsible for the administration of the Cree Indians in the area. That position had been appointed by the Federal Bureau of Indian Affairs. One of the major problems that seemed to be increasing was the consumption of illegal whiskey. The Inspector and Bright Cloud talked guardedly about the problem. It was a chronic abuse that required constant vigilance on the part of the police and the Tribal Council.

"Captain Leroux," said Bright Cloud, "Tomorrow, if you would like, I can show you our settlement here at Fort Lewis. I help run the infirmary with another nurse from the missionary branch. A doctor is available only on call from Lac St. Jean, so we're busy most of the time."

"I'd enjoy that. I've never been this far north. The land has a rugged, natural beauty that's hard to resist. The winters must be long and harsh though," answered Mark. Bright Cloud was not the kind of person he expected to find in this secluded wilderness.

"Yes, they're difficult. Spring brings swarms of mosquitoes and black flies. If we didn't have to contend with them, it would be paradise in the North Woods." Bright Cloud was relaxed and easy to talk to. She radiated warmth and sincerity.

Mark was impressed with her intelligence and directness. Many of her mannerisms were similar to ones he had observed in Flying Eagle, such as turning her head slightly away from the person who was talking to her as if she wanted to hear better, and at the same time keeping her dark eyes locked on the speaker. Throughout the evening she continued to press him for anything he could remember about her brother. He had put a lot of effort into forgetting that portion of his life, so he had to concentrate in order to recall things. She seemed to be searching for anything she could find about what Flying Eagle had planned to do after the war.

Flying Eagle had not talked much to Mark about his personal feelings. He talked some about Bright Cloud's education and his own. Neither he nor Mark divulged a whole lot more about their families. Home and family were usually reserved for those quiet moments when they could escape from the reality of the front, which was rare. During and after many discussions, Mark often looked at Flying Eagle and wondered just who the real person was behind the proud face. One topic that was often discussed was the future of the Cree nation and what contributions Flying Eagle could make to alleviate some of the hardships that were endemic to the tribe and to the northland.

Bright Cloud seemed especially pleased to hear about those discussions pertaining to her people. Father Dumont brought the evening meal to a close with a toast, raising a wine glass above his face, and asked for the occasion ahead of them to be blessed with God's Grace. Bright Cloud glanced at Mark as she rose for the toast. Her eyes betrayed a weariness that she had successfully hidden up to that point. They seemed to be searching for answers that Mark feared he could not give, and he had an uncomfortable feeling that he may have let her down.

"I'll see all of you tomorrow. We've a number of patients at the infirmary, and I must go over my rounds one more time tonight. It's been a wonderful evening, Captain."

"My dear, Bright Cloud," interrupted Father Dumont, "You look tired, my child. You work too hard, yet I don't know what I'd ever do without you. But we understand and will see you in the morning. Bonsoir, my angel of the north."

Bright Cloud said her farewells to the other guests and left the room. Mark was a little puzzled by the sudden interruption of Father Dumont. Tomorrow should prove to be an interesting day for everybody, he thought.

Mark and the Inspector started the ritual of filling their pipes with tobacco. Soon the air above the table was filled with smoke from the two contented participants. Father Dumont suggested that they go over the ceremony for tomorrow.

"This is how we've planned it. The tribal council agrees that the ceremony should take place immediately after the memorial Mass for Flying Eagle. You'll be able to talk to the congregation from the pulpit. I expect about 100 people. Some will have traveled from far away. We'll make sure that the Mann family sits at the front. How much time do you need, Captain?"

"I need only ten to fifteen minutes. I have a medal and a framed scroll with a description of the action that earned the citation for Flying Eagle. Both Mr. Holden and the Inspector have assured me that the family understands English. What about the other members of the congregation?" asked Mark.

"They'll be fine," Father Dumont said. "Our mission schools have been very successful with the students over the years. Most will understand enough to know what is happening. Perhaps this is one of our great sins, because we have made many members of the tribe more like us than is good for them. I've talked with Mr. Holden about these things and I don't see any problems with the presentation to Running Deer. Do you have anything to add, Inspector?"

"You've covered it all very well, Father. After the presentation the schedule is up to you and Bob. If the weather holds, we can fly you out late tomorrow or whenever you wish. We're at your service." The Inspector seemed relaxed and content.

"Why don't we see what tomorrow brings and tentatively plan to leave on the day after the presentation," Mark suggested. "I'll be a civilian by then."

"What are your plans for the future, Captain?" inquired the Inspector casually.

"I can't answer that with any certainty. These past few days have taken me from Washington to Maine to Quebec City and now to this beautiful spot in the North Woods. I really don't know what I'm going to do. I would like to do something with my forestry training. However, my highest priority is to overcome and cope with the problems I acquired from the war. I've tried to be honest with myself about my limitations. Therefore, I've got to find myself first before I can be of much help to others."

"I admire your honesty and candor in confronting your priorities, Captain. Self evaluation is not something man does very well," admitted the Inspector.

"May God be with you, my son. If there is nothing else to discuss, with your permission, I'll excuse myself." Father Dumont did not sit still for long. As he passed Mark's chair, he gave him an affectionate pat on the shoulder.

"He surely has to be one of God's most tireless workers. He has been heroic in his labors for the flock," remarked the Inspector. "Never have these people been better served than they are right now. The energetic priest is also, surprisingly, a leading spokesman for the preservation of many of the ancient Indian customs. I must say with all due respect and a certain amount of envy, he's a consummate politician." They all nodded in agreement.

The evening drew out the weariness of the woodland travelers who soon retired to their respective rooms. The Inspector left Mark and Bob to stay at the police quarters next door. The first thought that came to Mark's mind as he stretched out on the bunk was, what am I doing here? He had a feeling it was more than an errand boy delivering a medal. He had also taken on the impossible job of trying to justify Flying Eagle's death to his people. Mark wasn't sure of his ability to accomplish such a task. The uneasy feeling that something besides a simple medal ceremony was afoot at Fort Lewis continued to plague him. He had sensed it earlier with Bright Cloud and Father Dumont. Mark wasn't so sure about the Inspector.

He could hear the anxious barking of a dog in the village. It was soon taken up by a band of wolves in the distant forest. The lonely primal sound echoed across the lake, giving Mark a compelling sense of loneliness. There was a part of Mark that responded to the cries of the distant timber wolves, a mythical kinship and an instinctive fear of being alone. Melancholic emotions flooded over him for no apparent reason. The land was working its spell upon him. He wasn't sure if the spell was going to be a charm or a curse. Entwined with the howl of the wolves, Mark also picked up the mournful call of loons talking to each other from across the lake.

Mark's final thoughts of the evening were about Bright Cloud. Never had he seen such simple beauty in a person. He tried to recall any conversations with Flying Eagle about her. At a young age, they were both uprooted from their surroundings and transplanted to the distant world of the white man. Academically, they both did very well, but socially, they were poorly equipped to handle the racial prejudices that existed in their new environment. He could remember Flying Eagle's reluctance to voluntarily get involved socially with the other officers of the company and battalion. One example was his habit of not speaking unless he was spoken to, and he never volunteered suggestions unless specifically asked for an opinion. Mark always attributed it to the inherent modesty and reserve that was a large part of his personality. Tonight, he better understood that part of him for the first time. It had been a natural defense system against rejection. Mark's admiration and respect deepened for the courage and perseverance required by Bright Cloud and Flying Eagle to seek education in the outside world.

The next morning, sunshine filled Mark's room with the promise of new and exciting experiences. A loud knock came at the door while he was still in that lazy state of mind between deep sleep and being awake.

"It's me, Bob Holden. Just checking to see if you're awake. I'll finish dressing and meet you soon. I hope you slept well, you snored enough to be heard through two doors," laughed Bob.

"I'll see you shortly," said Mark, jumping out of bed, checking his watch. He wanted to look his best for today, so he hurried to get shaved and ready. He met Bob Holden in the large dining room within twenty minutes.

"Good morning, Bob. I would have overslept if you hadn't been my alarm. I slept like a log once I got to sleep."

"I'm an early bird by nature. Some of the sounds outside kept me awake. Did you hear those wolves howling?"

"Yes." Mark silently chuckled to himself, amused at Bob's reaction.

"I'm not accustomed to that type of thing. I came from Philadelphia where we have wolves only in zoos. I'm glad to hear you rested well. Today will be the end of the trail for your project. I talked to the Inspector and he agreed to go out tomorrow as long as the weather holds. I told him it was up to you. As for me, I'm flexible."

"What did you think of Flying Eagle's sister last night?"

"Mark, I can tell you one thing," Bob Holden announced enthusiastically. "I've seen a lot of pretty women in my short career, but she is by far one of the loveliest persons I've ever met." Mark nodded in agreement. "She's attractive, and that natural modesty, typical of her people, is very becoming. I liked her very much and was impressed with her honesty and integrity. Quebec City and Montreal would be hard pressed to find a match for her."

"You've put my own thoughts into words. I remember Flying Eagle talking about her, but he never mentioned her beauty. These people are lucky to have such a dedicated person working for their welfare," Mark answered.

As they talked, two Cree women entered the room carrying a large pot of coffee, a plate of muffins, and several containers of spreads. They were shy at first, but Bob made them feel at ease with a handshake and a smile. They made a hasty retreat to the kitchen area as soon as they served the two men at the table.

"Father Dumont asked me to tell you that he would return in plenty of time for the Mass. He's gone to deliver communion to an elderly couple that cannot travel. That man is a bundle of energy. I could never keep up with him, and I'm forty years younger!"

"He certainly keeps on top of things," Mark mumbled, stuffing his mouth with a warm corn muffin topped with apple jelly.

"The Inspector and the Father have their hands full. Life here must be difficult. Long periods of isolation along with the despair that comes with subsistence living are fertile grounds for alcoholism," Bob replied with a concerned look on his face.

"You're right, Bob." Mark replied. "As soon as I finish this coffee, I'm going to take a look around the village. Want to come along?" asked Mark.

"Sure. I'd like to stretch my legs. It looks like another good day. You must realize, Mark, that you're bringing more than recognition to these people. You're reinforcing their pride in themselves, also. It'll add to their sense of self-worth. You offer a valuable gift that will help them find a place in our more complicated world. This is another good example of the hands across the border between Canada and the United States."

There was a flurry of activity outside the door. Mark and Bob could see Father Dumont in a very animated discussion with Bright Cloud. He was gesturing with his two arms in mid-air. He finally shrugged his shoulders in a last measure of displeasure as Bright Cloud quickly bolted through the door holding the hand of a small child. With a reluctant glance towards the priest, she defiantly walked directly to the table and greeted them.

"Captain Leroux, Mr. Holden," she acknowledged, standing the young child on a chair directly in front of them. "I hope your evening was a restful one. I came here early this morning to introduce you to a young lady of four years old that has captured the hearts of everybody at Fort Lewis. We call her Bright Star because she has been a ray of hope in the same way the North Star is a beacon for my people. It's fitting and proper that you meet her now, because she is Flying Eagle's daughter!"

Chapter Six

Mark and Robert stood up from the table as Bright Cloud approached with the little girl. Mark did not know that Flying Eagle had a child, or had been married. He didn't know what to say. Kneeling before the little girl, Mark took her small hand in his. Her dark eyes shined intently at him from a tiny round face. She was not afraid of these strange men, but she was not totally comfortable with them either. Bright Star still clasped her aunt's hand as if it was a lifeline.

"Hello, Bright Star. My name is Mark. I'm happy to see you this morning." She was dressed in a combination of traditional and modern clothing. Her colorful red wool shirt was tucked into blue corduroy pants such as could be purchased at the Hudson Bay Store. On her feet she wore moccasins decorated with beads and porcupine quills. Her shining black hair was loosely woven into two long braids with a red ribbon tied at the end of each, much like Bright Cloud wore again this morning. The child was adorable.

Mark smiled and turned to Bright Cloud. "I didn't know about Bright Star. I'm surprised your brother never mentioned her to me. Her name is appropriate, she's precious. I'm glad you brought her to meet us."

"Star, you go along to the good Father and listen to him. I'll be with you shortly." Star happily skipped away to find the Priest beyond the entrance.

"We call her Star for short. I had a feeling you didn't know. It was typical of my brother to keep such things to himself. Please, sit down and continue your breakfast. With your permission, I'd like to take a moment of your time to tell you his story so that you can better understand the whole person. My brother was a visionary in many ways. I'm sure he would have been successful in whatever he attempted to do in life, if he had not been killed. You must have seen that side of him too, Captain. From the time he was a young man he yearned to do something that would make life easier for our people. He knew that down through the ages changes were made to accommodate circumstances. The Crees were traditionally nomadic hunters. When the tradesmen came to these lands, a change took place that turned the Crees forever towards the path of the white man. Pelts were traded for goods and more permanent homes were established. Many of the old ways were ignored and forgotten. That was fine as long as the animals were plentiful. When the animals were scarce, poverty and starvation became a part of our daily life. Dependency on outside resources was a necessity for the first time in the history of the proud Cree Nation. That is not to say it is good or bad, only that it's the real situation. Fear of the future, dependency on the government, and loss of pride have been heavy burdens for my people.

"Whiskey has also become a problem for those that are without hope. The very future of the Crees is threatened by this despair. Our people are at a crossroad that will affect the future. I apologize for telling you these things, but I think it's important for you to better understand the world in which we live," she looked warily at the two men.

"Bright Cloud, believe me, we're interested. Please continue," Mark replied. Bob nodded in agreement.

"My father learned to read and write from the Jesuit missionaries, and he was determined that Flying Eagle and I should have the chances that he never had. He thought that the way to strengthen our culture was through education. That meant adapting to the white man's world in some ways; but, in doing so, maybe some of the traditions of the Cree people can be kept alive. It's hard to be both, for you could lose your identity and maybe end up being neither." She paused for a second, with a forlorn look of weariness on her face. "My father received an offer for the two of us to be educated in the United States. He was proud of us both when we accepted. We both went to Syracuse University, my brother obtained an engineer degree, and I studied nursing. There was some animosity within the tribe about this, but it soon disappeared when it was known that we would be back to help where we could.

"Flying Eagle went through the ROTC program, as you did, Captain. The last time he came home before going to France, he married a girl he has loved since childhood. They were together for just a few days and were so happy. Star is a true love child in every way. Her mother died in childbirth at our infirmary. Writing the sad news to Flying Eagle was the hardest thing I've ever had to do. I had a feeling you didn't know, Captain. It would be like him not to say anything about his personal problems. I never had a good chance to tell him how proud I was of him, or to say good-bye." Sadness once again touched her face.

Mark was concerned and surprised, yet it also angered him that Flying Eagle chose to suffer such devastating news all by himself. Bright Cloud seemed relieved for the opportunity to unburden herself in front of the two strangers. Mark could feel the pain she tried to hide.

"I never knew about his wife or Bright Star. I'm amazed to think that he endured such a tragedy on top of all we went through together. He was a strong man, that's for sure. It's a blessing to have little Star."

Bob Holden had been as engrossed in the story as Mark. He added softly: "That's one of the saddest stories I've ever heard. What a legacy for the child."

"Father Dumont and many others in the village thought it would be easier to simply say nothing. I disagreed with them. It's a part of my brother's life and I thought that you, of all people, had a right to know the whole truth."

"Thank you for your candor and for bringing me into your circle of confidence. I appreciate the gesture. Flying Eagle treated his men the same way as he would members of his own family. I tell you this because he worked and functioned in an atmosphere of trust and respect. Every man that served in his command had nothing but praise for him. It was a sad day when Flying Eagle left us." Mark looked directly at Bright Cloud. He saw the hurt and grief she was carrying and hoped, somehow, he was not adding to her burden.

"Thank you, Captain, for the kind words. Now, if you'll excuse me, I've got to care for Star. After the Mass, I can show you around if you like." Bright Cloud got up to leave.

"That'll be fine. I look forward to it," answered Mark.

"There goes a remarkable young lady," Bob said.

Mark and Bob went outside to walk down the path towards the wharf. The morning air had the sweet feel of Spring. You could smell the spruce and fir distinctly. Mixed with it was the sweet cinnamon aroma of large-toothed-aspen. The natural world was springing back to life after a long winter of dormancy. The sun was warm, but the air still had a chill to it in the shade. The float plane rocked gently at the dock. Beyond the dock was another one wider and longer, belonging to the Hudson Bay Company store south of the police station. The store was a large structure made of cedar logs positioned near the end of the dock closer to the water than any of the other buildings. A smaller cabin was constructed near the main building with a platform connecting the two. This was where the Hudson Bay Factor lived.

They were amazed to find such a large variety of goods and foodstuffs available on the well-stocked shelves. It was the first Hudson Bay Store either had ever encountered. Past the store to the south, away from the village, the trail narrowed to a single path.

One thing Mark noticed was the absence of black flies. It was still a little early for them. When the spring hatch eventually takes place, a person could be driven mad without protection from the relentless little creatures. Noting that it was not wise to venture too far, Mark and Bob turned to retrace their steps when they saw the Inspector coming towards them in long powerful strides.

"Good morning, gentlemen. I see you're up and about early this morning. From what you've seen, are your impressions favorable towards our little village on Lac Diamante?"

"One word to describe it is peaceful. That's a state of mind as much as a description of a place. It's an idyllic setting at this end of the lake. A person could certainly be content here," Mark exclaimed.

"I was hoping you'd find it that way," the policeman replied. "I come here as often as I can on my own patrols and I stay longer than at other outposts. I've always been welcome here, and I can assure you that policemen are not welcome in many places. Most of the French speaking citizens in the Province view the police with skepticism simply because we represent authority by way of Britain instead of from France."

"Things aren't so much different here in Canada as they are in the States. It probably depends more on the man than on the uniform," said Mark as the Inspector fell in step beside them.

"I'm going to get ready for the Mass. You should also, Mark. Father Dumont runs a tight ship; he tolerates late arrivals, but he doesn't like it."

Back at the church hall, Mark put on a fresh set of Marine Corps greens for the ceremony, giving himself a final check in the mirror on the wall. The two Marine emblems on his high collar were a gift from his father when he received his commission. He wore all of the ribbons he had earned in the Corps on his left breast. This special occasion was important enough to justify them. Snapping his leather Sam Brown belt in place completed his preparations. He was ready for the morning's work. Perhaps, he thought, this would be the only time these people would ever have a chance to see a marine from the United States of America in full uniform.

"Time to go, Captain," announced the Inspector, entering the room in his bright red tunic.

"I'm all set, Sir," Mark replied.

They collected Bob Holden in the hallway and headed for the church, entering it from a side door. Father Dumont asked them to follow him into the sacristy beside the altar. Three chairs had been provided for them. The priest and the young server boy took their seats opposite the three guests.

Mark had never been to a civilian Catholic service before, and he felt slightly out of place. It seemed much more formal than the Methodist services he attended as a young man with his father and Aunt Maddie. The church was already full of people curiously watching Mark. He recognized Bright Cloud in the front row. Little Star sat between her and an older man with white hair, whom Mark assumed to be Running Deer. He did not want to stare, but Flying Eagle's father fascinated him.

Running Deer was about the same size as Flying Eagle, maybe a little heavier around the chest. His Cree heritage was evident. He was looking piously at the altar with a rosary in his hand and was praying, apparently unperturbed by the presence of strangers. Mark was nervous, because he wanted to do the presentation so that everybody could understand what he was saying. He kept telling himself to be calm for a little longer. All eyes in the church still seemed to be bearing on him. There was no way to avoid them. He understood their curiosity and concern. Mark did not detect animosity towards him, but neither did he feel acceptance.

Father Dumont made some announcements from the pulpit first, then proceeded to conduct the Mass at the altar. Mark thought it was beautiful. Bob Holden had provided him with a missal so that he could follow the Latin liturgy a little easier. After communion, the Priest introduced the Inspector who was encouraged to say a few words. Inspector Clough effortlessly climbed the two steps to the pulpit and with a pensive air looked out at the crowded church, pausing for a moment, as if to recall what he was about to say to the congregation.

"You people already know who I am and why I'm here, but let me remind you that not too long ago I was far away in a land where death and destruction was taking place on a scale beyond your wildest imagination. As a Canadian soldier, I had the opportunity to visit several units from the armed forces of the United States, our neighbor to the south. It was a privilege for me to observe such fine men fighting our common enemy. One of the best troop commanders I observed is here with us today. Those same qualities that made him a popular officer will be apparent to all of you shortly as you get to know him.

"Flying Eagle was a Canadian Cree Indian, yet he served in the United States Army because it gave him the opportunity to rise to his fullest potential. The enemy he fought was a common foe of all men who value peace and freedom of choice. It's my pleasure to introduce Captain Mark Leroux. He has traveled on a long journey to bring a message of hope and appreciation to our small village. His presence among us brings great honor and tribute to one of our own. My fellow villagers, take this young man into your hearts and welcome him with the warmth I know you are capable of giving." When the Inspector finished with his introductory message, the small church was deathly silent. The congregation drank his every word, and were now ready to hear what the stranger among them had to say.

"Thank you, Father Dumont and Inspector Clough," Mark acknowledged the two men with a large knot in his stomach. "It's a privilege for me to be here in your beautiful village on the shore of Lac Diamante. We're gathered here, today, to honor the person whom you called Flying Eagle. I knew him as First Lieutenant Joseph Mann of the United States Army, who commanded one of the platoons in my company of four platoons. The government of the United States has asked me to come to your village to pay tribute to his courage and pay homage to the selfless warrior that he became. It's an honor and a privilege for me to be the bearer of this message of appreciation. I first met Flying Eagle when he was ordered to our regiment in France as a platoon leader. I was his company commander and within a short period of time, we became close friends. I admired his profound goodness. He was a great leader to his men who, in turn, respected him for his solicitation on their behalf. I cannot adequately describe what the conditions were like in the fighting trenches of France, so I will not even try, but you should be aware that any man subjected to the brutality and to the terror that is a daily occurrence at the front, is marked forever as a member of that select fraternity of warriors. Only the strong or lucky survived. The gentle and caring nature of Flying Eagle was tormented perhaps more than others who cared less." In his mind, Mark could still see the two of them on that last day of combat. They were exhausted physically and spiritually. It took concentrated effort to say something when the spirit has been so completely purged. It was like being in a dream, but the smell of cordite and the filth in the trenches along with the screams of the wounded quickly brought you back to reality. No, Mark thought to himself, I cannot tell these people what it was really like and maybe, it's just as well…

"In the gentle rolling hills of France, the prevailing north winds caress the beautiful final resting place of Flying Eagle and his brother warriors. The guns are now silent, and if you listen closely, you can actually hear birds singing in the summer sun. Peace and solitude have finally come to the battlefield. It is not an empty place, for the spirits of thousands of young men, who will remain forever young, grace these sacred resting places with their silent pleas to all of us...do not forget their sacrifice. Nobody can appreciate the tranquility any more than those fallen soldiers buried beneath the well trimmed graves. It's truly a beautiful place, and I think you would all agree with me if you were to see it. I had the opportunity to visit the location before I left France. The graves are being permanently memorialized with a large monument, under construction at the time of my visit, by a thankful French people, and a saddened American nation. One inscription I saw being chiseled into a granite marker simply said: 'Virtue and Courage Are Their Own Monument and Reward'.

"Flying Eagle sacrificed his own life to save mine. It was not something he had to do, but it was a measure of the man's devotion to others that made him come to my aid during a violent enemy attack. I survived the onslaught; he did not. His death was one of thousands on that same day, yet his unselfish bravery will always be an inspiration for me. His short life and legacy of service to others is a memorial to the human spirit's abounding ability to perform noble deeds.

"I'm not able to answer your inquiring eyes. I wish that I could ease your loss and lighten your heavy hearts. The victory of winged death is complete. I can understand your sorrow. He was one of your own, and he was like a brother to me, too. Though he has gone from our midst, he still remains in our hearts. With these thoughts I extend to all of you my own hand of fellowship.

"The Army of the United States of America takes pride in awarding the Distinguished Service Cross in recognition of Flying Eagle's heroic service to the cause of freedom. I personally bear witness to that bravery above and beyond the call of duty. It's an inadequate tribute to the sacrifice he has made, but it's given in order for his loved ones to share in his deeds, and for future generations to honor his valor.

"I'm a humble bearer of this symbolic tribute to your son, Running Deer. Please accept it as a part of Flying Eagle's enduring legacy."

Mark carefully stepped from the pulpit toward Running Deer and Bright Cloud. Mark's hands trembled slightly as he opened the blue felt case of the medal and held it in front of Running Deer. Uncontrolled tears streamed down Running Deer's bronze face, clouding his vision. Mark held out the case for him to take and extended a hand across the pew. Running Deer took the case and the handshake and said in a barely audible voice, choked with emotion, "Thank you very much."

Mark was having trouble controlling his own emotions, too. He felt the eyes of Bright Cloud upon him, and without another word or gesture, returned to his seat between the Inspector and Bob Holden.

The beautiful medal was striking to Running Deer. It had a blue ribbon with small red and white stripes on both edges. Hanging beneath the ribbon was a bronze cross with an eagle perched at the center of the cross ready for flight. Beneath the eagle on a scroll was the simple phrase - For Valor. Running Deer passed it on for Bright Cloud to examine more closely. He wished that he could say the words his heart felt, but they did not come to his lips. He thought the young Captain understood what was in his heart when their eyes met.

The Priest completed the service, asking Mark to accompany him to the front of the church so that he could be personally introduced to the members of the congregation. The tireless Father Dumont seemed to know everybody by their first names. Anxious to get a closer look at the young marine, the villagers greeted him with warmth and sincerity, and thanked him for coming. Men with grips of steel not knowing what to say, let their hearts speak through their eyes. These hardy people had accepted his presence. Some young teen-aged girls took his hand with shy smiles and suppressed giggles.

Running Deer was at the very end of the procession. He spoke directly to Mark: "You bring great honor to me and to my family. I thank you for that. I also thank your government for recognizing and paying tribute to my son's bravery. I'll remember this day for the rest of my life. My son wrote about you in his letters. You have made a sad day a little less sad for me, young man. Thank you for making the journey to our village."

Bright Cloud stood quietly beside him with little Star's hand in hers. Her eyes had a questioning look that surprised Mark. "The beautiful medal will be revered in our home, Captain Leroux. Thank you for coming. Maybe now the healing can begin."

"I'm pleased you've found some comfort by my visit. It's been an emotional experience for all of us," Mark replied.

Bright Star was restless under the tight control of her Aunt, so Bright Cloud passed her hand over to Running Deer who gladly accepted it with a smile. "We'll head home soon, Star. You must visit our home before you leave us, Captain."

"I promise to come before I leave, Sir," answered Mark.

"Father," announced Bright Cloud. "Yesterday, I promised Captain Leroux a tour of our village. This seems like a good time if he wishes."

"Yes, it's my pleasure."

"Before you two leave," the elderly Priest remarked. "I want this young soldier to know that he brought a large measure of pride to this tiny hamlet. Your visit has impacted their lives more than you can imagine. Thank you, my son. God bless you for caring."

Mark blushed under such lavish praise and was glad to be on his way with Bright Cloud.

"Father Dumont is right, Captain. Today will be a special memory for those of us who remember and honor the past," Bright Cloud said in a soft voice beside him.

"Your father is just like Flying Eagle described him. Your brother was very proud of him and talked about him often. He also spoke of you with a lot of admiration and affection."

"Did he ever talk to you about the problems facing our people?"

"You must realize that about the only time we had for quiet talk was during the lulls between shelling and actual combat. We were in the last stages of the war and there was a ferocity of effort on both sides that took on a life of its own. When we did talk, it was about the horror around us. We all found some release in remembering the pleasant things in our past, yet everybody had his own private wall built around him that prevented anyone else from knowing what he thought about many things. Friendships could frequently be a source of pain when one was killed. It became easier to accept what was taking place around us if we didn't get too involved. So in answer to your question, no, he didn't talk much about the plight of your people."

Mark and Bright Cloud walked north along a wooded path barely wide enough to squeeze a wagon through. Log cabins were spaced at short intervals along the walkway on the left. The log cabins reminded him of the cabin his father and uncles had built on Moosehead Lake for hunting and fishing trips. They looked sturdy and comfortable; most had a wisp of smoke curling from the chimneys. On the right side of the track was the church, next to the infirmary where Bright Cloud worked, and two other cabins directly on the shore of the lake.

"There's still a coolness in the air. I don't mind it because the black flies are not out yet," commented Bright Cloud.

The path came to a fast running stream with large logs placed across it for a bridge. Another trail turned west along the bank of the brook and disappeared from sight. "This spring," said Bright Cloud, pointing to a small pond-like area to the right of the path, "is our water supply for the village. It forms a pool below the bridge for storage of the water. That path to your left leads to a large ridge that helps protect the village from severe winter winds from the north. At the top of the hill is a formation called Lookout Rock where you can see for miles to the east and south. My brother and I used to play there a lot when we were small. My father's cabin is over the bridge and to the right."

She pointed to a small cabin similar to the others in the village, except that it occupied a beautiful location on the water's edge. Two or three cords of dry wood were neatly stacked against the north wall. Bright Cloud did not attempt to walk towards the cabin. She was acting different, but Mark did not know her that well and thought nothing about it.

"Captain," she finally blurted out in desperation. "Do you have any plans for yourself after today?"

It was such a direct question, he was unable to give an answer immediately. He looked at her and for the first time since he had met her, she avoided his eyes.

"I don't know for sure. A lot of things have crossed my mind. Why do you ask this of me? I'm a little baffled by your inquiry." Mark answered in a firm tone.

"Oh, I haven't handled it well," she cried in a nervous state of mind. "Sometimes my boldness gets me into trouble. Forgive me, Captain, please excuse me. I'd like very much to go back to the Mounted Police station, where you'll be able to, understand…" She ran back down the trail with Mark at her side, wondering what kind of problem he had stumbled into.

They hurriedly made their way past the church to the RCMP Station. The Inspector held the door open for them shaking his head and smiling, as he patiently closed the door.

"You two look like you're in a hurry and in search of some explanations."

"That's an understatement, Inspector," said Mark, snatching his hat off and placing it on the table in the middle of the room.

"I'll explain," started the Inspector.

"No, Inspector, it's my place to ask the Captain. I owe him that courtesy," demanded Bright Cloud wearily sitting down at the table.

By this time Mark was losing his composure. He was angry at both the Inspector and Bright Cloud for such treatment. "Won't someone tell me what's going on! I'm not enjoying this mystery in the least, you know."

"I'm sure you're not, Captain," confessed Bright Cloud with a distressed look on her face. "Please, sit down and accept my apologies. We certainly didn't intend to make this day anything but what you have already made of it for the whole village. I feel ashamed for my impulsive timing." Mark sat down opposite her, as she continued: "From the very first moment we knew that it was you who was coming with the medal, it was our intention to ask something of you when you arrived at the village. Our little conspiracy has spread far, I'm afraid, and that's why I wanted to speak to you before anyone else slipped with our secret. We're a proud people and do not ask for favors easily.

These hard times have made us even more desperate than ever before. We need help from you, not just because you were a friend of Flying Eagle, but because you're a professional forester." Bright Cloud blurted out the last sentence, relieved that it was now out in the open.

The Inspector quietly took a seat beside Bright Cloud and watched Mark's reaction. Anyone would have been surprised at such a request under the circumstances, and Mark was no exception. He searched for the right words. "Let me explain something, Captain," he said, looking at a flustered Bright Cloud. "I was hoping you wouldn't spring this on him out of the blue, Bright Cloud."

"Inspector, I'm beginning to wonder! Why do you need the services of a forester?" Mark had finally found his voice.

"Simple question, Captain. It deserves a simple answer, but that's not possible. In essence, the Crees here in the Lac Diamante area have been granted a large area of land for the tribal council to own and manage as official tribal lands. Normally, land is not deeded to Indians, but the federal government has given the provinces the right and obligation to settle the grievances of the different tribes in regard to traditional hunting and fishing regions. They're not farmers because the soil will not support crops. They've always been a hunting people. That is slowly changing. The tribes are becoming more and more like the whites as a means of bettering their way of life. I'm not going to debate the merits or the dangers of the trend right now." The Inspector could see that Mark still had not received answers that meant anything to him.

"I know you're bursting with questions, Captain. Let me impose upon you for a little longer and they'll soon be answered. Without any more background, the fact remains that the Lac Diamante Crees have about thirty thousand acres of forest land that may be taken from them if they don't develop a forest management plan for it and convince the Provincial authorities that they are dependent on it for a part of their livelihood. Bright Cloud's people need someone such as yourself to document that need and to develop a workable plan in order to satisfy the Provincial authorities and to utilize some of the labor of the local tribe. It's a task only a professional could do. Therefore, Captain, we hoped that you could be persuaded to accept the task."

"What do you mean? I'm a stranger not just to their homeland but to their culture. I'm also an American national," Mark answered sharply. He did not know if he was being hoodwinked or being honored by this consideration. Flying Eagle had saved his life, but now...

"I think it must sound bizarre to you," cried Bright Cloud in a wavering voice. She made another one of those hand gestures that was a part of her spontaneous nature and continued, "I hope you're not offended by our request for your assistance. The original idea came from my brother in a letter to me. I've kept it in my heart as a dream for my people since the day I received it. I shared it with the Inspector one day, and he suggested that we see what could be done." The strain and the tension in the room was giving Bright Cloud grave misgivings about being a party to the conspiracy.

At this point, without hearing another word from the other two people in the room, Mark thought he saw how it all came together! He had been dubbed into making the trip on the pretext of honoring Flying Eagle. It had been nothing but a conspiracy from the start. Mark nervously left his seat because he could no longer remain calm and sit idle. He felt used and betrayed, and it hurt.

"Captain, I understand your feelings, but our reason for not soliciting an answer from you any sooner was out of consideration for your health," the Inspector was talking as fast as he could. "Once you were here, we thought you'd understand the need for your services. Duplicity was not our intent. Our respect for you is the same as Flying Eagle's respect when he was alive. I felt it was better for you to come here first. When we heard about the medal, it was your friend Major Korsman who suggested you as a courier. I'm sorry, my friend. I apologize for my insensitivity; I see now that I was wrong." The Inspector was stunned by Mark's reaction and sat motionless at the table.

"The fault is all mine," cried Bright Cloud. "This has been handled so badly. You've earned my respect and I feel terrible that I've been responsible for making you feel distrustful of us. You, of all people, do not deserve to be treated with any ill will. I'm sorry and I ask your forgiveness," Bright Cloud pleaded. "This is a letter from Flying Eagle to me. It was his last one and I treasure it more than anything in the world. You're mentioned in the letter, and maybe it will help explain how things worked out, and why we placed our last hopes upon you, Captain. I only ask you to look at the purity of our intentions."

Mark carefully read the letter in silence.

Somewhere in France

Dear Sister,

I hope and pray that the peace and tranquility of Lac Diamante are the same as when I left. I can imagine all of you safe there and it gives me comfort. I'm saddened still by the news of Minnie, she was a wonderful person and I loved her dearly. Little Bright Star helps to overcome the loss of her mother; but, to be honest, it doesn't make the pain go away. It isn't fair for someone so gentle as Minnie to be taken from me. She had become my world and now all our dreams are for nothing. If I sound bitter, it is because I am. I apologize...

As for you, Bright Cloud, no brother ever had a more loving, generous sister than I do. Thank you for your care of Star. It must be a burden on top of your work building the infirmary. Someday I'll make it up to you, I promise, but for now all I can say is thank God you are there. I'm so proud of your accomplishments, especially going to school and returning home to help our people. I hope everybody appreciates what you do for them.

My platoon is busy at the front. The fighting is intense, and I am glad we have Captain Leroux as our company commander. He's a fine officer that makes everybody do their job. I admire him and respect his judgment. I'm glad to call him a friend. He's unique in the Army because he's a Marine officer. He once told me there are several others like him because there is not enough Marine units to go around. Lucky for us!

The other day I found out that he was a professional forester and plans to return to Maine after the war and work with woodland owners. Maybe I could ask him to develop a system of management for the tribal lands. I haven't had a chance to mention this to him, yet, but I shall very soon. I know that I could work with him and accomplish much for our people.

I don't want you to worry about me, I am in good hands. I don't think much about death, but it must be faced honestly. If it is my fate to be called I want you to know that my last thoughts will be of my wonderful family. In that event, tell little Star that her father will always be watching over her. I will be as close to her as death allows.

Thank you, Sis, for being all that you are. I send all my love to everybody.

Your brother,

Flying Eagle

Bright Cloud watched Mark read the letter with anxious, searching eyes and could see that the letter had opened up old feelings to the point where Mark seemed to be having difficulty maintaining his composure in front of her. It was as if he was still at the front with Flying Eagle. Mark's neck muscles flexed with tension. Perspiration formed in tiny beads across his forehead as he finished reading the letter and placed it on the table. He was seized with emotion and avoided Bright Cloud's searching stare because he was uncomfortable having her see him in such a vulnerable state. She instinctively reached for his hand as he released the letter. It was a simple act of compassion on her part. Mark responded by taking her slender hand in both of his, and for the first time since receiving the news of Flying Eagle's death, Bright Cloud lost control. She wept unashamedly, silently thanking God for the release that had come to her troubled soul.

The Inspector was a reluctant witness to a true catharsis for two different people from two different cultures. He may even have been witness to a miracle worked upon the lives of two people burdened beyond their years. He had known Bright Cloud ever since she was a young girl, and he marveled at the energy and dedication she put into her work, rarely taking a moment for herself. He thought she overdid things by running the infirmary, and caring for her father and Bright Star all at the same time. Maybe there wasn't sufficient time for her to grieve. Now it all came out in a torrent as her slender body convulsed in emotional release. This incident with Mark had opened the pressure valve, and it had to run its course…

The transformation on Mark was subtle, but nevertheless positive. After several minutes of silence, except for Bright Cloud's soul wrenching sobs, Mark felt better. This experience with the Inspector and Bright Cloud had an intimacy that touched him with the power of their mutual feelings. The room was filled with raw emotions so strong that they touched everyone's heart. It was a sharply intimate display of human grief and compassion.

"I'm sorry that I proved so difficult to approach with this request," Mark admitted haltingly. "In answer to your request, yes, I'll take the job if you still want me. The honor of helping to fulfill one of Flying Eagle's dreams would be a pleasure, as far as I'm concerned."

Bright Cloud turned away from the table with handkerchief in hand to collect her thoughts. She was still speechless but nodded her head in acknowledgment of his offer to help. She was exhausted and drained of energy. She avoided the looks of the two men, and remained quiet in her chair.

The Inspector had not said a word for fear of breaking the spell that hung over the little station. He knew that he had been a spectator to a very special event. "I have maps of the area here at the station. We would also be glad to have you bunk here with us if you wish, Captain. I know this is a sudden move on your part and you may want to take time to think it over. In these latitudes, the summer is pleasant and short, but the flies and mosquitoes are bothersome. They're usually gone by the end of July, at which time it's great to be in the forest. Winter, however, comes early and can be harsh and long."

Mark did not respond to the Inspector immediately; he had a lot of things spinning around in his head. He was interested in assisting the Cree Nation, but he needed time to think about it and examine the magnitude of the commitment he was undertaking.

"Obviously, I'm unprepared to do anything immediately. How far is the tract from Lac Diamante, anyway? "

The Inspector pointed to a wall map and placed his finger on one spot. "This is the Tribal forest area right here."

It was a vast parcel of forest land outlined on a Provincial map with black ink, approximately a ten mile square. Mark hadn't realized that they were as far north as the map indicated. He understood now why the air outside was so brisk for this time of year. The area was a maze of rivers and ponds, with no roads whatsoever. The nearest one was at Lac St. Jean. At a quick glance, it appeared to him that the only way to move logs to market would be by water. The Inspector read his mind.

"There's a direct flow on the Swift River that cuts the tract in half, through the land of Quebec Paper Company, to meet up with the Diamond River from the lake here. As a matter of fact, I believe the riparian rights to these two rivers have been secured by Father Dumont for the tribal council. That gives water access directly to Lac St. Jean." Inspector Clough continued with a somber tone. "These people are in need of any help they can get. The most important thing I can impress upon you is that they value their traditional way of life above all else. Sure the native Crees have taken advantage of many things from the white man's world, but it is not their intention to lose identity in the changeover. The change started long ago with the new markets available for their furs. They just simply adapted to a way of life that was easier and more productive for them. However, the reality is that the Crees still need water and land to survive."

"You're a noble spokesman for them, Inspector. If I had known about this sooner, I would have come more prepared. As it is, I've packed only two uniforms with me and no field clothes. Before I can do anything I need access to a forestry library, and some special forestry instruments. The more I think about it, the more I'm beginning to like the idea," Mark answered with a sparkle in his eye.

Suddenly, there was a flurry of footsteps at the door when a young boy burst into the room without knocking and cried hysterically, "Old Louie is at the infirmary and is breaking everything up!" The Inspector was out the door before the frightened boy could finish.

Bright Cloud had regained some degree of calmness and ran through the door, calling to Mark, "Come Captain, this is not pretty, but you may as well see it now." They both ran as fast as they could toward the infirmary. Bright Cloud beat him to the dwelling.

When they entered the front door they saw a slovenly dressed Indian of powerful and heavy set dimensions threatening the Inspector with a scalpel in one hand and a hunting knife in the other. Bright Cloud grabbed Mark's arm and kept him from entering the room. "It's best this way," she exclaimed excitedly.

Mark had seen his share of fights between men, and it looked as if the Inspector might need some help. "Inspector…"

"Not now, Captain. I've done this several times with this man. He knows the drill. If he doesn't drop both weapons, I'll hurt him, and he knows it." Before the words were spoken, the Inspector lurched at the huge man with both hands, grabbing the assailant's arms, thrusting them upward and inward at the same time. The movement was followed by a swift knee jerk to the groin of the assailant with all the speed and strength the powerful policeman could muster.

Mark could not help from wincing at the potent maneuver. As expected, it instantly dropped the large man to the floor senseless with a muffled groan on his heavy lips.

"Is he all right?" asked Bright Cloud. "You can put him in the bed by the door if you like."

"He's all right now," remarked the Inspector slightly out of breath. "When he wakes up he may be a little weak, and probably as humble as ever. Captain, can you give me a hand with him? He weighs a ton."

They both had all they could do to lift the dead weight of the Indian onto the bed. It was one of several arranged so that each patient had a view of the lake. The infirmary was immaculate with the pungent smell of disinfectant hanging heavy in the air. Several patients were occupying the beds. A slight figure was bent over the patient nearest the ruckus in case protection was needed. There was something familiar about the movements of the frightened nurse that caught Mark's attention. In the excitement of the situation Mark racked his brain trying to place the person and was shocked when she turned towards them. It was Michelle Gurney.

Chapter Seven

Two people could not have been more surprised than Mark and Michelle Gurney. A chance meeting in a remote wilderness hundreds of miles from their last location was amazing. She recognized him immediately and rushed, smiling, to take his hand. The excitement about Louie was enough for Michelle, but the shock of seeing a person she had only briefly met under vastly different circumstances a few days ago, flustered her normally well-composed self.

"I'm so glad and surprised to see you again, Mark," exclaimed Michelle still shaken. "I recognized you coming through the door with Bright Cloud. So you're the one the whole village has been talking about! Imagine, our meeting again this far away from Boston. It's really amazing. I'm glad that the Inspector could come when he did; I was afraid for the other patients. I thought I could handle him, but he got out of control."

Holding her hand firmly, Mark stammered, "I never dreamed of meeting you here. It's wonderful to see you again so soon. I see that you're doing what you were hoping to do. What a coincidence." Even though there was pleasure in seeing a familiar face in Michelle, Mark felt awkward. He did not actually know Michelle any better than he did Bright Cloud or the Inspector, and he did not want to go beyond the familiarity level of good manners in expressing his joy at such a reunion. He had the feeling that Michelle felt the same way.

The Inspector curiously watched the two for a moment and said, "This goes to show you what a small world it's becoming. I remember meeting a young soldier in France that was my closest chum in grade school. He had moved far away when we were small. We lost contact with each other until I recognized his name on a roster. In the middle of France we became little boys together again. It was a glorious experience for me. I'd say that this occasion is a good omen."

Bright Cloud was quiet throughout the commotion. She still looked drained and her uncharacteristic lack of enthusiasm made Mark feel somehow responsible for her discomfort. She was relieved that no one was hurt by Louie's actions.

"I'm so sorry this had to happen, Mike." Bright Cloud used the name for the first time in reference to Michelle. "Old Louie can be a handful at times and I should never have left you alone with him in this condition. I'll help you straighten out the mess."

"Come, Captain, let's leave the two ladies to their work." The Inspector nudged Mark's arm towards the door.

"Thanks for being so helpful, Inspector. I don't know what might have happened if you had not come. I'll see you before you leave, Mark, when we can talk again." Michelle's eyes were aglow and her face still flushed.

"Thank you both for such a memorable day," Bright Cloud told him, thinking of all that had taken place. Once again, Mark saw that touch of sadness in her eyes that he had seen earlier. They said their good-byes and hastily left the infirmary. Old Louie continued to moan from the bed.

Mark shook his head. "That maneuver you used on Louie was a guarantee that he would not be in a fighting mood for a while. Ugh, that must have hurt!"

"He's been warned enough times. Now he has to suffer the consequences of his actions. I didn't mean to hit him as hard as I did. Michelle could have been hurt seriously. She's the new mission nurse that Father Dumont has been trying to get for quite some time. How did you two meet, if I may ask?"

"I met her on a train coming home. She got off at Boston after we had visited with each other for a few hours. I promised to write to her. I still can't believe it," Mark explained.

"I know that everybody likes her a lot," remarked the Inspector casually. "What you saw back there is an example of our main problem up here. This rot gut cheap booze is tearing down many years of fine family and tribal traditions and values. Everybody suffers from it. The afflicted men are trouble, and their families suffer even more from the after effects of the curse." The hardy policeman worked himself into a state of indignant rage just thinking about the situation.

"We try hard to disrupt the distribution, but it's such a large area for so few men to patrol that we make only a small difference. When I catch a whiskey agent, believe me, he gets swift justice from the law! The hardest part is to see what it does to the family. This is one custom of the white man that has damaged their culture, even though some of the finer parts of our western civilization have enriched them in many ways. However, alcohol, diseases, and welfare checks have all helped to deteriorate the fabric of an already fragile society. The church has been a strong influence, helping to maintain the spiritual traditions. The church has also taken over most community functions that benefit everybody. Father Dumont is an eloquent spokesman for the Indians and their struggle to retain some of their ancient values. He distributes federal and provincial aid, while we enforce the law and represent the government. The people respect authority, which makes our job easier than it would be in the United States, where you have a long-standing tradition of defying authority."

The two men returned to the RCMP station. People they met along the way greeted them warmly. It pleased Mark to feel accepted by the people in the community. The Inspector expertly kindled a fire in the small stove, and soon the aroma of coffee filled the room. Both men smoked their pipes enjoying an informal interlude with each other that lasted several hours.

"Well, Inspector Clough, it's been quite a day for me! For one thing, it's brought me to the end of a Marine Corps career. I have to honestly say that I take off the uniform with a little reluctance. I've been proud to wear it. The service has been good to me. I'll always consider my time as a company commander as the high-water mark of my life. No matter what happens from this point forward, I'm sure it will be anticlimactic and pale compared to the intensity of my involvement with the company. Is that the way you felt when you left Army service?" Mark asked Inspector Clough with interest.

"Very similar in most ways. We can never be as we were before the war, but I've established a new direction for my life that I'm enjoying. Of course, our police organization is paramilitary by design and I like working in a structured atmosphere. The war has helped me set priorities easier than I ever did before. It also taught me that our time here is fleeting at best, and I'm constantly redefining what's important in my life. The Mounted Police is more regimented than the Army with stricter rules of conduct. It's not for everybody, but it suits my temperament just fine."

"I can understand that. I wouldn't trade the last few years for anything, but I have no desire to repeat them either. I've a strong feeling you've been instrumental in getting me here. If that's so, I would like to apologize for my angry outburst with you and Bright Cloud. The forestry proposition sounds challenging, and I'm glad for the opportunity."

"I must confess that I did have a small hand in asking for you; however, it was Flying Eagle that first saw the possibilities for the tribal lands. If there was a key person in the conspiracy, as you call it, it would definitely have to be your good friend Major Korsman. He was responsible for having the Marine Corps and the State Department draw up your orders. I'd call him a real friend," said Inspector Clough, cleaning his pipe over an open stove lid.

Mark thought about the Inspector's statement for a while. He was pleased with the behind-the-scene manipulations of Arlo, the doughty Finn in Kittery. "It's just like him to pull a stunt like this. I had a feeling, right from the start, that he played a big part in my coming here. I've got to write a report of what took place here, and then he'll handle my mustering out papers. The forestry project will be good for me spiritually and physically. I never deceived myself that my highest priority is a recovery from the effects of the war and all of its problems; otherwise I'm doomed. This forestry plan may very well be part of the answer. I work at my best with a full load of responsibilities. It helps me cut a path through the priorities. Without realizing it, this project for the tribal land was made to order for me!"

Appreciative of Mark's enthusiasm, the Inspector said, "This forest operation will be an invaluable source of tribal pride. They need it as much as they need economic assistance. By taking the responsibility for the plan of the forest, you'll automatically become a part of their inner circle. Your consulate man, Mr. Holden, is at the rectory waiting for us. In the excitement of everything I forgot about him. We're invited to have dinner with Running Deer. It'll be a little cramped at their cabin, but we'll fit. It was my plan to bring up the forestry situation to you at that time, but Bright Cloud's enthusiasm, typically, got the best of her. She could not wait. I'm anxious for you and Running Deer to become better acquainted. He learned English from Jesuit missionaries and is familiar with the Indian and the white man's customs. But make no mistake about him - he is now, and always will be, an Indian at heart and proud of it."

"How's he made a living up here in the wilderness?" asked Mark, anxious to find out all he could about the natives of the region in general, and specifically Running Deer.

"You can't equate the work habits of the western world to the customs of the native people. They're driven and motivated by the weather; seasonal habits of the animals they depend on for food; shelter and livelihood, and the limitations of extreme winter conditions. Their world evolves around the winter. To be unprepared for it is to perish. They spend their entire life in the pursuit of necessities to daily life, but we can discuss that at some other time. Let's pick up Bob Holden and go see Running Deer?" inquired the Inspector, slipping his pipe in his pants pocket.

"Sounds fine to me."

Mark had to walk fast to keep up with the Inspector's long stride. They found the priest and Bob deep in conversation. The Inspector informed Father Dumont what had transpired at the infirmary and he promised to look in on Louie's problem. He was pleased to hear of Mark's acceptance of the tribal forest plan. "Running Deer has been looking forward to this day, and your decision about the land will surely make him happy. I've just had a most enjoyable visit with this young American diplomat," said Father Dumont, pushing himself away from the table. "Run along now and enjoy your visit, gentlemen. I've got to see old Louie, once again!"

After the priest had left, the Inspector turned to Mark and Bob with a gleam in his eye and said, "I almost feel sorry for old Louie. He's about to taste the good Father's wrath."

The three men casually walked along the path Mark had taken with Bright Cloud. Continuing over the bridge past the pool, they came to Running Deer's log cabin. The air was heavy with smoke from the evening fires of the nearby cabins. Running Deer's cabin was neatly kept with a large centrally located great room, which served as the sitting room, dining room, and the kitchen combined. The floor was well-worn spruce boards that had been scrubbed until they shined. Bright Cloud met them at the door. Mark could not detect any residual ill effects from their earlier encounter. He was relieved to see her smiling face again. A huge stone-faced fireplace with a crackling fire warmed the room, creating an atmosphere of informality. On the opposite wall near the entrance, a stone chimney had been built for the cast-iron cook stove where Bright Cloud was diligently working as they came in.

"Welcome to our home. I'm pleased for you to have the chance to better understand and know my father. He's gone outside for another armful of wood," Bright Cloud warmly greeted them.

The orderly cabin had a natural feel of informal practicality. The huge fireplace on the north wall dominated the room. It was constructed from rocks held together with mortar, with a large half log mantel that stretched all the way across the structure. On the mantel was a picture of Flying Eagle in his army uniform, and a picture of a younger Bright Cloud in her white nurse's uniform. On both sides of the room was a doorway that, Mark assumed, went to the bedrooms. At the center of the room was a large tavern table covered with a white tablecloth and a multitude of food. Running Deer came from a side door with his arms piled high with wood for the fireplace. He emptied it in the wood box, brushed his arms of loose chips and extended his hand to Mark.

"At last, Captain, we meet again. Welcome to our home. My daughter has taken over our cabin and runs it as efficiently as she does the infirmary. I'm glad to see all of you, Inspector and Mr. Holden." His greeting was sincere and heartfelt.

"Thank you, Running Deer," replied the Inspector. "I could not very well turn down an offer to enjoy Bright Cloud's fine cooking. When the alternative is Corporal Haynes or myself on the old barrack stove, your daughter wins by a mile."

"Thank you again, gentlemen, for accepting our invitation. Father has been lucky enough to obtain a plump goose for the occasion." Bright Cloud replied, busy tending things at the stove.

Bob Holden was singularly silent until now. He was touched by the atmosphere of warmth and informality. "My participation in this presentation has been one of the most rewarding experiences of my life. Father Dumont just spent much of the afternoon telling me about your Cree legacy in this region of Quebec Province. To be able to share such hospitality is, indeed, a privilege. Your work at the infirmary is most admirable, Bright Cloud. I'm pleased to share your table."

"When we first started the medical care facility, Father Dumont insisted on treating all of the people regardless of race. Many people travel for long distances to have care, and some white people still refuse to come because of my presence. I'm unhappy about that, but maybe now, with Michelle Gurney, we'll be able to serve everybody. She's a marvelous person, and so full of energy," answered Bright Cloud. "Everything seems ready, gentlemen. Why don't you sit at the table so that we can judge Father's goose." She had an impish way of handling her father, who would never admit it to anybody, but he loved being the object of her concern.

The goose was well plucked by the time they finished eating. Bright Cloud enjoyed seeing them eat with the kind of ravenous appetite that the North Woods produces. For dessert, she made it simple, like the last bars of a symphony, an apple cobbler with strong cheese. Mark would have called it an upside down cake. Whatever it was called, he thought it was a perfect ending to a wonderful dining experience.

Bright Cloud insisted that they remain seated while she removed the dishes and served more hot coffee. "If you'll excuse me for a little while, I want to check on the patients. The pot of coffee on the stove is full. I'll be back shortly."

The men soon had a dense cloud of smoke from their pipes floating into the rafters of the cabin. The atmosphere was congenial and restful. Mark was enjoying the company of Running Deer. He was well informed, articulate, and spoke better English than many Canadians.

"Our Village, here on the shore of Lac Diamante, is not only an isolated outpost far from your western form of civilization. This is an important place, not just because of my daughter's work at the infirmary, or because of the Inspector's police station, or even because of the church, which is the last for many miles. The true significance of this place is that the Indian and the white man meet here; neither one or the other dominates.

"North of here, in the land of the silent forest and clear lakes, the Indian is in his element. Even though it has been hard on us, we have conquered the northlands and survived as a people. Being able to continue with our traditions has been our greatest reward.

"South of here is your world that has not always been kind to my people. I'm an Indian. My dead son was an Indian even though he

91

embraced your way of life. It is the same for my daughter and probably will be the same for my granddaughter. They will always be Indian in spite of the education. What I'm trying to say...no matter what things we copy from your world, we are never allowed to be white. Many things from your world have been good for me and for my tribe, and I've seen much goodness in the hearts of white men. It's hard to understand that many of your people still judge us on the basis of their own values, not on our values as Indians. We are judged as people that are inadequate by your standards. Even though we have adopted many of your ways, we don't want to lose our identity as Crees." The men listened without comment as Running Deer continued his monologue.

"Much of our hurt and confusion originates within our own breast because we're not one or the other. We have a foot in both cultures and are afraid of losing our identity as Indian; on the other hand, we cannot find acceptance as white, which we are not! It's a true dilemma. The main difference between the white and red man can be simply stated. We believe that everything on this earth has a soul - the trees, the rivers, the rocks, the animals. They are here to be used by man and must be appreciated. Whites believe that only man has a soul, the difference is that simple, and that complex.

"I think of these things often and I see no change in our problems. That saddens me. But now you have come with a comforting message of hope, Captain. It's most welcome. We ask only for a chance to live in peace and harmony. We can never go back to the way it used to be before the traders came, and we would not want such a harsh life again. However, we want to hold our heads high and be proud of who we are and have a voice in controlling our own destiny. That is most important to us right now." Pipe smoke filled the still air as Mark and Bob listened with rapt attention. The Inspector, who had heard it all before, observed the other men as Running Deer spun his message through their consciousness.

Running Deer paused to clean and light his pipe, then he continued in a slow and deliberate manner that made the listeners feel that he was measuring every word for its greatest impact. "It's important for you to understand where we have been in order for you to help us through tomorrow. My daughter has told me of your acceptance of the forestland project. We thank you for your generosity. It's important to us because it will become an annual source of income for the tribe, and a well thought-out plan will also prove to the government that we are responsible heirs to the land that we have always claimed as a birthright. It is a symbol that takes on a far greater importance than the actual size and value of the land in itself. My son talked of forest husbandry. It is not foreign to us. To the contrary, it's a concept deeply ingrained in our people. We have survived in this land by not being destructive of those things which support our way of life."

Bright Cloud quietly returned to the cabin while her father was in the midst of his speech. She suppressed a smile. Her father was up to his old habit of dominating the conversation. She used the moment to observe the men at the table. The Inspector was tolerating her father with silent respect. He had heard these stories before and was not about to enter into a debate. Bob Holden gave the impression of listening intently, but she felt he was being professionally courteous to his host in a detached fashion.

Mark, however, was a different study. His face presented as many questions as it did answers. It was apparent that he had fallen under her father's spell. Mark saw Bright Cloud take a seat at the far end of the table and returned her smile. She thought the smile came easy to him. Bright Cloud saw glimpses of something else that concerned her. For reasons even Mark could not understand, on occasion, a detached sensation would come over him as if he had escaped from the reality of the moment. It never stayed for long, and the lapses were becoming less frequent and less intense. He knew that it was noticeable to others, and it always embarrassed him. It was through these experiences, however, that Mark was able to measure the extent of his progress. They no longer left him in a painful sweat like they used to. Bright Cloud was angry at herself for observing him at one of his most vulnerable moments.

Her father stopped talking for a breather. The Inspector was quiet until now. "You may not be aware of it, Captain, but before your Spanish War took place, we had a serious uprising against the Dominion of Canada. It was led by a half breed called Louis Riel. The rebellion opposed the decision of the government to build a railroad across Canada to open up portions of the North Country that were inaccessible up to that time. Such a decision involved lands that had been used by the natives for many generations. Riel was a very intelligent and charismatic leader of the protest that became a full blown rebellion.

"Running Deer was a young man at that time and was a part of it. He had joined forces with a powerful chief called Poundmaker, who in turn allied himself with the metis (half breed) leader, Riel. The final confrontation took place in 1885. It was the one and only war between Canadian officials and the Indian population. I know that Running Deer sees this conflict from both sides, even though he was a participant with Chief Poundmaker when General Frederick Middleton defeated them. I think that Running Deer would want you to understand this part of his life. He's still concerned about the welfare of the native people and is active in that role." The Inspector deliberately finished his coffee and nodded an approval to Bright Cloud.

"I'm amazed at the contrast between the United States and Canada in the way they handled the native population. I guess we did very badly," commented Mark.

"The western expansion in your country, Captain, was on such a large scale that the displaced Indian lands were already a fact before the government could act. Your main problem was the large numbers of homesteaders. It was more a matter of rapid growth than any malicious intent or incompetence from the government. If we had had the same numbers of people looking for land, then our problems would have been very similar. It's easy to see how the situation became so tense for everybody." The policeman settled back in his chair stretching his long arms to the back of his head.

"Ah, Inspector, you speak with much wisdom." Running Deer was a great admirer of the policeman, and turned the subject of the conversation back to the situation at hand. "You know, Captain Leroux, the forestry project has been a dream that we have wanted to make a reality ever since my son was in school. It was his idea to help us adapt to those things that could help us and at the same time preserve as much of our culture as possible. It was his desire to bring you here to Fort Lewis after the war. Your presence is the fulfillment of his dreams. I can tell by the way my daughter is silent, that she is going to scold me for talking so much." Running Deer beamed with pride as he confronted his daughter.

"Father, you embarrass me!"

"I think both of you have been very thoughtful and gracious with us, and this evening has been interesting and informative. If I'd known about your need for something that I could provide, I would've come sooner. My memory and my respect for Flying Eagle is such that I would've dropped everything to come to your assistance. We never talked about the forest project. We simply were not at that point in our relationship where we could ask such a thing of each other," Mark told them.

"You would've liked his wife, Minnie. My heart has been heavy since her death. Then, Flying Eagle's untimely death was almost too much to bear. Through all of the grief and sad times, my wonderful daughter has not wavered in her support. She's an angel to this old man. I see her with little Bright Star and my heart glows with pride. I have never been one to boast, but God has blessed me with my Bright Cloud," Running Deer threw an arm in her direction. Bright Cloud blushed and turned away from everybody's eyes.

"Your father has spoken the truth, Bright Cloud," the Inspector continued. "In all of my travels and stations, I've never met a person who accomplishes as much in a day's time as you do, young lady. I wish I had your energy!"

"Come, come, now. You're all getting carried away with yourselves. I don't like that. Little Star will be home in a while. She's been at a friend's home so that she would not be a distraction from your visit with my father. Which reminds me, Father, have you forgotten the box of papers we spoke of?" Bright Cloud mentioned, pointing towards the mantel.

"No, no, I've not forgotten them," said Running Deer, slowly getting out of his chair to pick up a large shoe box from the cupboard beside the fireplace. "This contains the original deeds made out to the tribal council and several letters from the Department of Indian Affairs. There is also a copy of the signed agreement for the land between the Tribal Council and the Province of Quebec. There are no maps, but the one on the wall at the police station is correct and generally accurate. You'll find that the boundaries of the tract are all marked using as many of the natural features of the terrain as possible."

"That's right," commented Inspector Clough. "I've seen copies of what you have there. There should not be any problem with laying out the perimeter of the tract. This part of Canada has not been extensively surveyed, so natural boundaries were used whenever possible."

"I want you to take these papers now, Captain. You'll need them for your plan." Running Deer placed the box on the table and pushed it in front of Mark.

"Thanks, Running Deer. I'll take good care of them and return them to you when I've completed the job. I'm not sure how I'm going to do the plan, but I expect that field work could be completed by August, and the plan drafted by September or October. However, I can't start any field work until I have access to instruments and a library. I also need a new set of clothes. I'll have to review the situation. Why don't you let me sleep on it tonight? I'll have a workable plan of action by tomorrow morning." Mark glanced around the table for any comments.

Bob Holden was thinking out loud to the group, "I'll have to leave tomorrow morning, Mark. My superiors have other plans for me, and the Inspector has promised that the plane is at our disposal for a return trip to Quebec City."

"Whatever you decide to do, Captain, the Mounted Police is ready to assist in any way possible. The Provincial Forestry Department is available in Quebec if you need access to them," offered Inspector Clough.

The time had come to break up the congenial evening. It had been a busy day for everybody. With the valuable shoe box of papers tucked under his left arm, Mark shook hands with Running Deer while Bright Cloud escorted them to the door.

"Thank you for a memorable day," said Mark. "You and your father have given me the gift of trust, and I promise to not let you down."

As they were leaving the cabin, Bright Cloud called after Mark, "I could never imagine your letting anyone down, Captain."

"If either of you need me, I'll be at quarters," said the Inspector with a wave of his hand.

"Thanks, Inspector, it's been a great day for me. I'm almost sorry to see it come to an end," said Mark. "See you in the morning."

"I've never been a part of such an occasion as this one has turned out to be." Bob Holden turned to Mark, "The folks here are some of the nicest I've ever met. I hate to return to so-called civilized society tomorrow. Whatever you decide, Captain, I'm sure it will be right for you. I also extend an offer to help if you need it. Rest well, and I'll see you tomorrow morning."

"Thanks, Bob, I'll let you know."

The soft breeze blowing over the village was scented with the promise of spring. Spruce and balsam fir mingled with the pungent smell of smoke from the chimneys in the settlement. Mark was not ready to turn in yet, so he slowly made his way to the wharf near the police station. It was pitch black outside. The only light available to show the way were the stars that shone more brilliantly than he had ever seen them. A few lights could be seen from the village. The Hudson Bay Store was dark, but the factor's house was awash in light from every window.

There was a tranquility to this place, Mark thought. The gentle splash of waves on the shore blended with the whir of the wind through the trees, creating an atmosphere of isolated well-being. He ventured out to the end of the dock where he could see the lights still shining from the infirmary and Running Deer's cabin. He was filled with emotions that needed to be sorted out. Mark felt great satisfaction at the completion of the job he volunteered for, and was pleased with the prospect of doing a forest management plan that he was trained to do. He never thought for a moment that the job was beyond his capacity to bring to a successful conclusion. This trip to northern Canada was changing him. He felt it in many ways that were impossible to describe. The chance of becoming more intimately involved with other people was a sensation he hadn't experienced for a long time. He was hopeful that the person he had once been would eventually find a way out of the darkness. It was time.

Sitting on the wharf in the middle of the night at this obscure outpost in the North Woods, Mark thanked God for the promise of tomorrow and asked for the strength to meet the challenge.

Chapter Eight

A new day dawned at Fort Lewis. The first rays of sunshine filtered through the tall trees that framed the lake, reflecting off the mirror-smooth water, making the small ripples on the water look as if they were dancing. Mark awoke to a room filled with sunshine and started to get dressed. He followed the tantalizing aroma of percolating coffee to the dining room, where he met Father Dumont sitting at one of the long tables.

"Good morning, Father."

"Ah, Captain Leroux, good morning. I understand that you're going to be with us for a while longer. It's a relief for me that you've agreed to do the forest plan. I'm sure everyone has been telling you about the situation, so I won't bother to duplicate what others have already said."

"Yes, they have, Father," answered Mark, helping himself to the muffins on the table. "I had supper with Running Deer last night. He went over everything in detail. I've come up with a schedule to accomplish our goals. Bob Holden is flying out this morning with the constable. I'm going with them to confer with the Quebec Forestry authorities in regards to equipment and other necessary information. I'll need several forest volume and growth tables for the area, and they're a logical source. I also need a set of field clothes. I'm excited at the prospect of going to work again.

"I'm not familiar with the silvicultural requirements of the sub-arctic boreal forests, and I'll need all the help that's available. If this project is as important as everybody claims, then it should be put together with all the skill possible. The quality of our labor will be judged by the next generation. Of course, that's true of all forestry activity. When I've found the right information and equipment, Father Dumont, I'll return to start work."

"I applaud your strategy and your reasoning, Captain. I'm sure the information will be made available to you. If you need a letter of recommendation from me, I'll be glad to write one," Father Dumont offered.

"Yes, that would be helpful, Father. I have one other request for you, and that's to call me Mark from now on. My commission is retired and I'm technically not a captain anymore."

"It's going to be exciting having you here, Mark. As you go about your business in the forest, I should warn you to be on the lookout for illegal activity such as peddling whiskey. It's a lucrative enterprise now. When the Inspector finds perpetrators, his justice is swift. I don't know if he told you or not, but he also regulates hunting and fishing laws. The lands belong to all Canadians, but the natives have special privileges because of their heritage which is as it should be. They resent the intrusion of regulations upon their lives, and to some individuals, the Inspector represents that disruption. The problem becomes more difficult the further you get from the village. You'll always have to be on the alert, because you are, like it or not, going to be perceived as a part of the regulation process. Don't let me alarm you, because your relationship with Running Deer will help you to get along fine, but it's wise to be prepared. Eh?"

"The Inspector told me the same thing. I'll be careful, Father. I appreciate your concern. In case I don't see them before the plane is ready, would you say good-bye to Running Deer and Bright Cloud for me. Tell them I'll be back in a couple of weeks, to start the field work."

Mark watched the lake shrink below them as the float plane climbed above the high ridge to the west of the village. Seeing the tiny hamlet from this perspective gave Mark a deeper appreciation for the meaning of community, and he better understood now why Flying Eagle was so proud of his homeland. Mark had a long letter from Father Dumont to the Director of Indian Affairs at Lac St. Jean tucked into his shirt pocket. The Inspector could not make the trip, so he was alone with Bob Holden and the pilot. Both seemed content to remain quiet and watch the landscape below as the plane sped southward.

Mark accompanied Bob to the American Consulate in Quebec City where he sent telegrams to Arlo and to his Aunt Maddie. He told them about the forest plan and the role he would be playing in its development. He intended to follow up with a more detailed letter.

Even though he was pleased with his new project, Mark found it difficult to take off the green uniform. Pride in the Marine Corps and all it stood for would always be a part of his life. The uniform was a symbol of his rite of passage. Mark and Bob selected his new wardrobe from one of Quebec's largest clothing outfitters. The clothes were comfortable and serviceable for use in the harsh forest environment during the spring and summer months. Since Mark was going to return to the forest and his own cooking very shortly, he and Bob went to a fine restaurant for a memorable dining experience which included a large steak and all the milk he could drink, topped off with apple pie a la mode.

The next day, Mark and Bob went to the main office of the Department of Indian Affairs, where they received an excellent briefing from an intelligent, caring young agent. The agent confirmed the sense of urgency that Bright Cloud and Running Deer had passed on to Mark. Mark learned another interesting fact about the Indian land. Rich deposits of aluminum and asbestos had been discovered nearby, indicating that the general area was worthy of consideration for potential mineral development. If rich deposits were found on the Indian lands they had the right to develop them, because the Tribal Council held the mineral rights.

In order for a forest enterprise to succeed, long term markets were a necessity. This truism is central to proper management on all commercial forestlands. Otherwise, the forest becomes a part of the rest of the landscape that holds the world together. Mark finished at the Indian Bureau and said good-bye to Bob with a promise to get together when Mark returned to Quebec. Mark's last night in Quebec was filled with letter writing to Arlo and Aunt Maddie.

Anxious to check on the marketing situation, Mark returned to Lac St. Jean by rail the next day where he made an appointment with a procurement forester in a large pulp and paper company located at the northern end of Lac. St. Jean. He met a heavy- framed middle-aged forester that was able to answer many of his questions. The two men were on common ground. The camaraderie of foresters superseded nationality. Mark welcomed the news that the paper company was interested in a steady supply of wood products, primarily pulpwood for newsprint. The quantity would depend on the allowable cut of the management plan and the manpower available to harvest the wood. In order to obtain access to the marketplace, an assigned quota would have to be agreed upon. Mark decided to postpone that commitment for a later time after he had talked with Running Deer and Father Dumont.

A second item that had to be resolved was transportation of the forest products to the mill. The paper company obtained wood for pulping operations on its own lands, other private landowners and the public Province of Quebec forests. All of the wood came to the plant via waterways. Logs were separated from pulpwood in large ponds or boomed areas in the lake and then channeled to a sawmill for breakdown into lumber. The two foresters studied a map of the area and came to the conclusion that the best way to transport the wood from tribal lands would be through lands owned by the Paper Company adjacent to the tribal land. The Swift River cut the tribal lands in half with an ample seasonal flow of water in the springtime. Several miles to the south, it merged with the Diamond River from Lac Diamante and then passed through paper company lands on its way to Lac St. Jean. The total flow was about a hundred miles. The company forester thought it was possible to drive the wood that far. It depended on the condition of the river bed and banks along the river. He was unfamiliar with them. They would grant passage rights of the wood quotas through their lands. Realistically, it was the only outlet available to the Council. Later, an agreement would have to be signed to spell out the details of the riparian rights.

Mark discussed the availability of forestry instruments and equipment to conduct a thorough forest inventory and growth study of the tribal lands. Again, he had come to the right place! The necessary tools could be borrowed from the company. They had a supply of their most recently computed volume tables for the spruce-fir forest type of Northern Canada. The tables and silvicultural guidelines that were available from the paper company were the same ones used by private and provincial foresters throughout the region as training syllabuses. Mark was informed that the northern limit of commercial forestry parallels the permanent frost line.

The accepted method of tree harvesting in the borealis forest type is the clear-cut technique. This method works well and accomplishes the goals of reproducing the cut-over area with a large percentage of spruce which needs full sunlight for its development. Seed sources in the form of large trees are left to the west and north of the cut areas so that the prevailing winds can disseminate the seed to the harvested area. It works well for even-aged management systems, that is, forests of uniform size and age. Examination of stands cut earlier will show a lush carpet of young and vigorous trees taking the place of harvested trees. The clear-cut system insured a steady supply of wood fiber, a lush environment for wildlife, and helped regulate the accumulation of snowfall, which in turn, insured a steady supply of high quality water all year round with a minimum input from man. Mark was more familiar with the partial cut system for white pine, where cuts over a period of years encouraged white pine seedlings to grow in light shade. In the spruce-fir region, however, balsam fir would dominate the site if partial cuts are used. Balsam fir is a less desirable species than the spruce because it has a shorter fiber length that produces a weaker paper product, so the clear-cut method naturally evolved from the silvical characteristics of the species involved. Balsam fir also has a shorter life than spruce and its subsequent loss in the mature stands detracts from the total productivity. In theory, there could be a cut taking place on the forest area every year in the rotation equivalent to annual growth minus losses from insects, disease and fire. The growth and harvest of the forest becomes cyclical and self perpetuating, producing a continuous supply of products forever if proper management techniques are intelligently applied.

The tribal lands were near the permanent frost line. Consequently, the cutting budgets should be conservative (fewer trees cut than were being grown per year) to build up the reserve in those regions. Another important consideration that further supported the clear-cut method was the lack of deep soils. The entire region had been scrapped clean to bedrock during the glacial advance to the south and east. Windthrow becomes an important factor in those areas of shallow soil. Partial cutting would contribute to the losses sustained from windthrow, thus depleting the total productivity of the stand. Clearcutting for the tribal lands simplified harvests because it concentrated areas of activity and encouraged more efficiency for the work crews. Productivity of forest products is of course greater using the clear-cut method of harvest. It has become an accepted technique of harvesting the forest and meets all of the requirements of a sustained-yield management system.

Mark was satisfied with the technical information he had secured from the paper company forester, who promised to be available for help if it was needed. Mark had completed most of his preparations for the project by the time he left the office of the pulp mill. It took a while, but he located a ride to the RCMP station on the waterfront at Lac. St. Jean. Before he could carry all of his supplies into the building, a familiar figure opened the door to help him. It was Inspector Clough.

"It's good to see you, Inspector. I was hoping you might be around," exclaimed Mark, glad to see a familiar face.

"I'm fortunate to catch you, Mark, because I came specifically with that in mind." The Inspector gave him an approving nod. "You look different out of uniform. That confident look in your eyes tells me you've had good luck so far."

"You wouldn't believe how great people have been. The forester at the pulp mill has been most helpful. He's going to collect the list of things I need and bring them to you. The most gratifying piece of news though, is the marketing possibilities to the paper mill at prices that should yield excellent returns to the tribe. The company has been very generous."

The Inspector nodded his head, "I thought you'd receive that kind of reception; they're good for this region. Now, about your supplies and other needs while you're on this project. I've been authorized to let you know that the Hudson Bay Company will provide you with anything you desire. Just sign for it and the Bureau of Indian Affairs will pay for it. I've got some equipment at Fort Lewis for you from RCMP stores. Do you have a firearm?

"Yes, I've got my service .45 pistol in an under-arm holster right now beneath this shirt," said Mark, pulling out a shirt tail to expose the automatic. "I was going to speak to you about it. Can I get some extra ammunition for it up here?"

"Yes, there are a lot of those surplus military weapons floating around since the war. I'd use one myself, but police regulations say I have to carry this .38 Webley. We have some ammunition here, and I'll see to it that the store at the village orders some for your use."

"I'm going to start back to the village in a day or two. I've decided to walk back along the water route of the spring flow. The trip will serve several functions. First, it will help condition me physically; second, it will allow me to observe the condition of the river for the logs and pulpwood drive in the spring; and finally, it will give me an opportunity to acclimate myself to the woodland community in these northern latitudes. I expect it will take me almost two weeks to reach Lac Diamante. I'll travel as light as I can." Mark watched the Inspector for some reaction.

"You're starting out with a bang, young man. You'll need some things from our stores here, and I want to go over your route very carefully. Don't forget, civilization and help will be a long way from you."

Mark had supper at the station with the Inspector and several other policemen. The station was a large complex that housed a complete troop as well as a warehouse and a radio station. After the meal was completed, the two of them went upstairs to a small room with a single bed and a table filled to overflowing with assorted supplies. Obviously, the Inspector had been expecting him.

"I knew you would be along sometime and I wanted to be ready for you." The Inspector laughed and snapped open a pack from the table. "This one contains our silk service tent. There's nothing better for this region. You'll need to cut poles before setting it up, but that's no problem with the small belt ax included. There's also a mummy sleeping bag and a headnet for the black flies, which you'll need more than anything else; trust me on that one. It'll be your most prized possession for the early summer months. Please help yourself and pick out what you want from the stores. For a two week trip, you'll have to supplement yourself with fish from the stream or the pack will be unbearable to handle for any distance. Let's take a look at your map, now, and maybe we can help you." They both knew it was a very serious business to take a prolonged trip alone in the woods of Northern Canada.

Mark spread out the map from the paper company and traced his proposed route with his finger. There was a cabin used by the RCMP and other woodland travelers at the intersection of the Swift and Diamond Rivers about ten miles from Fort Lewis.

"We could leave you a cache of food at the cabin," said the Inspector, pointing to the cabin marked on the map. "I'll see to it that you have enough food to continue from that point into the tribal land if you want to follow that route. Leave a note of your intentions at the cabin. After seven days, I'll have a man check the cabin every day. We have a motor launch that can take you up the river several miles from Lac St. Jean. How does that sound?"

"I'll be glad to hitch a ride up to the first rapids with your motor launch, and your plan to leave a supply of food at the cabin is sound strategy. I'm anxious to do this, so the sooner I start the better I'll feel about everything. Don't worry about me, Inspector, I'll be okay."

"My concern is not as unselfish as it may sound. If something was to happen to you, it would be my job to try and locate your whereabouts. I hate organizing lost-person searches. I'm not as young as I used to be," answered the policeman.

"I'd settle for being in your condition when I'm as old as you are, Inspector," Mark replied with a smile.

"Then it's decided. I'll have the launch ready for you early tomorrow morning. That will give you a chance to get your packs together. Anything you don't want to carry in your back pack, leave here, and I'll have it sent to the village, for your return." The Inspector started to leave the room; then, as an afterthought, said, "A final word of caution, Mark. The hooch peddlers are driving us to the limit. Be careful out there, keep your pistol loaded and be wary of strangers. Nothing in the forest can hurt you; only people can do that."

The next day Mark was up at an early hour ready and anxious to begin his new adventure. The backpack filled with supplies was as heavy a load as he dared to begin the trip. The powerful motor launch easily carried him towards the outlet of the Swift River at the northern end of Lac St. Jean. Mark was happy with another warm, sunny day. It reinforced his optimism for the journey ahead. As they got closer to the river outlet, he could feel the currents against the hull of the launch. The motor worked harder to make headway in the powerful rush of the river towards the lake.

A large ledge loomed overhead from the eastern shore on the right. Upstream they could see rapids in the center of the flow. The young constable seemed to know where he was going. Shortly past the ledge, he quickly pulled the boat to the right into a cleared area and partially beached it.

"This is as far as we can go, Sir."

Mark picked up his pack and jumped out of the boat. "This pack has some heft to it!"

"They always do at the start, Sir. The load lessens as each day goes by, and your stamina increases. But, that doesn't help for the beginning, does it?" The constable shook his hand and was soon back in midstream out of sight, the sound of the boat swallowed by the roar of the raging river.

Watching the boat, his last umbilical cord to civilization, disappear around a bend in the stream gave Mark a fleeting moment of panic. He asked himself if he was out of his mind to be in the middle of an unlimited wilderness all by himself? He came face to face with a North Wood's reality in a hurry. Mosquitoes and black flies in his native Maine could be severe, but the onslaught he was now experiencing was beyond anything he had ever expected. The air was literally full of swarming hungry insects feverishly looking for a meal on his blood. They filled his ears, his eyes and any opening that they could find in his clothing. They stunned him with their ferocity. Thankfully, the Inspector had prepared him for this unpleasant fact of life. Mark donned the lightweight head net as fast as he could.

The head screen was long enough to drop to his shoulders and as soon as he brushed away the few that got under the screen he had welcome relief. With his pack in place, Mark started his long journey to the north. The forward movement helped lighten the black fly attacks, but even a slight pause was enough to revive their interest and increase their numbers. A fan made out of short balsam fir boughs helped clear the flies from the front of his face. The urge to have a smoke presented a problem with the net around his head.

Mark solved the problem by making a small opening at the base of the mesh with a safety pin from his pack. The hole was large enough for the pipe stem, yet it eliminated the possibility of black flies getting through. He felt better now that he could enjoy the contentment of his pipe and good tobacco. Excessive smoking had not been one of his faults; however, in the open out-of-doors, the enjoyment of smoking contributed to his sense of well-being. The smoke also helped to keep the pests away.

A well-traveled path threaded its way along the river bank. His main purpose in traversing the river was to observe the flow of the water for obstructions to a potential spring drive of logs and pulpwood. The roar of the water was strong and continuous. The big spring flush had long since passed, but the rivers were still being fed from small watersheds of melting snow further north. They were higher now than they would be in the summer, yet not as high as the spring flow that would start the movement of wood from the concentration yards packed on the ice.

After several hours of making good progress, Mark began to falter and question the validity of his judgment for attempting such an effort. He had overestimated his physical condition. He realized that his endurance would improve as each day went by, but the trek back to the village was not going to be easy. The physical demands of his body were actually a welcome phenomenon. It was something Mark could feel and overcome, which gave him the satisfaction of accomplishing something tangible. It was a small thing, but any improvement over the status quo was progress, he thought. Here in the solitude of the forest, Mark was able to focus on his inner self and become better acquainted with his own strengths and weaknesses. He didn't realize how much he needed this until he got underway. Each step northward pushed him closer to his physical limit.

Mark had thoughtfully stuffed several candy bars in his jacket pockets to eat along the trail. They satisfied his monumental sweet tooth and provided additional energy. The Hershey chocolate bar made the hours on the trail a little easier. A slower steady pace for the afternoon seemed to be a wise course, especially for the first few days. In general, Mark had planned the trip so that he would not stop until noontime when he could eat whatever was quick and convenient. Once he was at the evening campsite, he could fish and cook a more substantial meal. The clear pools of the stream were full of fish. Mark's pack was loaded with the bare essentials for the trail. The sleeping bag and tent took most of the space. Food took up the rest except for a few changes of socks and underwear. Among his food stores was a large loaf of fresh bread which had been tempting him all day. It was one concession he allowed himself for the first day or two. The comment of the young constable about the pack getting lighter as the trip progressed was of little consolation at this stage of the trip. The only other articles he carried were the pistol under his jacket and a knife and a camp ax on the same belt. Of course the most important supply items such as matches in waterproof containers and a compass, he carried in his jacket pockets.

The forest was composed of pole-size trees forming a continuous canopy of green needles above the trail beside the stream. The heavy tree crowns kept the dampness of the river confined to the river basin area, forming a micro climate that was cooler than the surrounding air. The mosquitoes did not flourish as abundantly in the cooler air as they did in the more open sunny spots. The forest floor was covered with soft textured sphagnum moss and delicate princess pines.

Mark came upon a convenient location where a breeze blew from the west and was relatively free of black flies. It was sunny and the rocks had been warmed by the noon sun, presenting an inviting place for his first break. It was a beautiful spot with flat ledges rising high above the river bed. He was relieved to take off the pack and stretch out on the rock outcrop. His shoulders hurt, but his feet were holding up in fine shape. Thankfully, the new boots he'd purchased continued to feel comfortable. He'd never been bothered with foot problems even in the muddy trenches of France. His legs were another matter. They ached from the demands being placed upon them. Only time would make the ache go away.

The loaf of bread that had been enticing him all morning, supplemented with a topping of peanut butter, proved to be a feast of the first order. Never had food of any kind tasted so satisfying to him as the peanut butter sandwich eaten on the sunny ledge in the middle of God's country. After a short rest, he resumed his trek to the north.

By three o'clock he was looking for a suitable location to make evening camp. Mark selected a site off the pathway near the river and started gathering firewood and cutting poles for the tent set up. The tent proved simple to erect, just as the Inspector promised, but it surprised him how small it really was. Nothing contributed to the enjoyment of camping any more than the friendly crackling of a fire. The temperature had fallen considerably since the sun set. The cool evening air eliminated the black flies as a nuisance. It was a relief to remove the headnet. After supper, he went through the familiar ritual of cleaning, filling, and lighting his pipe. He'd bought a new corn cob pipe for the trip. Shortly, his weary body required rest.

There was barely room in the tent for him and the pack, but he managed by propping it under his head as a pillow of sorts. In no time at all, Mark fell into the deep sleep of exhaustion. The night settled over him so completely, that he was oblivious to the distant call of wolves and the hoot of an owl above his campsite. The thunder of the river blocked out all other sounds. The steady noise was soothing to his ear as he lay in the shelter of the tent. He could not get the memory of a forestry classmate by the name of Brown out of his mind. It had been a long time since he recalled their camping trip of many years ago. It brought a smile to his lips, yet, there was a tinge of sadness, too.

Mark thought of the time when he and three other forestry students climbed Mount Chocorua in the White Mountains of New Hampshire. It was a two-day affair with an overnight stay at the summit. All of the supplies and equipment were evenly distributed among the students. One student, called Brownie, was boisterous, heavy-framed and extremely powerful. In the spirit of good fun, unknown to Brownie, the others decided to give this good-natured behemoth an added burden of a fifteen pound rock secretly placed at the bottom of his pack.

It was a grueling climb to the top under ideal conditions, but with the added weight, sweat beads started to appear on their comrade's brow. Nonchalantly wiping them off, Brownie said nothing. The others could barely contain their laughter. Two-thirds of the way up the mountain, Brownie was noticeably tiring, but never said a word to his friends.

During a break at the side of the trail, Mark casually mentioned how well conditioned everybody was from the strenuous summer workouts in the forest. They unanimously agreed that such a spirited climb as they were having could only be attributed to the stamina they had developed over the grueling summer weeks. This was, after all, their working environment, and they had to be able to handle it. Brownie loudly agreed along with the rest of his friends.

The top finally came into view and was conquered. The beautiful panorama at the crest was worth the effort, especially to the west where a setting sun bounced its red and orange radiance against the soft cumulus clouds overhead. The beauty at the summit squelched any tendency for idle chatter. Brownie sat on a rock in utter exhaustion, while Mark and the other students silently admired the view. It was decided to make their evening camp just below the peak so that the heavy winds would be less severe. Within a short time, Brownie announced that he was hungry and proceeded to empty his pack.

The tranquility of the summit was suddenly broken by the roar of an outraged bull of a man. Brownie was so furious that he was speechless. He waved the maverick rock in his powerful hands uttering unspeakable retribution. His eyes were wide with anger, and he was on the verge of doing bodily harm. Then, as quickly as his anger came, it subsided into a long deep-in-the-belly laugh that echoed off the mountain top. Only a stout heart of immense proportions could have seen the humor in the situation. They laughed about the joke way into the night, with Brownie vowing to get revenge. Graduation and the war in Europe prevented Brownie from obtaining his revenge. He was killed while leading a patrol in France.

It was a different world back in those days. He could still hear his classmates laughing on the mountaintop. It had been easy to laugh together then. Brownie's death was announced in one of the papers that his Aunt Maddie had sent to him in France. The war had certainly taken the nation's best. Mark often wondered if the price the nation had to pay was worth what it got in return.

Every muscle in Mark's body complained in protest as he prepared for another day on the trail. A quick wash in the ice cold river water started his blood thumping in short order. The water was so cold that it masked the pain of his aching muscles. The stubble of a beard on his chin would be useful in combating the black flies. After breakfast he broke camp and resumed his walk upstream determined to equal the time of the first day. It would take some Herculean effort to match the first day. Traditionally, the second day is the most difficult of all. By that time the leg muscles have used up all of their reserves. He made a note in his journal that the paper company had chained a few bumper logs near some rapids to keep the moving wood in the center of the channel.

Even though Mark was plagued with sore muscles and a general deterioration of physical conditioning, an experienced eye would be able to detect that the mark of the forest was still with him, after all these years. His steps were light and silent with fluid movements which became easier and easier as time went by. The tranquility of the forest was reposed in him, and for the first time in years, he felt at peace with himself. Mark was feeling good about his progress, but he was most proud of the fact that he was regaining an increased awareness and alertness to things around him. When his senses were able to perceive sounds, movement, and smells that a year ago would have remained unrecognizable, he knew that time and the recuperative power of solitude in the forest environment he loved was working its magic upon him.

On the third day, Mark stopped earlier than usual for evening camp because he wanted to catch some fish for supper and breakfast. He chose a location with deep pools close by, and within fifteen minutes had caught two large whitefish, one of them over twenty inches long. The evening meal of roasted fish surpassed any delicacy his taste buds had sampled in a long time, contributing to his sense of well-being.

At the end of each day, he sat in front of a blazing campfire and contemplated where he had been and where he was going. Flying Eagle was never very far from his thoughts. What a great experience it would have been if he and Flying Eagle could have worked on this land together. Frequently, Flying Eagle's angular features seemed to appear in the dancing flames of the fire before him. It was almost as if he was trying to show his approval.

Sometimes Mark wondered just who his dead friend really was. Flying Eagle had taken advantage of the opportunities the western world had made available to him, yet he proudly proclaimed himself as an Indian. Flying Eagle would have succeeded in any endeavor of his choosing because he possessed the universally admired characteristics of motivation, honesty, and intelligence which transcends all societies. His sister, Bright Cloud, was richly endowed with the same qualities. Mark thought often about her. He could still see the sadness in her eyes when she let Mark read Flying Eagle's letter. That look haunted him every day on the trail.

The night was as black as the ace of spades and contrasted with the burning embers of the campfire, creating a dark ring of the unknown around the oasis of light. Mark placed one more log on the fire when he heard the loud crack of a dead branch in the darkness behind him. His conditioned reflex allowed him to move quickly outside of the fire zone so that his eyes could become adjusted to the night's darkness. He crouched beside a tree and waited with every nerve of his body alert for whatever was out there. All was quiet except for the steady hum of the river. After about fifteen minutes of watching and listening, Mark heard the sound of rapid movements through the trees with the dry branches on the forest floor making their unique snapping sound. Something or someone had been watching him at the campfire!

If the visitor had been a human being, he thought, it was very likely that they wanted to avoid contact for any of a number of reasons. It was also possible that it was an animal, such as a deer or a moose. He was determined to continue the same routine he had already established for the trip. The only concessions that he would do differently was to select his future sites for the evening camp further from the river in a dense stand of trees and to set up his tent so that it would be outside of the circle of light from the fire.

That night, Mark waited until the fire was totally out before he finally turned in. During the offensives in France he developed the habit of sleeping with his nerves still reasonably alert while his body replenished itself in a deeper slumber. It became an acquired instinct that never left him. His body was tired, yet his nerves refused to let down the vigilance that conditions required of them. He decided to load a round of ammunition into the chamber of the pistol, carefully lowering the hammer before returning it to the holster. Now, he only had to cock the hammer to fire. In the morning he would remove the bullet from the chamber. It was foolishly unsafe to carry the Colt .45 pistol with a round under the hammer once he started walking!

Morning came too soon with a light rain! Mark decided to continue. If he got too wet he could stop and dry out, but the prospect of getting wet was a welcome tradeoff to not wearing the bothersome headnet. Besides, his wool clothing would protect him. Mark also realized that he should not take the chance of making himself sick with the prospect of pneumonia. He'd always been conscious of his limitations, and being alone in the wilderness, he was not about to go beyond reasonable risk. Mark decided to continue in the rain, stopping when necessary, and keeping an eye out for a more sheltered site for the evening's camp.

Massive rock formations ahead of him rose forty or fifty feet in the air. The cliffs impressed Mark with their majestic thrust to the sky, so he decided to locate a campsite for the evening near the top of the rocky outcrop where a large formation hung several feet out over the river. The steep incline up to the top was covered with large maple and white birch trees. He found a good spot at the top and quickly set up for his fourth evening. The fish from the river were once more a welcome supplement to his diet. He ate his evening meal relishing every bite, even in the rain.

Each day that passed, Mark's body found it easier to travel further than the day before. The high protein diet of the fish along with the nights of sound sleep was making a new man out of him. It had been three years since the blackout, and he was acutely aware of the transformation now taking place.

In the middle of the night, he again heard the sound of rain drops against the tent roof. It increased his appreciation for the cramped comfort in the warm dry shelter of the Inspector's service tent. The late spring months of northern Quebec are often a combination of every season. The days had been unusually warm for this time of year, so a return to normal was not unexpected, and that was one reason Mark took advice from experienced woodsmen and wore wool field clothing. The threat of rain did not bother him as much as the incessant black fly attacks. He had decided to eat in the tent whenever it was set up to avoid fighting the insects at mealtime. Man is not the only one that is afflicted by the bloodthirsty pests. Large animals such as deer and caribou are often the object of feeding frenzies that turn their bodies into bleeding pulsating masses of flesh. This in turn draws other swarms of flies to the feeding ground where they partake of more flesh and blood. Often the tormented creature dies from loss of blood and exhaustion.

On the ninth day of his journey, Mark found himself at the edge of a chasm looking down into a small stream that entered the Diamond River from the east. The roar of the water cascading through the gorge drowned out other sounds. The rush of the smaller stream over the rapids at the bottom of the chasm as it met the larger force of the Diamond impacted the entire area with the restless power of unharnessed energy. He leaned against a rock to eat his last chocolate bar and to enjoy the awesome show of force below him. Small wisps of mist rose from the bottom of the gorge. The distance to the other side was about forty feet, so he decided to turn east along the southern bank of the stream until he found a crossing point.

Mark located a passable spot not too far from the junction of the two streams where the stream fanned out to a depth of about two feet. He estimated that by tomorrow night he should make it to the cache at the cabin. His pack was lighter now and his performance had improved appreciably.

He wrote in his journal that the river from this point southward required no additional work in stream bed improvement. However, he was not as optimistic about the flow from here to the Indian lands. He decided to continue along the Diamond River until it met the Swift River, then proceed north into the Indian lands scouting the Swift's banks. The additional supplies the Inspector promised for a cache should be enough for a few more days of travel to complete his riverbed review.

The day that Mark left the juncture of the two rivers, he stumbled and caught his foot on a stick. It quickly threw him off balance, throwing him head first against a rock. His hands instinctively reached out to protect his fall to the ground, but his head struck the protruding rock first before the outstretched hands could avert his fall.

Blackness overtook him...

Chapter Nine

Inspector Clough was uncomfortable about Mark's unescorted trip over such a long distance. Nine days had already passed and Mark should have completed the distance unless something had happened to him. Inspector Clough made up his mind that, first thing in the morning, he would personally go to the cache cabin to see if Mark had left any messages.

At the break of dawn, Inspector Clough feverishly canoed to the outlet of Lac Diamante with powerful strokes of the paddle. He was concerned, and when he felt the way he did this morning, his intuition was generally correct. A warm breeze gave some relief from the black flies. The water was high, so river travel would be easier without fear of striking rapids that could endanger the fragile bark canoe. Within an hour, he arrived at a small waterfall on the Diamond River, where he had to portage a short distance. Beyond the falls the river would carry him directly to the cabin he had pointed out to Mark. The Inspector's anxiety increased. Mark was nowhere in sight and there was no message at the cabin.

Fear of potential mishaps gripped the Inspector. "How could I have been so stupid as to let him go alone?" He berated himself out loud. The only logical thing to do was retrace the route Mark was supposed to have taken. One location in particular came to the policeman's mind, a chasm on the eastern side of the Diamond where a tributary flowed into the main river bed. It was a tricky area that could be dangerous. He knew it well from past patrols. The potential for tragedy frightened the Inspector and he paddled to the rapids without regard for his own safety.

Leaving the canoe on the shore, he hastened down the river bank on foot in order to carefully examine all of the terrain. It could be an unforgiving land and a person could easily disappear, never to be heard from again. The North rarely divulged its secrets. He was thankful it was not colder. The chasm Inspector Clough had in mind was just ahead. He dreaded to think about the possibilities, then, suddenly, he almost tripped over an inert figure lying beside a bloodstained rock.

It was hard to determine how badly Mark was injured. The Inspector knew that he had been unconscious for at least a day because the bloodied area of his head was already dark red and completely dry. The black flies had been busy at the wound but the headnet protected the rest of his face. The policeman carefully removed the backpack from Mark's shoulders, checked his body for broken bones, and then gently rolled him on his back.

Mark's face had landed in a patch of sphagnum moss, some still clung to his skin. A closer examination of the moss under Mark's face showed evidence of a small amount of vomit and his left ear had a small pool of dried blood. The Inspector did not think it was excessive bleeding, but whatever happen inside the skull he had no way of knowing. The worried policeman gently plucked the pieces of moss from Mark's face and felt for a pulse. His face was warm to the touch. Recognition would have been difficult with the ten day growth of beard on his face. Relieved that the pulse seemed strong, Inspector Clough again checked to determine if any bones were broken, and found no evidence. Mark's wool clothing had protected him against the chilling evening air.

He decided to carry Mark in his arms back to the canoe, returning the way he had come. Someone could come back for the pack later. Carefully lifting Mark so that they faced each other, Inspector Clough slung him over his left shoulder with ease, much as he would a sack of grain. The strong muscular frame of the policeman proved equal to the task, even though Mark weighed about one hundred and fifty pounds. Slowly the mile-long walk to the life-saving canoe was traveled by the powerful Inspector without once stopping to rest. He knew that concussions could be serious, even fatal, and he winced at the possibility of his newfound friend being permanently injured or dying from such a blow to the head. Concussions required that the patient be kept warm and comfortable in order to avoid further shock. Here in the forest there was little he could do until he got Mark in the canoe.

Moving the patient was a judgment call on the part of the Inspector. He could have built a shelter for Mark and left to get help, but he believed that the infirmary was the best place for Mark, calculating that he could be there within a couple of hours. Mark's new warm clothing may have saved his life! The fact that the headnet stayed in place also saved his face from being savaged by the flies.

Inspector Clough deposited Mark's limp body in the center of the canoe and rushed to the nearby cabin where he got some warm blankets to wrap around him. Each stroke of the paddle propelled the canoe closer to the infirmary. At the end of each stroke, the craft slowed slightly against the opposing current of the Diamond. The hardest part of the river was going to be the section around the waterfall. After the portage, it would be much easier paddling. Inspector Clough left Mark in the canoe at the portage and dragged it around the falls along the heavily-used walkway. A short distance from the falls the river widened into the main body of the lake where there was little current to hold him back. Inspector Clough strained his eyes to pick up the light color of the wharf near the police station and pointed the canoe toward it like an arrow. Long steady strokes propelled the fragile craft along the water's surface as fast as it had ever traveled. Beads of sweat dripped from the Inspector's chin. He could not see anybody near the shore, so he continued recklessly towards the infirmary instead of the wharf. The light canoe had enough momentum that when it touched land its full length rode up onto the sandy shore.

The perspiring Inspector effortlessly picked Mark's limp body out of the canoe. Nobody had noticed him yet, so he let out a loud yell to attract attention from whoever was inside. It did not take long to cover the distance up the bank to the infirmary steps, where Bright Cloud opened the door wide for them.

"What's wrong? Who is it?" Bright Cloud asked anxiously. Before she could continue, the exhausted Inspector ran through the door opening and deposited Mark on the nearest empty bed.

"It's Mark Leroux. He's been unconscious for a long time. Apparently, he tripped and banged his head on a rock. I found him only hours ago," gasped the spent Inspector.

She recognized the face in spite of the misleading beard.

"Oh no, not him!" she cried out loud. It was a spontaneous reaction. Panic ran through her body as she reached for Mark's hand to check his pulse. She broke out in a cold sweat. Thank God, she thought, his pulse was higher than normal. She was completely unprepared for such an encounter. Feelings deep within her consciousness reacted to Mark's serious condition. The Inspector was standing beside her breathing heavily after the strenuous ordeal. He had witnessed her response.

"I don't think he has any broken bones, Bright Cloud. I noticed some blood in his right ear and a small amount of vomit residue was still on the ground. He hasn't regained consciousness since I found him, and I don't think he has at any time since the fall," cried the Inspector rationally. "My guess is that it happened sometime yesterday, so he's been out for twenty-four hours, at least."

Bright Cloud's professional instincts finally took command over her impulsive anxiety. She removed the headnet and unfastened Mark's jacket so that she could examine him thoroughly. She carefully straightened his head on the pillow and noticed the uneven pupils in his eyes when she pulled the lids back! He definitely was suffering from a concussion, she admitted. With the Inspector's help, she removed his outer clothing and checked further for the possibility of broken bones. Mark was lucky, nothing was broken!

"I hardly recognized him with the beard and different clothes. I left his pack in the forest and will send someone out to retrieve it as soon as I can. What do you think, Bright Cloud, should we try to bring him around?" The Inspector asked wearily. He was still exhausted from the experience.

Bright Cloud took some extra blankets from a closet and carefully tucked them around Mark. All that could be done now is keep him warm. "There isn't much we can do, Inspector. I'll clean his head injury and sterilize it against infection. Maybe smelling salts would help to bring him around, but we shouldn't give him anything by the mouth."

Inspector Clough silently watched the way Bright Cloud attended to Mark. She was always the professional who analyzed the situation and prescribed treatment, but he could see that she was upset by his condition. This young marine had made an impression upon Flying Eagle's sister, and she was unable to hide it even from herself! At this crucial moment the Inspector admired her as never before. The whole North Country saw her as the compassionate person that she was, and took for granted the role she chose to help her people. What she thought as a person was rarely considered by the people she served, and the Inspector was frequently guilty of that inconsiderate assumption, also. Now, for the first time since he had known her, the

Inspector saw her vulnerability and a glimpse into the world of her private feelings.

"When he left, I knew he would come back. I never dreamed it would be so soon or like this," said Bright Cloud, frustrated with her helplessness. "His temperature is normal. I think we should let him rest after such a trip. Sometimes concussions take a long time, and sometimes they..." She didn't finish the thought, but the kind Inspector understood what she meant.

The Inspector reached out to comfort her in his arms, for she seemed so terribly alone. "He'll come out of this, Bright Cloud. He's a fighter with youth and a strong body on his side. Don't be too negative about the future. Thank God you're here. Take care of yourself, young lady, for we need you," he said, not wanting to intrude any longer into her personal feelings. "If you don't need me anymore, I'll be at the station. I'm tired and hungry." He was almost to the door when Bright Cloud spoke in a hushed tone.

"Thank you again, dear friend, for being there when needed. I don't know what we would do without you. May I ask something of you?"

"Please do."

"Just between the two of us," she cried. "I know that you've discovered one of my secrets today, and I want to keep it that way, a secret between the two of us. Right now I'm confused and unsure of myself. I can't explain what I feel...I haven't had time to think about it."

He had seen a part of what was in her heart, and understood. "Bright Cloud, what I saw was the deep concern you show for all of us. If it was an admission of feelings beyond what you've given to others; then of course, your secret is safe with me. Right now, I'm concerned for him, too. It's only natural to feel bad that this misfortune happened to Mark while he's working on a project for the council. However, Bright Cloud, and I speak as your friend, I would caution you to take note with your head, and if your heart is telling you the same thing, then you should listen carefully. Much sorrow can come to you if it is not meant to be." The Inspector regretted the words as soon as he uttered them. If he had the power to retract them he would gladly have done so.

She turned away from the Inspector, avoiding his eyes, and looked towards Mark's bed. She didn't know what was happening to her world! It had been so structured and orderly before Mark came to the village; now it was in disarray because he had returned and needed her care. He may even be dying and there was nothing she could do to prevent the disaster. She was admitting the dormant feelings to herself and never felt so desolate and helpless in her life as she did at this hour of discovery. The possibility that she may never be able to express her feelings to him only added to her anguish. The revelation of those feelings aroused mixed emotions of turmoil and euphoria, all at the same time...

She felt a strong arm around her shoulder and a reassuring voice from the Inspector. "I didn't mean to hurt you, but we've been friends for too long not to be honest with each other. If I had been blessed with a son, I would have felt proud if he could have been like Mark. I can't think of any other person more worthy of your feelings from the heart, if that is what it truly is. He's from another world, Bright Cloud, and there's a danger of heartache for both of you! I hope you'll realize this, too."

She found some comfort from his words. Then, dutifully motioned him out the door. Once again Bright Cloud showed herself to be the ultimate pragmatist, angry at herself for letting her feelings become so obvious. The Inspector was correct; after all, they were really strangers.

Bright Cloud watched the Inspector from her window at the infirmary. Michelle had gone on a house call at the far end of the village leaving Bright Cloud alone at the infirmary. She was thankful for that. She pulled a table closer to Mark's bed for the things that she needed to dress his head wound. She had to cut some of his hair around the infected parts of the scalp. Later he could have it cut more evenly. The antiseptics must have hurt some, but Mark's inert body showed no response to the treatment. After cleaning the open wounds, she bandaged his head leaving only the eyes open. There was nothing else she could do. She pulled a chair beside his bed and sat quietly with him. She thought carefully about what the Inspector had said to her. Maybe she had been infatuated by the drama of the presentation; she did not know. It was of little comfort to analyze her own feelings, because she always came back to the same premise: if it was not her heart speaking, why did it hurt so much?

Later in the afternoon, Michelle Gurney returned to the infirmary, aghast to see Bright Cloud with a distressed look on her face.

"What's wrong?" demanded Michelle.

"It's Mark… he's been injured. The Inspector found him in the forest by the river and carried him here a few hours ago. I think he has a concussion from a bad fall on a rock. I've cleaned his head wound and made him comfortable. He hasn't regained consciousness yet. I'm afraid for him. I've sent for Father Dumont," Bright Cloud answered, avoiding Michelle's searching look.

Michelle checked Mark using the same procedures Bright Cloud had used. His pulse was still faster than normal, and the eye check confirmed his uneven pupils. She then placed her ear against his nostrils and listened carefully for several seconds.

"He should be okay; his breathing is steady and slower than the high pulse would indicate. You're right, Bright Cloud, he's got to remain quiet for a while. The hard blow to the head made the skull swell abnormally, thereby squeezing the brain. You've already made him comfortable, Bright Cloud, yet, you look worse than our patient here. What's wrong? Is there something you're not telling me?"

"No, nothing important. It was just so unexpected to have him show up like this. A short time ago he seemed so strong and formidable in his uniform. I feel responsible for his condition by asking for his help," she replied hesitantly.

"Now, that kind of self-abuse is uncalled for and accomplishes nothing; you know better than that. This accident could've happen to him under any circumstances, anywhere. Let me fix you some tea. I'd like some myself, its been a trying day so far. Well, I see the good Father coming up the path, so I'll put out another cup for him, too."

"Thanks, Mike," said Bright Cloud, thankful for Michelle's reassuring presence. The infirmary and the people of the village were well served when Michelle volunteered to help at the request of the church missionary group. Her competence was matched by her boundless energy and good nature that always seemed to be in control. Right now, Bright Cloud was not thinking rationally, and she was relieved to have Michelle's support.

The Inspector had already told Father Dumont about Mark. It did not take the priest long before he came to the infirmary to check his condition firsthand. "What's your opinion on the condition of the young American, Bright Cloud?"

"I'm not a doctor, Father, though I wish we had one here right now. He's still unconscious and has been since the accident. He's in the hands of your God…"

"He's your God also," replied the priest sharply, noticing her distress. "Is there something I don't know that I should?"

"No, it's just that we're only nurses, not doctors. Sometimes the hardest part of the job is when we can't do anything except wait and observe. It makes us feel so helpless. Come, Father, Mike is preparing tea. We're thankful for your company." Bright Cloud led him into the next room. The two nurses worked under his directorship, but he never put them in a position where they felt subordinate to him. His support for their efforts was complete and sincere.

"One thing is certain, our young American friend is in the hands of God, but up here he uses you two as a surrogate to do his healing for Him. I'll pray for the Captain's speedy recovery, and for our two angels of the North Woods."

Evening shadows enveloped the outpost village, and the tempo of daily life slackened. The sun sank from view behind the high ridge to the west where the rays still reached for the clouds, reflecting a beautiful halo of colors along the top of the ridge just before it disappeared from view. Bright Cloud watched the sunset from her vigil over Mark, and gladly accepted it as a good omen. Michelle had turned in for the evening after soliciting a solemn promise from Bright Cloud that she would be called if there was any change in Mark's condition.

Bright Cloud relaxed in the chair and thought about her life. She was a young lady so much in demand by the people she served, that there was hardly any time left for her to have a private life of her own. When she was at school in New York State several young men expressed a strong desire to want to know her better. Even though she was popular with all of the students at school, she did not encourage the young men because of her intense dedication to her studies. It seemed to her that she had always been busy to the point of exhaustion from the time she was a young girl. She thought it was the way life was supposed to be.

She was content with her life at the infirmary; it gave her a satisfying sense of fulfillment. When Mark came to the village, she discovered a part of herself that had been long ignored and unfulfilled. New feelings and emotions she had never felt before began to stir within her. They were unsettling and disruptive. She felt, for the very first time, that something important was lacking in her life. The Inspector had spoken the truth with much wisdom. There could be no denying that he spoke from experience. She herself had experienced several instances of mixed courtships that ended in unhappiness or, sometimes, tragedy. She did not deceive herself of the cruel facts.

There was nothing wrong with having the feelings, she thought. It would, however, be wrong to make too much of them. If they are to be fulfilled or not, the future held the answer for her. She had enough faith in her God to leave it in His hands. In the meantime, she found comfort acknowledging the reality of her emotions and in the perceptions of those feelings. She could never apologize for having had them in the first place!

In the middle of the evening a ray of light from the moon overlooking the lake beamed through the window casting a shadow across the room. Bright Cloud finally succumbed to the needs of her weary body and dozed off to sleep with her hands clasped together resting in her lap. Light from the moon illuminated her white smock. Sitting in the chair beside the bed, the shadows of the night hid her face from view.

Mark stirred once without being detected by Bright Cloud. As a matter of fact, he opened his eyes several times, but could not see anything except a bright light shining into a room. Not knowing where he was or what had happened to him, Mark's initial reaction was that he had died. Laying on the bed with warm blankets around him was a comforting sensation. Slowly, as if in a dream, recollection of the fall came to him. He had a headache and could feel the heavy bandages wrapped around his head. His first thought was that he was still in France at the hospital.

Mark studied the moonlight in the room, noticing that someone was sitting in a chair beside him. He did not know who it was. Her head and the upper part of her body was hidden by the dark shadows. The sudden movement of his arms as he tried to pull free of the blanket was detected by Bright Cloud. She was quickly on her feet ready to light the lamp. Mark was blinded by the sudden light from the kerosene lamp. Out of the harsh blindness came a clear voice beside him that Mark would recognize anywhere.

"You've scared us, Captain," whispered a relieved Bright Cloud in his ear. "Do you hurt anywhere?"

Mark's voice was faint and the words came slowly from his parched lips. "Could I have some water, please?"

Bright Cloud rushed to get a glass of cold water with a straw and gently placed it between his dry and cracked lips. His response so far was encouraging.

"Are you in pain, Captain?" she softly asked, holding the glass while he sipped through the straw.

"Oh, yes." The sound of his voice was strange, even to himself. "My head throbs and it's hard to focus my eyes."

"Drink slowly, you're at the infirmary. The Inspector found you on the trail and brought you here. You've had a bad fall," Bright Cloud explained in a soft voice.

Mark fell asleep again. Bright Cloud felt for a pulse and was relieved to find that it had returned to normal. She checked his eyes again and the pupils were both the same. She could hardly contain her joy; a crisis had passed. Bright Cloud pulled the blanket closer to his neck and tucked it around him. Normal color would slowly return to his ashen face. Father Dumont's optimistic prediction had been right, she thought, turning off the lamp to resume her lonely vigil until Michelle came in the morning.

Several days had passed since Mark's injury. His recovery was complete with no complications, except the large cut on his head, which still required a change of bandage every day. He was on his feet the first day he woke up from his coma. After the second day, he gave in to the Inspector's urging to move into the barracks with him.

The infirmary was busy, as usual, with many patients coming from long distances to get help from the two nurses. Mark was surprised to see how many children came to the infirmary for injuries and normal childhood diseases such as chickenpox. Pregnant women were common, too, and the care of the newborn child was a task both Michelle and Bright Cloud looked forward to. Michelle fitted in to the routine with compassion and grace. She brought her own style of selfless service and her own high level of professionalism to the isolated and obscure facility. There were many things about the forest people that she respected, and her sincerity was reciprocated by those who got to know her. She soon developed a reputation far and wide on following through on a promise or a commitment. Mark found her easier to talk to than Bright Cloud.

Mark was not as successful at figuring out Bright Cloud. She had changed since his first visit, and he had the distinct feeling that she was trying to avoid him. She would not engage him in long conversations when he was at the infirmary like she did when he first visited the village. He never doubted her concern for his welfare. When she changed his head bandage, she was especially gentle. He had no right to expect anything more from her, yet, she seemed to be less willing to spend time and talk to him the way she did before his injury. Now, she even seemed a little uneasy in his presence. He tried, on several occasions, to make eye contact with her, but she quickly avoided him. This led him to believe that he may have said or done something to offend her. He didn't know. The Inspector was out most of the day and returned by canoe on the lake to find Mark sitting at the shore watching him approach the dock. It had been four days since the Inspector carried Mark to the infirmary. "Hello, Mark," hailed the policeman from the canoe. He was trailing a fish line behind the canoe and pulled it out of the water for Mark to see. It contained a half dozen whitefish.

"This is our supper, and it can't come any too soon for me." The Inspector laughed heartily, walking towards the station.

"Inspector, you're an excellent provisioner of the larder," exclaimed Mark, admiring the string of fish.

"I'll get the fire going if you'd like to clean these up," suggested the Inspector with a grin.

"My pleasure," answered Mark, checking the sharpness of his belt knife. "They're nice ones. We never get fresh water fish this large in southern Maine."

"This land is blessed with cold waters and large supplies of fish. Good thing too, because it's the main diet up here. The Cree and the Montagnais would be hard pressed to survive without the fish now that they no longer follow caribou herds for foods like they used to. These whitefish are tasty though!" said the Inspector, chopping small pieces of kindling from a dry cedar stick. A few moments later, the dry wood was snapping and cracking under the frying pan.

"Inspector, I've been thinking," said Mark pensively.

"I could tell you had something on your mind, young man."

"In a day or two I'm going to go back in the forest and start what I came up here to do. I'm feeling better and will go easy at first. There's a lot to be done and I'm restless to be at it."

"I don't see any problem with that; you know your limitations better than anyone else. I've taken the liberty of checking out a cabin for your exclusive use on the Swift River almost in the middle of the forest tract in question. I've even had some of the men in the village provision it for you. They're cutting a supply of firewood for your cabin as we speak. That way you can spend your time doing the important things you came to do. The cabin is in good shape and ideally located for your needs. The trail north through the village, past lookout rock goes directly in front of it. I've used it myself many times. It's about ten miles from the village. Word has already been spread throughout the region that it's yours to use as you see fit."

"I didn't expect that, Inspector, thanks for your help again." The two ate the rest of the meal in silence. There was something about the solitude of the forest that made men not talk as much as they do in more civilized society. It was the mark of the woodsman to say little and do much.

Mark broke the silence first. "I've got a crazy question for you. I've heard it from different people and I'm still not sure if there's any truth to it."

"If you ask a crazy question, you end up with a crazy answer," said the Inspector with an impish grin.

"Well, here it is. If a person starts out in a straight line at a normal walk and carries a rifle in his right hand for a long enough distance, the weight of the rifle will be responsible for his body to take shorter steps on the right side. Thus, he'll end up walking in a large circle," Mark finished with a twinkle in his eye and half expected the policeman to call it nonsense.

"Yes, I've heard that one, too, and I'd be inclined to believe it, if the terrain was relatively flat without trails. However, it's a real good riddle over a few too many drinks. If you try it and it works, let me know!" said the Inspector with a grin and a shake of the head.

"I've wondered about it for a long time," said Mark with a broad grin.

"On a more serious note, do you have any lasting effects from the mustard gas used by the Germans?" questioned the Inspector. "Did any of your exposed skin get a prolonged dose of the chemical?"

"Not direct exposure, but I did get burned quite bad under the arms, around the groin and a couple of other places where there was moisture. I was lucky, mine cleared up after a year or so. Do you still have problems from it?" Mark asked of Inspector Clough, who had not talked very much about his war experiences.

"When I first arrived in France with the Canadian Brigade, about April, 1915, we were involved in the first use of gas by the Germans at Ypres. We were attacking along beside some Algerian Zouaves when the gas hit us. Evidently the mixture was not correctly concocted, so it was not as successful as the Germans had planned. It was too heavy and settled in the low spots. We got away from it by seeking higher elevations. I was splattered with wet mud from a mortar shell and the gas reacted rapidly with the moisture, as everyone soon found out. I had some ugly burns that kept getting infected, and they bother me some, even after all these years. I was just curious if others had the same reaction to the gas." The Inspector drew on his pipe, blowing smoke rings in the air over his head.

"I'm sure some soldiers did. My own wounds were just not as visible as some. However, I feel stronger than ever, thanks to you and the good people here at Fort Lewis," Mark replied with a sense of pride and accomplishment. He felt his confidence level growing daily.

"You've changed since I first met you a month ago, Yank. These North Woods can help a strong man find himself, but she can be a fickle mistress, too, and destroy him just as easily. I've known of men driven mad by the isolation and the loneliness, or even the constant cry of the wind in the winter." The Inspector spoke with conviction, looking out the window.

"When I started out on the walk by the river, I knew that I needed some time to myself. I was fortunate that you came looking for me when you did, Inspector. I owe you my life."

"I'll admit you gave us a scare that time, Yank. I'm glad I found you quick enough. If our situation had been reversed, you would've done the same thing for me or anyone else. It's what we do for each other up here in the forest. All of us who do our jobs in the wilderness eventually develop a kinship with one another that transcends all races and cultures. It's a sign of strength to be self-reliant and independent, but it can be foolish to carry it too far. We're never really alone." Mark thought he saw a hint of sadness come over the burly policeman. The room fell silent for a few seconds.

"I don't mean to pry, Inspector, but do you have a family out there? I've only seen you at your work."

"The Mounted Police has become my family, Mark. I was married and my wife waited for me through four long years of war. Before I could get home to see her, she died from the influenza epidemic." A veil of sadness slowly came over the Inspector's face. He looked across the lake in order to avoid Mark's glance.

Mark regretted bringing up such a painful subject. "I'm sorry, Inspector, I didn't know. I understand some of your loss. My father died from the same thing before I returned home. We have that in common."

"Don't feel bad because you brought up the subject. It's not my way to talk about myself, so I don't bother to volunteer information. My wife was a dear person who filled my life with love. She was a tower of strength, especially during the war. Frankly, I had a hard time picking up my life without her. I'm still thankful for the memories that we shared."

"I'm sorry, Inspector, it was not right for me to pry."

"No, Yank, it was not for you to know, and I apologize for burdening you with my sorrow."

"When I was a patient at the hospital in France, it took me a while to sort things out. My feeling of self-worth was at a low point. I feel different now and am content with the direction my life is taking. Some time in the future I would like to go back to France and visit the places where I fell apart. Only then will I feel that my life has come full circle."

"Perhaps that would be beneficial. You're young and have a long time ahead of you. We should not dwell on the things that depress us. Life goes on. The only hand we have to play is the one we've been dealt. You're about to embark on a new assignment and my police work continues to be a source of satisfaction to me. There is much to feel good about in life, if we care to look for it. I'll be leaving tomorrow for a few days. Corporal Haynes can take care of things in my absence. Your pack is in the stock room behind me here. He went out the same day to retrieve it," said Inspector Clough, changing the subject. "Your forestry tools have not come in yet. As soon as they do I'll make sure you get them. Running Deer and Father Dumont have taken care of the supply details of the cabin. There's another cabin located at the northeast corner of the land which they're also supplying for your occasional use if you need it."

"I'd like to start back again soon. Tomorrow sounds about right for me to check out the center cabin, as you call it. I'll see what Bright Cloud and Michelle have to say about my wound," commented Mark.

"I'm sure she'll try to limit your activity for a while longer. That's her nature with everybody. I guess I've already sort of adopted our two nurses. I never had any children of my own."

"They're fortunate to have such a benefactor, Inspector."

Nighttime comes to the village of Fort Lewis much quicker than it does in the lower latitudes. The darkness of the night has to be experienced in order to understand just how completely it blocks out the ability to see objects. The stars make very little difference to the blackness of the night. In the distance, a dog barked and was answered by others at the opposite end of the village. The Inspector had already turned in and Mark planned to follow suit very shortly. The more he found out about the Inspector, the more his respect grew for the gentle policeman. Mark soon fell asleep.

The next day came with scattered clouds and partial sunshine. Mark was up early and ready for the walk to the center cabin. He shaved off the stubble of beard and headed for the infirmary to see if anyone was in. Some patients were still at rest in the main wardroom, so he checked in the small kitchen to find Bright Cloud tending the fire with her back to him. A board on the floor squeaked and startled her. Bright Cloud turned to see who it was. She looked tired and drawn, yet relieved to find that it was Mark standing there.

"I didn't mean to surprise you. I'm sorry," Mark apologized.

"No, it was nothing. Would you care to join me in a cup of tea? I was just fixing some." Bright Cloud seemed genuinely glad to see him.

"I'd like that," answered Mark, taking a seat at the small table near the stove.

"I hope you slept well. Your color is an improvement over when the Inspector carried you here, but I see that your wound is still bleeding," observed Bright Cloud, taking a seat at the table beside Mark with two tea cups. "As long as it continues to bleed, the possibility of infection exists."

"It has to be getting better, I'm feeling more like myself, maybe a little weaker, but that should be improving soon. I wanted to see if you would change the bandage for me, because I'm going out to the center cabin this morning. I could take extra dressings if you think it's necessary."

Mark looked up from his tea cup to find her looking at him in the same manner as a scolding mother to an unruly child. She quickly replied, "But a trip alone is not wise. Your wound is still draining and you should wait for it to heal completely."

He did not disagree with her statement, but she saw that her protests fell on deaf ears! He was restless and wanted to start doing something worthwhile. His mind was already made up. She loaded a small piece of wood in the stove, and left the room to get some bandages. There was an awkward silence when she returned.

"What are you going to do when you get there?" asked Bright Cloud. She did not want to interfere with any of his plans, but it was not wise to take on too much at such an early stage of his recovery.

"I'd like to get settled in the cabin first. I need a chance to study the information I've already collected from your father and others. I need to study past land use patterns of the area. If I know what has been done in the past, I can prepare for the future better. Most of all, I need a place to focus myself without interruptions so that I can design a forest management system that will work for the tribal land. I guess what I'm trying to say is, I need a place to lay out the project in an atmosphere where I can concentrate on it, and not be in the way of other people. The cabin is a great idea, it can be my office as well as my bunk," he explained.

Bright Cloud seemed pleased with the logic of his answer. She finished wrapping the bandage around his head, testing its tightness with a gentle tug. "The cabin is small, but you'll be able to do your work there. I'll give you some extra bandages to take along, and some sulfa and hydrogen peroxide. Change the dressing every day. The wound is looking good, and should heal without complications provided you keep it disinfected."

"I promise to change it as you have instructed," Mark finished his tea and reluctantly started to rise from the small table. Then he abruptly changed his mind and sat down to confront Bright Cloud with something that had been on his mind these past few days.

"Bright Cloud, I don't wish to offend you or be a burden in any way, and I mean that most sincerely…" he was having trouble finding the right words.

"You could never be a burden to me, Captain," she replied, without meeting his questioning stare.

"I'd like to be your friend, but, lately, I've sensed a reaction, on your part, to my presence these past few days that has made me feel uneasy. It has not been the same as my first visit and I want to ask you if there is something I've done or said that has hurt you. If that is the case, I'm truly sorry and I apologize. The last thing I want is to hurt you," he cried.

Bright Cloud not only heard his voice but carefully recorded every word he spoke in her pounding heart. If she was not careful now, she would betray herself. She frantically hunted for the right words to explain her position and answered without looking at him.

"You've nothing to apologize for; it's I who must ask for your forgiveness. I share my father's happiness that you've returned to us. That joy turned to fear when the Inspector found you. I'm sorry if I've distressed you; I didn't intend to do that." Mark could see that she was distraught and waited for her to continue. "I owe you an explanation for my actions. You, as a stranger to our culture, must understand that we live beyond the edge of the civilized world up here, and there is no room for chance or unpreparedness. Death and tragedy are daily occurrences here to my people, and sometimes I have to turn a cold heart towards it or I could not continue to be of help. I try hard to be objective and professional. Often it's the only defense against tragedy that's available to me, and I have used it more often than most. If I led you to think that I didn't care, then I'm sincerely sorry. It was never my intention to do such a thing. Now, please, I must return to the patients, they're waiting for care. I wish you 'bon voyage' on your walk to the cabin. Go easy and you should be fine."

Anxious to not be questioned anymore, Bright Cloud impulsively reached out and touched his shoulder in a farewell gesture, and left the room. Mark remained seated for a while not quite sure what to think. This morning was a new experience for him. He left the infirmary with more questions in his head than answers!

It took Mark an hour to gather what he wanted for the trip. After a visit to the Hudson Bay Store, he shouldered his pack and headed towards the center cabin. Walking abreast of the infirmary, he caught a movement in one of the windows. The front door opened shortly and the slender form of Bright Cloud appeared. She must have been watching for his passing.

"Be careful, Mark," she hollered to him in her clear voice.

"I will, Bright Cloud, thank you for everything," he replied with a wave of the hand.

By the time he was past the bridge over the spring Mark looked back to see her still watching him. A slow wave of the hand from her made his step a little lighter. Bright Cloud was consumed with emptiness. Michelle saw Bright Cloud at the door, and being the astute observer of human behavior that she was, understood what was in her heart. She placed a sympathetic arm around Bright Cloud's waist and helped her back inside the infirmary.

Chapter Ten

The path leading from the village intersected the trail which led to the dominating ridge west of the village. Lookout Rock was poised at the edge of the escarpment towering over the village like an ancient sentinel. Mark walked past Running Deer's cabin and saw no sign of him. A short distance from the village, the light on the trail was blanked out by the overtopping canopies of the spruce trees. The forest stands here were still a part of the organized township of Fort Lewis. The trail leading to the Northeast was wider than a single-person foot trail, but could not be used as a roadway for horse-drawn carts without further improvements.

Mark learned that the Cree forest tract was one of many scattered throughout the province. The Native Americans had exclusive hunting, fishing and trapping rights on most of the lands. However, on these special tracts, ownership was absolute. They controlled the mineral rights, riparian or water rights, and whatever forest products could be harvested from the land.

The center cabin was about ten miles from the village. The boundary line for the tribal land was about half way between the village and the center cabin and was well marked where the trail intersected it. Mark noticed the recent ax blazes defining one of the boundaries as he passed into the tribal forest tract. The line was marked out in a north-south azimuth. Running Deer had assured him that the complete perimeter had been documented and blazed. He was reassured to know that it had been completed because it eliminated the need for him to do a boundary survey prior to completing the forest management plan. The survey would have meant additional manpower and equipment. The balance of the field work for the inventory and growth determination could be done by himself without additional assistance.

Mark observed that the forest was well stocked with coniferous species, mostly spruces and balsam fir, but a scattered number of eastern larch grew on some of the drier sites. There was also a mixture of deciduous trees, maples and birches being the most common, along the streams and poorly drained areas. The trees were vigorous and normal size where the soil was deep enough for stability. For one thing, the stands were densely populated with more stems per acre, making travel difficult. The thick stands made the understory relatively darker, giving them a forbidding atmosphere. The mature trees retained their dead branches, unlike the white pine stands further south, which have a tendency to self-prune themselves. Mark could feel the vastness of the northern coniferous forest he was entering. It added to the haunting desolate feeling of being alone in a landscape without end. There is a primal majesty to the northern forest that the pine forests do not have. Part of the majesty comes from the extremes of weather and its threatening magnitude.

Some of the more productive stands on sites where the soil has greater depth produce excellent quality spruce trees of 16-24 inches dbh (diameter breast height = 4.5 feet above ground). The balsam fir does not grow as large, because it has a shorter life span than the spruce. Generally, scattered on some of the poorer soils, was a small amount of banksiana pine, which Mark had never seen growing in a natural state. Another species he encountered of commercial importance was jack pine, which was confined to the lighter soils, but nevertheless was an important component of the northern forest community.

Within a mile or so after entering the tract, Mark came upon an area the Inspector described in great detail to him. It was a low lying area that was flooded by beaver many years ago. It had once been a dense stand of mature trees; then the busy beavers constructed their dams and flooded the section, thus killing the standing trees. Near the trail, Mark was introduced to his first example of the Cree Indian's memorial to a person that was held in reverence. They were called "lob-sticks", which were created from the large spruce and cedar trees killed by the flooding waters. The Crees then pruned all the branches on the dead trees to the precarious top of the tree creating a unique spike or plume. This wooden spire was their cenotaph or memorial to a person buried somewhere else. It was a striking tribute created to the memory of Flying Eagle. The spiked "lob-sticks" towered over the area like church spires towering over a town. It was a hallowed spot to the members of Flying Eagle's tribe. A fitting tribute to a beloved warrior, Flying Eagle would have been pleased. It was simple and elegant. There was a peaceful presence within the area, and Mark had a peculiar feeling that he was not alone.

Mark decided to take a break beside the trail at the site of the cenotaph. He took off his pack to enjoy a candy bar and a strip of dried meat similar to what he used to eat at home, his father called it "jerky". It was tasty and easy to carry on the trail. Wildlife was plentiful in the beaver-flooded wetlands. Birds were everywhere. He recognized a snipe and some thin beaked plovers in the meadow area nearby. In the depths of the forest Mark heard the yipping of foxes. It was a sound that added character to the cacophony of the deep wilderness. The irritating noises had driven many wilderness dwellers mad. The wily scavengers of the boreal forest were capable of maintaining their irritating bark for long periods of time, day and night.

Windthrow, Mark observed, was definitely a problem on the shallow soil of the Canadian shield. Whenever the wind velocity reached a certain intensity, the soil was incapable of supporting the trees upright. That of itself, indicated the desirability of using small size clear-cuts as a harvesting tool. Keeping the openings small and seed-bearing trees to the west and north would adequately regenerate areas of several acres in size with seedlings, and it would help to dissipate wind velocity. It also solved the problem of trying to reproduce more spruce which is the longer lasting more valuable species.

The sight of Bright Cloud waving good-bye to him from the infirmary remained vivid in his memory. There was something almost spiritual about her. Mark could not determine if it was a quality which radiated from her, or if it was a figment of his own imagination.

The remainder of the trip to the center cabin was uneventful. Mark made it by mid-day. When he first saw the cabin from a rise on the path he noticed a few "lob-sticks" around it. The cabin was sturdily constructed of cedar logs heavily chinked with clay mixed with moose hair. It was approximately twenty feet by twenty-five feet with the door facing to the south next to the river. One window faced west which made the interior dark for the morning hours. The stone fireplace was beautifully constructed with a large hand-hewn half log serving as a mantel. The large stone chimney and fireplace took up most of the north wall of the cabin. It was intentionally placed there, because it was difficult to drive heat north if the heat source is at the southern end of the room. The interior had a warm, comfortable feel to him. Leaving the door open to let more light into the dark interior, Mark noticed a note on the table. It read as follows:

"We hope that you will like the cabin, Captain Leroux. It was a special place for Flying Eagle and myself. There is a storage cellar under the floor near the hearth for canned foods and supplies. The bedding is in a roll suspended from the ceiling near the bed. This helps to discourage rodents should they get inside. The cupboards are filled with food and utensils. We hope this cabin will be a safe refuge for you. We are indebted to you and glad to have you with us, good luck."
Running Deer

In the dry sink near the door was a fresh pail of water drawn from the river outside. Mark could not have been more pleased with his "homecoming". The small lean-to on the south wall beside the door was filled with a large supply of dry firewood. Beside the hearth stood the wood box, piled high with dry logs. The tribal elders had thought of everything. An unwritten law of the woods was that you left the cabin as you found it with a good supply of dry wood ready for instant use in an emergency.

Before the day passed, Mark was anxious to test his luck fishing in the Swift River. Within a short time he caught a string of fish large enough for several meals. He had developed an appetite for the whitefish that populated the northern Canadian waters and looked forward to creating menus to satisfy his appetite. Fish was a diet staple in the north, supplemented by geese in the spring and fall when they followed their migration routes. Caribou, deer, or moose were taken any season whenever the opportunities presented themselves. One did not have to live in the wilderness very long before you understood that hunger was the dominant motivating force in the region. Constant diligence in the search for food was required for survival. One misjudgment or stretch of bad luck could be disastrous.

The Inspector had told him about the tragic famine and pestilence that had been the curse of 1910. That year the snows broke all records and accumulated to such heights that nothing was able to move. Many perished from hunger. Remembering the terrible winter of that year was part of the reason behind Running Deer's decision to educate his children and to prepare them for the future so that they would not have to bear a similar ordeal.

Another item on Mark's agenda for the day was a curious desire to make bannock bread. He checked his food supply, and the main ingredients of barley flour and/or oatmeal was available in the well stocked cabin. In order to sweeten the unleavened bread he added some molasses to the moist mixture and poured it into a greased cast iron frying pan. All he needed now was to get the fire going to cook his creation for the evening meal. The thought of fish and warm bread made him hungry again.

His bannock bread did not turn out as well as expected — it was soggy. Nevertheless, it satisfied his hunger. The next time he would use less water in the mix. Experience was the best teacher.

Mark's first evening in the central cabin was one of satisfaction with himself and the way his life was going. Contentment was a part of his satisfaction, and it felt right. The bandage on his head was no longer bleeding so he decided to let it go until the next day before he placed new bandages on the cut. The trip and excitement of settling into his new home was tiring and the small bunk felt good to his tired body. The only sound he could hear was the rush of the river. The restful sounds reminded him of his home in Maine beside the brook. One night, when Mark was a small child, his father told him that if the rocks are removed from the river bed, the music is removed from the river. Tonight, on the eve of his new adventure, it would have been nice to share this experience with his father, the way he had so many other things in his life.

Nocturnal animals take over the landscape from the daylight creatures, and the night becomes a noisy cacophony where life, death, and survival co-exist in the forest. The fight for survival in the North Woods is its singular constant, and survival of the fittest is the law of the land.

Mark approached the new day with a shout that must have been heard for miles in the stillness of the morning. It was his intention to check the map he had been given by the Bureau of Indian Affairs against what was actually on the ground. The thirty thousand acres was approximately ten miles square. In order to traverse the circumference he would need a minimum of two days. A perimeter patrol would do several things for him. First, it would orient him to the tract before starting the forest inventory cruises. Second, it would give him the opportunity to make personal observations of the physical condition and location of the boundary markers. Another important result of a perimeter reconnoiter was a chance to observe the physical disposition of the tract in relation to the surrounding distinguishing landmarks and obtain a feel for the terrain. He needed that.

Mark packed a supply of food, his tent and blankets for at least two days on the perimeter. A good spot to start would be the line running north-south near the "lob-stick" cenotaph that intersected the same trail he had used yesterday.

The lines had been cleared for compass sightings a few years ago, which made the boundary line relatively easy to walk. He did freshen up some blaze marks and added more where he thought it was appropriate. The line ran perpendicular to the pathway leading to Fort Lewis on a north-south axis, climbing higher and higher onto the ridge that dominated the village to the west. The slope was long and steep for about two miles where Mark found an established corner. From that corner the line ran due west up the steepest portion of the ridge. It leveled off at the top where he decided to call it a day and spend the night on top of the ridge where the black flies were less of a problem.

The panoramic view from the top of the northern shoulder was breathtaking. He could not see the center cabin, but he could make out the "lob-sticks" beside the river nearby. The rock formation was a good location for an overview of the tribal forest tract. The only drawback to the forest management enterprise is the existence of the Canadian Shield, which is famous for its acid soil and shallow depth to bedrock. Mark was concerned about the long range effect of harvest operations on the productive sustainability of the soil. Neither government nor private industry had any answers to such a potential problem. It may prove necessary to modify management plans to reflect the response of boreal forests to harvest techniques, and to make changes that reflect the experience of prolonged intensive management. Further to the south, the paper companies had been operating with satisfactory results for many years. Water quality and water retention do not suffer, provided the cut-over openings are kept reasonably small. More native species of birds and animals frequented the cut-over areas than the mature forest sites.

Shortly after Mark had stopped for the night at the top of the ridge, a shot rang out across the still evening air. It came from somewhere in the northeastern corner of the tract. There was a cabin in that area that Running Deer told him he could use if necessary. Hunting continued all year round in the vicinity, and he would not be surprised that some hunter would use the advantages of lights at night to attract the game.

The ledge outcrop Mark was standing on obstructed his view of Fort Lewis, so in the fading light of dusk he walked south until he could pick up the lights of the village and the dark mass of the lake. The scene gave him a feeling of detachment, even a twinge of loneliness. The picture of Bright Cloud waving to him, and the angelic expression of her concern when he first woke from his coma still played on his mind. Her sudden coolness towards him was somewhat baffling, and perhaps he was as much troubled by his own response to Bright Cloud as he was to her detachment whenever he was around her. More and more she was beginning to dominate his thoughts. Acknowledging that simple fact was easy for him because he did not deceive himself. He continued to be captivated by a very beautiful woman he hardly knew, and it bothered him. Whatever the future held for him, one thing was certain, if carrying the image of the beautiful copper-skinned maiden, somewhere below him at Fort Lewis, enhanced his chances to renew himself, then maybe there was no harm in listening to his heart!

The next day, Mark continued to walk the most westerly line north of the ridge where he came to a species that he had not encountered in such large numbers as he now witnessed. Mark had seen some pine north of the Saint Lawrence River, but not on the scale he found in the northwest corner of the property. There was an extensive stand of jack pine and banksiana pine of all sizes; however, a large percentage of the trees were large sawlog size. These indicated the presence of more productive soil, because the trees had grown to a large size without windthrow damage. Generally, jack pine is absent from sites with deep fertile soils where the spruces and balsam fir are able to express dominance and are more aggressive in their initial stages of growth.

In the pine stands the ground was covered with a thick buildup of needle litter. In places it was a foot thick. By contrast, the spruce-fir stands are predominantly covered with club moss and a sprinkling of lesser species such as Labrador tea, sheep laurel, and snow berry. Some of the understory of the jack pine stand is composed of aspen and white birch on the more moist sites. The drier sites have a high density of jack pine reproduction.

Discovering the pine sites was exciting to Mark because he could write the management plan and prescription of treatment with more certainty of success than he could for the spruce-fir type. The two forest types would require different management and harvesting methods, and the silvicultural requirements of the two species were distinctly different.

There are two basic methods of managing forests for maximum production, the all-age system and the even-age system. Mark had already decided, as a result of his reconnoiter of the bounds, that he would handle the pine as an all-aged system for management, and that he would recommend the selection system of partial cuts for harvesting the forest products. That meant that on every acre, theoretically, there would be an even distribution of trees from one year old to 100 years old, and every five years you could harvest the oldest stems to make room for the younger trees. The ideal model would have an even distribution of the different age and size groups. Thus the forest becomes self-perpetuating and yields a continuous supply of products without depleting itself, provided all things remain equal.

The other basic system of management is even-aged management, whereby harvests are made in small clear-cuts to regenerate a larger percentage of spruce all in the same age class. The principle of sustained-yield is upheld by meticulously implementing the planned scattering of the harvest. In the ideally managed forest, after 60 to 100 years, depending on the rotation of the forest in question, you can go back to the original harvested area and continue the rotation cycle again, forever. The size of the cut area in both systems is governed by the total size of the tract and the rate of growth. If the harvest is maintained below the net growth, then the forest is building capital for the future much like a bank account builds capital with interest. If the forest is overcut, harvesting more than the net growth, then depletion of the forest resource is taking place. Mark believed his role to be the creation of a management document consisting of the following: (1) examination of past uses and the application of those uses to the present; (2) documenting what the present forest is composed of to the best of his ability; (3) establishment of a reasonable set of goals to be obtained: and (4) to set a standard of performance that will obtain the greatest number of goals, yet preserve the integrity of the total land resource. Most foresters by their very nature are long-range thinking people because the work they do bears fruit, primarily, for the next generation. Therein lies the fascination and the reward of the profession – the opportunity to serve and make a difference in the quality of life for mankind. Stewardship of the natural resources benefit from his professionalism.

The northwestern corner of the tract was a pile of rocks in a pyramid shape. This most northerly corner was beginning to look like the other spruce-fir stands near the center cabin. The pine stands ended less than a mile from the corner. Wet areas, bogs, ponds, and streams abounded throughout the northern part of Quebec Province.

With some luck Mark hoped to be at the second cabin on the tract by late afternoon. The Swift River was running high and living up to its name. He plunged into the frigid water and swam across. His food resources were getting low. Mark ate his last candy bar while he dried out from the swim.

Following the line to the cabin near the northeast corner of the tract, Mark had the uneasy feeling of being watched by something or someone. He didn't feel threatened, but he did find it disquieting. Maybe it could be explained by the fact that other forest travelers may have the same feeling about his presence. If it somehow involved those individuals that were selling whiskey, Mark believed that they were no threat to him, and it was to their advantage to remain unknown.

Mark could feel his physical strength returning. It was exhilarating to get back to the forest again. He kept the bandage on his head for insect protection as much as for the wound, which had stopped bleeding. The two weeks previously spent on the trail by the river had conditioned him very well; however, that level of stamina disappeared quickly during his recovery from the concussion.

The northeast corner marker of the forest tract was the same as the opposite corner in the west with the same type of boundary marker of stones in a pyramid. Now, he turned southward along the eastern boundary and walked for a couple of miles when he came to a trail that ran east-west, and was well packed from frequent use. Leaving the boundary, Mark followed the trail westward where his map indicated the location of the cabin.

The cabin soon came into view from the trail. It was similar in size to the center cabin but was covered with a vine that had a small reddish lavender flower, that upon closer examination looked like miniature spruce trees. He had never seen such a stunning display of color. It must be the fireweed he had heard so much about. At a distance, it made the cabin look as if it was painted red or was on fire — hence the name fireweed.

Otherwise the cabin was a duplicate of his center cabin, but Mark did not have the same feelings towards this dwelling. Maybe it was the vine covering, but it had a more sinister look and feel. Mark's main concern was the food cached inside. He was famished! Mark opened the door to a rather untidy cabin with dirty dishes on the table and dried foodstuffs left in pans on the fireplace grill. Ashes in the fireplace were still warm probably from the night before. The messy bunk had also been slept in. All of this left Mark with an uneasy feeling, confirming his premonitions of being watched for the past few days.

Most of the provisions that Running Deer cached at the cabin seemed to be intact, so Mark went about fixing something for a meal. First, he started a fire to make coffee. Two days without coffee was all he could stand. A can of warmed beans with crackers and marmalade satisfied his hunger.

Noting the disarray of the cabin, Mark made up his mind that he had to be more alert to what was going on around him. Not knowing what to expect as the evening settled in, he slept fully clothed and kept his pistol under his arm if needed in a hurry. He slept in short spurts in order to maintain some vigilance as the night wore on, fully prepared for the unexpected. The night ended without incident.

Mark set the cabin in order and left it as he would want to find it for his own use. He set out to pick up the eastern boundary of the forest tract, then head south toward the center cabin with an anxious urgency. He wanted to be sure that the cabin filled with his forestry papers and effects were safe from unwelcome intruders. His step was determined and brisk.

The woods had a unique smell of cedar and spruce. Further south in his pine forest of Maine, the pine smell was never as pungent or heavy. Mark almost missed the east-west trail that ran past the central cabin door. It was not as heavily used as the one further north at the fireweed cabin. Mark turned west and picked up the pace for the last few miles to the Swift River on the eastern side of the cabin. The "lob-sticks" on the riverside came into view before he got to the fast flowing river. The water continued to be high at the crossing. Mark plunged without hesitation into the stream up to his chest. It was cold and his legs were instantly numbed. The river was swift and he had trouble keeping his balance. By the time he climbed from the river bed on the other side, a slight figure dressed in fringed doeskin shirt and pants confronted him. It was Bright Cloud!

Chapter Eleven

Bright Cloud wore a white headdress around her forehead accented with red and green designs alternating with white bands around her head. Her doeskin shirt vibrated like waves on the ocean when she walked. It was covered with the same design as the headdress, with long fringes extending down her two arms and around her waist. The tight fitting doeskin pants were fringed like the shirt. His heart pounded when she called his name in a loud voice so that she could be heard above the thundering of the river.

"Hello, Mark," Bright Cloud cried, kneeling beside the river bank, offering him a helping hand.

"What a surprise to find you here, Bright Cloud. I was in a hurry to return to the cabin today, and now I know why." Watching her walk in light fluid movements with the long single braid of hair to the middle of her back, he thought that she was the most beautiful girl in the world. Seeing her again stirred the feelings he had been trying to suppress for days. He had to be careful. He was still a stranger in a strange land!

Her habit today emphasized her proud Indian heritage. There was a mystical air about her that was enchanting. This was a new Bright Cloud, and she looked more Cree Indian than ever.

Bright Cloud saw a different Mark, also. He still had the soldierly bearing without the uniform. The small beard made him look older. He radiated more self-confidence out here in the forest that he loved. His relaxed manner and ready smile was as disarming and infectious as always. Mark's head net had shifted on his head and hung at a comical angle over his left ear.

"I've taken the day to myself and came to see if you needed anything. The Mounted Police received a letter for you; I left it in the cabin on the table. You seem to be settled in and working well already. I didn't find you at the cabin and was about to leave when I saw you enter the river on the other side. How's your head?" Her voice rose above the drone of the water.

"The cut has stopped bleeding. I left the bandage on to discourage the mosquitoes."

Mark led the way back to the cabin where he was anxious to shed his pack and head net. "The first thing I want to do is change into some dry clothes and remove these wet, squishy shoes full of water." They laughed at the sound of the water in his shoes as they walked towards the cabin door.

"You go inside to change and I'll wait here for you."

It took a few seconds for Mark to become accustomed to the dark interior of the cabin. He saw that Bright Cloud had left more food on the table along with his letter. His curiosity got the better of him, so he picked up the letter to see who it was from. It was from Arlo. Mark worked as fast as he could to discard the wet cold clothes and replace them with dry ones.

"You can come in now, Bright Cloud. The letter is from an old friend of mine. Thanks for the additional food and for the letter. The way is long and you must be tired from the trip," said Mark. A warm feeling came over him as soon as she entered the cabin, filling it with an air of tranquility.

Bright Cloud seated herself at the table near the window. "No, I'm not tired. I walk a lot whenever I have a chance, and it was good to take a leave from the infirmary. I was wondering about your wound and the letter seemed to be a good reason to come and see how you're getting along."

"It's a relief to get away from the flies, isn't it?" asked Mark, unable to keep his eyes from her. "When I first arrived at the cabin and saw the generous preparations and thoughtfulness of your people, it made me feel welcome. I'll be comfortable here to carry out the work. I've checked the cabin to the north with all the fireweed covering it. It was well-stocked with supplies, also. However, I was surprised to find that someone had used it recently and left a mess behind. That's why I was in a hurry to return here to make sure my things would be untouched."

Bright Cloud blushed at the mention of some intruder at the other cabin. Avoiding Mark's inquiring look, she said, "Sometimes people take refuge in the shelters and are not appreciative of such things.

When I return I shall ask my father to spread the word that these two cabins are off limits except in an emergency!"

"I'm a stranger to this land and I wouldn't want to have special changes made just for me. The traditional customs of the region should prevail," he quickly told her.

"I'd feel the same way if I were you; however, my people are your host and we feel that you should have the right to conduct the work in an atmosphere of peace without distractions of any kind if they can be avoided. What you experienced at the other cabin I hope will not be repeated. The council will see to that." Bright Cloud stated her case with a firmness that left no doubt in Mark's mind that something would be done.

"My position as a guest is appreciated. Believe me, Bright Cloud, I'm pleased to be here. My life has been enriched already compared to what it was right after the war."

"It's not good to always be alone." Bright Cloud said in a whisper.

"The hardest thing is to be lonely and not be alone," Mark replied.

The conversation was turning personal and both of them felt uncomfortable with it. He had to be more careful of what he said. He was delighted that Bright Cloud was more outgoing and candid like she had been on his first visit. There was an air of serenity about her that touched him more than ever. Yet, at the same time, she was a person full of vibrant energy who expressed herself forcefully and honestly.

"Does the letter from your friend bring good news?" Bright Cloud asked, glancing at the letter on the table.

"I haven't read it yet. If you'll excuse me for a few minutes, I'll see what he has to say. This is the same person responsible for my coming in the first place. I've known him for several years."

The letter swept Mark along into another world with the incredible suggestive power of its message. When he finished reading it, Mark did not know what to say. He handed the letter across the table to Bright Cloud:

Dear Mark,

You may be surprised to hear from me, but I have been following your progress from a distance with great admiration for your efforts. I will send this out by diplomatic courier, assuming that you will receive it soon.

I wanted to let you know that the President of the United States has recently signed a bill to establish a monument to all soldiers that died in combat; specifically, it will be a monument to those fallen comrades that are unknown.

The significance of the monument is that all the families who have a loved one in an unmarked grave could, correctly, say that there is a chance the body of their loved one will be selected for the crypt. It will be dedicated to all of the dead who have no names on their headstones.

Since hearing of the project, I thought of you and Flying Eagle. Nobody will ever know for sure, but it could be his last remains that are selected for the marble tomb where the whole world will pay tribute to our Unknown Soldier. The inscription on the tomb will be: "Here Rests In Honored Glory, An American Soldier Known but to God!" It's a powerful possibility to contemplate.

Call on me if I can help you in any way, Mark. Our relationship has always been like two brothers. I hope your burden has been lightened by this expedition. All my best to you old friend.

Arlo (10 June 1921)

P.S.

I have a lot of leave time coming to me, so if I can be of any help to you, I'll be there. I visited your Aunt Maddie the other day and ate enough to last me for days! She is fine and sends her love.

Bright Cloud placed the letter on the table and looked out the window. The letter created a contradiction within her. It was unsettling and calming at the same time. She asked herself what did this thing in Washington have to do with her family? She had just reached the point in her life when she was able to live with the memory of Flying Eagle and his loss, before Mark came with the medal. Now, once again, it all seemed fresh and new, when all she ever wanted was for his spirit to be at rest. He had died in such violent discord, and she prayed every day for his soul to find peace and harmony. She cherished the legacy of valor and hoped that she was worthy of his sacrifice. Bright Cloud also hoped with all of her heart that he was free at last from earthly strife, and was now soaring with the eagles.

"What do you think of this tomb for an unknown soldier?" Bright Cloud asked, not wanting Mark to see her so unsettled. She honestly did not have an answer to the letter and looked to Mark for direction.

"I don't know how I feel about it." Mark was aware of her indecision. "It brings back a lot of feelings I thought had been settled. Arlo is a dear friend, and he's truthful about the possibility that it could be Flying Eagle's remains that are selected. It could be any of the thousands of soldiers that were killed and remained unidentifiable. Symbolically the monument represents all of them. As an American, I'm proud to see such a memorial contemplated. It's a beautiful idea and I'm sure it will give comfort to a lot of families such as yours. My own feelings are that it's a fine thing to do. Succeeding generations have a tendency to forget the sacrifices made for their freedom. This memorial could be a powerful reminder of our debt to those who have died in our defense."

The noise of the river filled the emotionally-charged room. Mark was touched by the poignancy of the moment. Bright Cloud had misty eyes that she was trying to hide. She finally responded, "It's a beautiful thought and it would always have a very special meaning for me and our people too. Your friend must be a very fine person to share such thoughts with you. I already like him and I've never met him."

"He's a special friend that has proved his faith in me in many ways. I can assure you that he would be proud to include you in his circle of friends. That goes for me too."

Bright Cloud knew what he had said was his way of being kind and courteous, yet, she was thrilled by the expression. Mark quickly changed the conversation by suggesting that they have something to eat. The mention of food eased the seriousness of the moment. Mark insisted on doing the cooking honors. She was his guest and he would serve her. They settled on canned salmon, peas and some large meal crackers with peanut butter and marmalade.

They ate slowly, enjoying light-hearted conversation. Bright Cloud told Mark about the first time she had seen a symphony orchestra give a performance. Even now a few years after the fact, Mark saw her enthusiasm and passion for the musical experience. The small talk helped to create an atmosphere of informality and naturalness. Mark was relieved to be with the same Bright Cloud he had seen during his first visit. Frequently her impetuous and natural self burst through the defenses she had built to hide her personal feelings. She laughed easily. At the end of the meal she insisted on helping Mark clean up and then told him that she had to return to the infirmary before dark settled in at the village. He anxiously informed her that he would accompany her back to the village in safety. She objected to that, so they compromised by agreeing that he would go as far as the "lob-sticks" cenotaph with her.

Bright Cloud led the way on the trail setting a pace that Mark was hard-pressed to keep. She seemed to flow across the ground with little effort. Her long black single braid bobbed from side to side as she walked. They didn't talk much. It was as if each of them was enjoying the company of the other and did not want to intrude on the special level of intimacy they had found.

Bright Cloud told Mark that the cenotaph was a tradition of her people and that it was considered a privilege to climb and trim the branches from the spire. It was a simple natural memorial in keeping with the customs of the North Country people. The letter from Arlo had stimulated fresh feelings in both of their hearts. Today, the tribute to Flying Eagle held a more timely meaning than ever before.

"The way is not long from here and I can manage myself. Thank you for coming this far and good luck with your work, Mark. Your head wound is doing fine. I know Father and the council members will see that your needs are taken care of." Bright Cloud stopped on the trail and faced Mark to say good-bye.

"Thank him for me and thank you for coming, Bright Cloud. The letter was good news and your visit has made the day special for me. The cabin will have lost its glow without you," Mark quietly admitted. He saw uncertainty in her eyes, and a look of sadness settled on her face, where a few minutes before there had been contentment.

Mark did not want to say good-bye. He was reluctant to see her go. Bright Cloud seemed to feel the same. They had enjoyed a few hours together, and during that time, discovered an unspoken attraction for one another. She broke the silence first, when she removed a small wooden cross from around her neck and held it out to him.

"I'd like for you to have this, Mark. It was carved by Flying Eagle when he was a small boy. He gave it to me when I left the village to attend nursing school in New York. He said it would always be lucky for me, and I believe it has been. I would like to share that luck with you."

The offering of one of her most treasured possessions from Flying Eagle made his heart pound. He accepted the cross, held it up to see it better, and was overwhelmed with thanksgiving. Without realizing what he was doing, Mark reached out for Bright Cloud and very tenderly kissed her on the lips. She did not resist the act. It was a manifestation of emotions he had been harboring for days. Her warm presence evoked strong feelings he never dreamed could be a part of his life. From that moment, his world, as he knew it, was changed forever.

He started to speak as he released her, but Bright Cloud gently placed a finger against his lips and softly whispered in her angelic voice, "Please, don't say anything now, Mark. Thank you for a most beautiful day."

Then, she was gone!

Mark wanted to sing out and share his new-found happiness with the world, but in that same instant, an empty feeling swept over him as he watched Bright Cloud disappear from sight on the trail. Alas, he told himself, now he knew that she cared for him. He had seen it in her eyes and felt it in the softness of her lips. His first urge was to race after her, but the whispered admonition to "not speak now" kept him from doing so. The solitude he had enjoyed could now be bolstered with hope. The possibilities for the future was enough to spring his soul from the darkness of yesterday to this moment of glorious discovery. His own feelings had at last been declared, but the supreme reward for him was the realization that she had similar feelings for him.

The cabin still radiated from the memory of her omnipresence. It would never be the same to Mark after her visit. The letter was her reason for coming, yet anyone could have conveyed the small envelope. Mark rationalized that her trip to the cabin had been by design. A smile came to his lips. There had been very few women in his life, some more serious than others, such as the nurse in France that had cared for him when he needed the support, but, the feelings faded quickly as he grew stronger. No other girl in his life had ever touched the reservoir of emotions that Bright Cloud had brought to the surface. He had traveled halfway around the world, went flying above the clouds where roads cease to exist, and in an obscure village in the middle of an unlimited wilderness, he had fallen in love.

The day after Bright Cloud's visit, it rained hard, so Mark spent the day snug and warm in his cabin cooking and organizing his field work. Once the boundaries were in place to his satisfaction, he would start the inventory and growth analysis of the forest stock on the property. The paper company forestry department had compiled volume tables for the different species of commercial importance in the area and Mark intended to use them for the computation of the volume by species for the tract. The concept of growth in individual trees and the large forest community as a whole, was a difficult phenomenon to quantify. Mark wanted to compose his own growth chart so that the predictions and projections would be based on facts obtained from the forest tract in question. Then the growth profile would accurately reflect the tribal lands' ability to produce. It would be impossible to measure every tree in the tract, so he decided to use a sampling procedure of about ten percent.

Once enough data had been collected, it could be expanded to represent the full acreage of the forest tract, then extrapolated to estimate future growth. There would be a statistical sampling probability error, but it would be negligible on the final figure. For planning purposes, the sampling error could be ignored.

Mark worked with a new enthusiasm since Bright Cloud's visit. As time passed, he began to worry that his impulsive act may have offended her after she had time to reflect on it. The image of Bright Cloud laughing with him at the small table was a picture which frequently came to his mind.

* * *

In the meantime, when Bright Cloud left Mark on the trail she continued to be unsure of herself. His kiss had been so sudden. Her instinctive response came from the heart and was beautiful. Her heart was bursting at her discovery! Never in her lifetime had she felt such overwhelming happiness as she experienced returning to the village on that eventful afternoon. She was assured with that one kiss that Mark shared similar feelings for her or else he could not have acted as he did. Now, she was feeling depressed and forlorn. The ecstasy of the memory was lost. The cruel, forbidding words of the Inspector kept coming back to haunt her. She felt betrayed and didn't know which way to turn.

She knew the potential danger that could lie ahead if things continued with her and Mark. She would probably give the same advice the Inspector did, if she was asked to council others in the same situation. But she could not help herself. When she learned of the letter for Mark, she was eager to volunteer and take it to him. She used his wound as a reason, and it worked with Corporal Haynes, who was glad to give the letter to her for delivery. She never deceived herself. She wanted to go; it was part of her impulsive nature. Bright Cloud was uncertain if Mark harbored the same feelings towards her. She had not been sure until he kissed her. Maybe she was putting more meaning into the act than he intended. Her life had been intensely focused on the formation of the infirmary. Now, everything was in disarray, and she felt pain that was incompatible with love.

Bright Cloud prayed for guidance in the uncertain days ahead, afraid that her dreams would just be a cruel twist of fate, that her hopes were out of reach. She was not sure exactly what she wanted her dreams and hopes to do for her, but she was certain that nobody had ever made her feel the way she did for Mark. What would she do when Mark finished the forestry work? Would he just disappear forever? The very thought filled her with more doubts and sadness. Life seemed so complicated. For the first time in her young life, the joy of loving someone was tormenting her soul. It wasn't fair!

The night of Bright Cloud's visit to the center cabin, Bright Star was especially active and energetic, and Bright Cloud was impatient and scolded her to be quiet. She loved the child as if she was her own, and she could not imagine life without her. Star was not a responsibility, but one of the great joys in her life. In her confused state of mind, Bright Cloud even had the terrible thought that the small child could be looked upon as an added burden by someone like Mark, and she was instantly ashamed of ever having entertained such an insensitive thought. She hid her face in the blankets and asked God to forgive her. It would be so easy if she was white instead of Indian. In her moment of grief, she prayed to be someone different and more like the white girls she went to school with. What started out as a warm glow in her heart when she left Mark on the trail, was now turning into a cruel memory. The realization that she and Mark could never be what her secret dreams hoped for, gave Bright Cloud several long tearful nights.

Running Deer heard his daughter in the bedroom and felt helpless to console her. He understood much about his proud daughter. She had been an inspiration to the village. Since the death of Flying Eagle, she was more than ever a role model of hopes and dreams for the younger members of the tribe. Because of her unselfish nature, she had been denied the carefree adolescent time of her life like other young people. She was quick to perceive her responsibilities to her own people, and she passionately embraced those opportunities as her way of life. The added work of caring for Star left her with little time for herself.

Running Deer puffed on his pipe staring into the dying embers in the fireplace with some misgivings for the future. It was difficult for him to think of Bright Cloud in despair. He realized that the source of her discomfort was the young American soldier. He liked and trusted the young man, but that was not to say that he knew very much about him. The shrewd old Cree had seen much of life. Only a select few men had ever passed his intense scrutiny and received his approval as decent, honest men with noble intentions. He had judged Mark to be from the same stock as his son and the Inspector, but reserved final judgment until he had a chance to observe him for a longer period of time. He wondered if Mark had similar feelings for Bright Cloud.

* * *

Scents from the forest filled the center cabin. Mark identified the source of the cinnamon-like aroma. It was the large-toothed aspen trees to the west of the cabin opposite the "lob-sticks". It blended with the spruce and balsam fir to make a distinctively intoxicating sweet smell. It was so pronounced that he could almost taste it.

Every night, Mark laid awake with thoughts of Bright Cloud. He reconstructed every move that she had made within the cabin, and come to the conclusion that he had been too hasty with her and possibly made a fool of himself. The rush of feelings over their first kiss had almost eclipsed the reason she came in the first place, the letter from Arlo.

He read the letter one more time before putting out the lamp. A part of him, also, protested against the disturbance of the remains of the soldier selected. Should the fallen be left in peace? The more he thought about the subject, the more he agreed with the memorial. The unknowns had earned their place in history. The monument would pay tribute to their ultimate sacrifice.

Mark worked diligently for several weeks on the forest tract, conducting the systematic inventory of the standing timber. His notes and field data were beginning to become a large portfolio. The small table in the cabin was covered with papers. He had been out in the field long enough and progressed far enough that his paper supply and other personal clothing items needed to be replenished. Packers from the village stopped by every week with his food necessities. Inspector Clough and Corporal Haynes made a surprise visit to the cabin one day with food and a rifle they thought he might find useful. It was a .35 caliber Remington semi-automatic carbine, a large enough caliber for most small game and deer. It was the Inspector's personal firearm, and Mark thanked him for the generous gesture.

Mark inquired about Bright Cloud and Running Deer, and was surprised to hear that Bright Cloud had been sick for several days after her visit. He immediately imagined himself responsible for the illness.

The Inspector noted Mark's concern and very quietly, so that only he and Mark could hear, said, "Whenever it's possible for you during your next visit to the village, drop by the station. I'd like to talk in private with you." Without another word, he and the Corporal left on their patrol.

The Inspector left Mark bewildered by that statement, knowing full well that it had to pertain to Bright Cloud. He watched the trail often to see if she would come again. He wanted to return to the tribal council with enough information so that they could start drawing up specific plans for tribal input. He did not want to return just for Bright Cloud, rationalizing that it would place her in an awkward position. Maybe it was fear of rejection, maybe it was the fear of finding Bright Cloud involved with someone else. Mark thought of many reasons why he should not go, and rationalized that his place was here doing the job he came to do. The last word from the Inspector sounded ominous. Now, he was anxious to find out exactly what was meant by the statement.

Physically, Mark never felt better than he did right now. The daily field exercises were responsible for a stronger, more muscular body. He had gained a little weight. He was proud of his endurance and his prowess in the forest, and attributed it to the exhaustive pace he had set for himself, along with the huge meals he consumed in the evenings. Most of his diet consisted of the whitefish and salmon he caught daily from the river. He slept the heavy sleep of the exhausted every night.

As the summer progressed, the warm days shortened noticeably. The mosquito and black fly population were less severe and eventually disappeared by early August. It was a welcome relief to be free of the bloodthirsty pests. However, this time of year forewarns of the coming of winter, and serious preparations had to be made. The winters were the great equalizers in the North Woods. You met the onslaught prepared, or you perished. Winter won every contest.

Mark added to the pile of firewood almost every day. Whenever he found a dry log or dead tree close to the cabin, he cut it into usable lengths and split the larger pieces. By midsummer, he had doubled the pile the council had prepared for him when he first took up residency at the cabin. He had not stored any fish or smoked any meat because he did not have time for such things. Consequently, he worked with diligence at the forest project, and was pleased with the progress to date.

The preliminary field work was completed. Mark had reached a milestone for the forest management plan and he needed additional information from the council members in order to complete the plan. He wanted to explore such things as basic goals and intentions, and what did the tribal council expect the forest to do for them? What type of manpower and skills were available to harvest the forest crop? The most important issue for the council was how much revenue did they need from the sale of forest products? What was their purpose of ownership? It was crucial for Mark to discuss these issues with the council.

Mark anticipated the trip to the village to seek the council's guidance with some trepidation, not knowing what the Inspector wanted. He also wondered about the kind of reception he would receive from Bright Cloud. He secured the cabin and headed towards Fort Lewis with an easy gait. Some of the preliminary notes and figures from the summarized inventory data were in his small pack.

It had been two months since Bright Cloud's visit to the cabin. He had worked hard to keep his mind focused on his commitment to the council, yet her memory was a constant companion. When the wind whispered through the trees he could hear her hauntingly soft voice say, "thank you for a beautiful day." It still gave him a warm glow. He wore the small wooden cross next to his heart.

The section of the trail near the cenotaph held a special meaning for Mark. Not so much for the memory of Bright Cloud and their first kiss, but for the memory of Flying Eagle, too. If it was possible, it would be logical to expect Flying Eagle's spirit to be free in the land he loved. The Cree believe that the mists of the forests are the spirits of the dead. Mark paused at the site and paid his respects as he always did, and once again, the strong presence of his dead friend gave him some comfort as he continued toward the village.

It was mid-afternoon by the time Mark arrived at Fort Lewis. The smell of fish was in the air, an indication that the people of the tribe were at work smoking and curing fish from the lake for the long winter months ahead. Mark removed his pack and knocked on the door of Running Deer's cabin with a tightness in his throat. Bright Cloud opened the door and stood before him.

"Hello, Bright Cloud," he said, his heart racing at the sight of her. She was as beautiful as he remembered, and her voice was like music to his ears.

"Mark, it's good to see you. Come in," she requested, surprised to see him.

"I've come to the village to speak to your father about a number of things before I continue with my work. He and the council need to provide me with more specific directions than I now have. Is he at home? Or is this a bad time?" Mark asked.

"No, it's not a bad time for Father," she said with a tremor in her voice. "He's at the police station with the Inspector. I've been wondering when you would be coming."

"I would have come earlier, but I felt it better to continue as I was until..." Mark ran out of words. He was ill at ease in the door, yet he could not enter the cabin. He searched for something to say and

156

thought of the small cross pressing against his beating heart, and reached in his pocket.

"You can see that your crucifix has kept me safe. I'll cherish it always. I want you to know that when you came to visit the center cabin, I didn't intend to insult you or cause you any distress. I apologize for my actions. I've thought of it often. My intentions were honorable and sincere."

"Your action was very beautiful to me," interrupted Bright Cloud. "I told you that and I meant every word of it. I'm honored to be the object of your concern. Please believe me when I say that I, too, have had feelings that I've never felt for anyone else. I've been frightened by them because, it can never be."

The words struck Mark like a heavy blow. He reeled under their impact leaning against the door jamb. Bright Cloud had even shocked herself, and could not believe that she had blurted out the cutting statement. She too turned for support against the table, and continued speaking without looking at him.

"I don't want to hurt you, Mark, for I have seen what is in your heart. A woman knows these things. I've often wondered what it would be like to be loved and to love in return. It's a new experience for me."

Mark stepped inside to the table and held up his hand to her.

"No, no, Mark, let me continue," she exclaimed. "If I don't say it now I'll never find the courage to say it again. Please bear with me, gentle Mark. First of all, my life has been full and I've been able to make a difference here to my people. The time I spent away at school was a wonderful opportunity for me to explore a whole new world. There has never been anyone in my life. I tell you this because I want you to know the truth. When you came to our village for the first time, I was infatuated by the possibilities, and I saw in you the person I had been searching for, but never realized until you came." She paused a second to catch her breath, turned to face him and looked deeply into his eyes. "Now that I have confessed to you and shredded any dignity I ever had, I can only conclude with the one thing which makes it impossible."

Bright Cloud quickly reached out to take his left hand, stripping away the sleeve to expose his arm. She did the same thing to herself, and held the two arms together exclaiming emotionally; "See, the color difference will always be there! Two different cultures will always separate us. It's hurtful, but it's the truth and you must see why it cannot be possible for us!"

"Bright Cloud, I don't know what to say except that my heart bursts to hear of your feelings for me. I have the same for you. I don't know what the answers are for us. It may be sudden and intense, but in time it can be beautiful and made to work because it's right. My heart tells me it's right, so how can you know that it can't be. Neither of us have given our feelings a chance." Mark was pleading against Bright Cloud's brutal logic. He was frightened. To have found an answer to his dreams, and to have it denied, was cruel. He never felt so dejected and alone as he did standing in the doorway of the cabin.

"That's not to say we cannot be friends, Mark. I'll always be your friend. As hard as it is to face reality now, in the long run, it will be better for us both." Bright Cloud spoke through tightly pressed lips without conviction.

"What you're asking is impossible, Bright Cloud," cried Mark, full of fear. "How can I ever look upon you as just a friend, when I've dreamed of being more. Can you honestly say that you really believe the words you're speaking? If you're already convinced that fate should keep us apart without giving it a chance, then you don't know me. In the past weeks I found what I imagined was the secret to life. I fell in love with you so completely that you permeated my every thought. Now, you tell me your feelings for me are the same, yet we cannot share the joy of that love. Nobody could ever love you and respect you as deeply as I do, Bright Cloud. I realize it's sudden, and that we're really strangers to each other. Within this short length of time my whole life has changed dramatically because of you. If this is the only way for us, then I'll settle for being a friend. I thought we were friends; I wanted it to be more." Mark abruptly left the room and headed with singular determination towards the police station.

Running Deer, the Inspector, and Corporal Haynes were sitting at a table in the police station and looked up in surprise to see Mark walk through the door in an unhappy emotional state.

"What's wrong, Mark, have you been shot? You look terrible," said the Inspector watching him closely, concerned about his young friend.

"Hello, everybody," said Mark dejectedly. "No, I just had to come out of the woods to get some things squared away. I stopped at your cabin, Running Deer, and Bright Cloud told me you were here."

Running Deer watched Mark as he spoke, and imagined what took place between the two young people. He had talked hard and long with Bright Cloud about her situation. He tried to discourage her because it had been his experience that the two cultures did not always work for the benefit of both parties. He anxiously left it up to her just how she should handle it. Now, he knew the answer after seeing the shaken young man before him. Running Deer's heart went out to Mark, for he liked the young American.

"The Inspector and I were just talking about you, and like magic, you appear. How is our new forester coming on the project?" asked Running Deer, trying to be a little more cheerful.

"That's what I came in for, Running Deer. I have to go over a few things with you and the council before I formulate plans for cutting and harvesting. The two of you can help me with some answers. I…" Mark realized he had forgotten the pack at Running Deer's cabin. "I seem to have left my pack at your doorstep, Sir. I'm sorry."

"Let me get it for you, Captain. Help yourself to tea. I'll only be a minute," said Corporal Haynes on his way out the door.

"Yes, by all means, make yourself comfortable. What happened to you Mark, are you okay?" the Inspector asked with a frown.

"It's not something I want to talk about, Inspector. Yes, I'm fine, and a cup of tea will be refreshing."

Running Deer was pleasantly impressed at the physical transformation of Mark. He had not seen Mark for months since he left for the center cabin. Long days in the wilderness had worked great things with him. Weak men do not do so well in the same situation. Running Deer's new appraisal of the young American confirmed what his heart had suspected when they first met.

"Earlier this summer, Bright Cloud delivered a letter to me from an old friend. You may remember it, Inspector," Mark stated, taking a seat at the table, glad to rest for a while. All of a sudden he felt tired.

"I do. She volunteered to take it out to you and examine your head wound at the same time."

"Yes, the letter was about a memorial in Washington, D.C., for an unknown soldier. As soon as Haynes returns, I'll let you read it." The warm tea tasted good; it was like a tonic to Mark. "Bright Cloud mentioned the letter to me when she returned," remarked Running Deer. "I have my own memorial to him in my heart. I'm not sure I feel

159

as you do. My Indian legacy cries out to leave the dead spirits where they have fallen."

Haynes entered the station and handed the sack to Mark without a word. The young constable had heard Bright Cloud in the cabin and called to see if she was all right. She came to the door and said that everything was all right. He could see that she had been crying.

The letter was passed around to the men at the table. After they had all read it, the Inspector spoke first. "It's a wonderful thing to think about, isn't it?"

"Someday I'll return to Washington just to pay tribute. It's a beautiful city," said Mark reflectively.

"I'd like that, too. I understand that France and other countries are doing the same thing," added the Inspector.

"Yes, probably," answered Mark.

"The North Woods seem to be agreeable to you, Captain," remarked Running Deer.

"Please, Sir, call me Mark. My military days are over."

"Mark then. You look no worse for wear after your stay in the forest," continued Running Deer. "Some men cannot handle the isolation and fall apart under such conditions. Others find inspiration and grow from the experience. This is what you seem to have accomplished."

"Thank you, Running Deer, but you misjudge me somewhat. I'm not a stranger to the forest, I grew up in the woods of Maine. Not the wilderness but the forest nevertheless. My experiences of the past few months have been productive and rewarding for me personally, and I want to thank you and the council for being such good hosts. If I had had to sustain myself in the woods, I would not have fared quite as well as I have under your generosity."

"Before you came in we were discussing an old problem up here that never seems to go away. More and more whiskey is finding its way into the region. Have you seen or heard anything suspicious?" asked the Inspector.

"Not that I can think of for certain, Inspector. When I first went to the vine-covered cabin, I swear I surprised someone who was using it, and they left in a hurry. I don't have any idea who it might have been, but they left the cabin a sloppy mess. During the first month I frequently had the feeling that someone was watching me, but it hasn't happened since that time. Nor have I ever seen tracks that were out of place. Of course I'm always looking up at the trees instead of at the ground."

"We're particularly concerned because somewhere out there is a recent supply of some potent rotgut that's a killer to the unwary," said the Inspector gravely. "Two Crees are already dead from drinking the stuff. We've got to give maximum effort to the problem before more damage is done. The word is out in the forest telegraph that your center cabin is 'off limits' to all concerned. You should not be disturbed; however, you should be armed for your own protection."

"I've been carrying my .45 service pistol ever since I returned," said Mark

"That's good," declared Running Deer. "We don't mean to be alarmists, but someone out there is causing a lot of trouble for my people. Normally the wilderness is as safe as any place, maybe safer than your large towns because the people understand their dependence on one another. Now we have an outside influence that is hurting us. As long as there is a demand for the hooch, there will be those greedy people who will take the chance to supply it for a profit. If the ones responsible are found out or challenged, they could be violent against you, Mark. Isn't that right, Inspector?"

"It is, Running Deer, and I mentioned this to Mark at the very beginning of his work in the woods. We're patrolling vigorously, yet we haven't curbed much of the supply. The penalty is severe, and rest assured that perpetrators will pay with maximum sentences," stated the Inspector.

Running Deer prepared to leave. "There's a council meeting tonight, Mark. Your timing for a visit was perfect; please come. We can go over whatever you need to do. Father Dumont will be present and the Inspector, too. Until tonight then, gentlemen."

Haynes excused himself shortly after Running Deer left, leaving Mark and the Inspector alone. Mark had not completely recovered from his confrontation with Bright Cloud, and he intuitively knew it was going to be discussed by the policeman who knew everything that was going on about everyone.

"I'm glad to have the chance to talk to you in private. Let me be direct in what I'm going to say, Mark. You're young enough to be my son, and I would like to be able to talk to you as if you were. When you came in the door, the look on your face spoke volumes about your distress. I assume it had to do with Bright Cloud."

"Let me warn you, Inspector, I'm a very private person. I think I know what's coming. I'm reluctant to discuss my personal business, but out of respect for you, I'll listen," warned Mark, irritated by the direction it was taking.

"I do understand, Mark. I'm the same way myself, and the privacy thing only gets worse as you get older. I just wanted to be honest with you and let you know that I've been aware of Bright Cloud's feelings for you ever since I carried you to the infirmary with a bang on your head. She swore me to secrecy which doesn't matter now that she's told you. You two young people are deserving of every piece of happiness you can find in this crazy world. It just happens to be my opinion that happiness for either of you can easily be crushed by the actions of others around you. Society does not take kindly to mixed couples.

"It's not right; it's not fair, but it's reality, and it's the truth," the Inspector continued. "I've seen this happen many times, and I will tell you now, in complete honesty, that I cautioned Bright Cloud the same as I'm telling you, Yank, against the feelings you have for each other. It generally leads to unhappiness. I would caution you to look down the road and see the potential for discord in your lives. If you decide to continue, I'll pray for harmony, but I would fear for eventual chaos.

"I don't want to see unhappiness come to either of you. My natural instinct is to protect Bright Cloud as much as it's possible. I've known her from the time she was a small girl and, believe me, there is much about her that is very special. I always wondered who the lucky man would be to win her affections; I think that she has chosen well."

Mark was still at a loss for words, yet he wanted the burly policeman to know that he harbored no ill will at this discussion of his private life. "A lot of good things have happened in my life. I see Bright Cloud as a blessing I would always be thankful for, Inspector. I can't give you the answer you would like to hear from me. If we lived in a perfect world, we would not be having this conversation, would we?"

"But, alas, Yank, it's not a perfect world!"

The Inspector stretched his large raw-boned hand across the table and with his best little-boy-face grinned from ear to ear. "Are we still friends?"

Mark found his attitude infectious and grasped the hand in the spirit it was intended. He could bunk at the station for the night. The Inspector volunteered to do supper for the two of them. Mark was famished enough to eat anything available.

The Cree tribal council met that evening at 7:00 o'clock. The Council hall was a one-room log structure inland from the police station. Father Dumont sat between Mark and the Inspector while Running Deer took his place at the head of the large table as the presiding head of the council. Ten or so other members were also present. Mark had seen most of them at the church or around the village earlier in the summer.

Several issues involving new hunting and trapping regulations were discussed prior to the whiskey problem. The debate got quite lively; even though he could not understand all that was said, he was aware of the main theme. Running Deer was in his element. He ran the meeting like a seasoned director. Sometimes he spoke English, and sometimes he used the Cree language.

When the time came to discuss the progress of Mark's work on the forest tract, Running Deer asked him to feel free to talk in his native English. He would be understood by most of the members.

"Thank you, Running Deer, it's a privilege to be here with the Council," Mark began, looking at each member around the table. "I've been over all of the land in the tribal forest tract. It's a very desirable parcel of land with a lot of potential. I've completed a forest inventory and a growth study, but have not computed all of the figures yet. However, enough has been done to point to the direction that should be taken. A market exists for softwood pulpwood and saw logs at Lac St. Jean. In order to get them there it will be necessary to collect and measure them on the snow and ice covering the rivers during the winter months. The spring melt will float them to the mill pond sorting area further south.

"There are several ways the forest material can be measured and I'll discuss that with you later in the year after I talk to the paper company. It's going to be easy to harvest and administer the forest products if you use small openings up to five acres in size and clear-cut every stem that is marketable. This will facilitate the reproduction of spruce over the more shade-tolerant balsam fir.

"There are two ways of getting the wood from the stump to the ice field. One is to cut the wood four feet long and pile it nearby where it was cut, so that yarding teams can pick it up for transport to the ice fields. The second method would be to use your own horses to haul the wood to the river. I'm not familiar with what you have available, but I haven't seen many horses in this area. That is one decision that you should resolve as soon as possible.

"Another item I wanted to discuss with you is an estimate of the number of men that would be available for cutting. If you could tell me, approximately, the number of man-days desirable in the form of work from the forest, it will give me an approximation of the allowable cutting budget to be proposed in the plan. You can harvest approximately five thousand cords from the tract each year and never run out of harvestable trees, provided it's managed properly in accordance with the plan." Mark hoped that he was not giving the Council too much information all at once.

"The most important principle in the plan is the manner in which the harvested areas are selected each year. Another consideration for the council is the development of woods crews, which also means housing and feeding for many men, and supplying them with tools to do the job. A lot of things need to be decided in a short period of time.

"The pulpwood does not need any brands placed on them. It's scaled for volume on the drey as it is carried to the river. The logs, however, will require a brand and are scaled for volume at a sorting pond as they are sawed at the mill located on Lac St. Jean. Payments can be arranged for the council through you, Father Dumont, in ways that best suit your needs. The company gives me the impression of being a fair buyer of forest products. I don't have anything else to report tonight, but if you have any questions I'd be glad to answer them if I can. Incidentally, I want to thank all of you for the very generous and thoughtful way you have kept me supplied. Your efforts have been appreciated."

Running Deer looked around the room for suggestions. Seeing none, he turned to Mark and said, "We'll discuss these things and let you know of our decision before many days pass. You ask us about organizing crews for work in the forest. We're not as familiar with such projects, and we require more time to decide things of importance. We're a people of great dependence upon one another; yet, the most treasured feature of our people is their independence of action. A little story may describe these dependent and independent truths of our way of life.

"Many years ago," Running Deer related his story, "two brothers were being chased by a hungry bear. One stopped to remove his pack and some heavy clothing. His brother said to him 'you can't outrun the bear anyway.' The other brother replied, 'I know, I only have to outrun you.'"

Mark's first impulse was to laugh at the story, but he saw that Running Deer was still very serious. Mark nodded to him that he understood the dilemma. The meeting broke for a recess, and everybody in the room shook his hand and thanked him for the job that he was doing. Father Dumont took him by the arm to a quiet corner of the room.

"My young American friend, I can tell by the look on the council member's faces that you've made a good impression. I'm so proud of your accomplishments. I have other things to say to the council this evening, but I wanted you to know that tomorrow is Sunday and I would be pleased to have you present for morning Mass. I pray often for your well-being, my son."

The frail priest turned and left to speak to Running Deer. Mark didn't answer him and continued toward the door. The evening air was filled with the smell of smoke and drying fish. The long wharf near the RCMP station looked like a good place to spend a quiet interlude listening to the water gently break against the shore. He hadn't gone too far on the dock when he realized that he was not alone. He could not make out who it was until she spoke. Then he recognized the voice of Michelle Gurney.

"Hello Mark, I was hoping to see you before you left for the forest."

"Hi, Michelle, you surprised me. I recognized you only after you spoke. The council meeting is continuing, but we finished my affairs. I would've felt out of place remaining while other things are discussed," Mark told her, turning to look back on the village from the vantage point at the end of the wharf.

"I'm sure they would not disapprove of your presence, but I'm glad to have the chance to visit with you. The light is not good but you seem to be doing well. I'm glad you stayed to help with the land. These people have so little to feel good about. When something positive does come along, they're easily filled with hope. I've found my calling here, and I hope it's been the same for you, Mark."

"I would not go so far as to say that, Michelle, but I've been able to find peace with myself again. I'm pleased with my progress of eliminating some of the demons I carried around since the war. I'm most thankful for that, and I'm grateful for the way these people have made me feel important to their way of life. By focusing on other people's needs, I looked less and less at my own. It's been a humbling and a rewarding experience," Mark admitted calmly.

"You exude an air of confidence that was not evident earlier. Many things have happened since our chance meeting on the train months ago! It was another world, wasn't it, Mark?"

"Ah, yes, things change," Mark replied. Michelle was visible only in outline against the moonlight, but he could tell that she had found contentment. She was relaxed and thoughtful, and radiated an enthusiasm for life that infected those around her. Mark was glad that they had become good friends.

"You're pleased about coming here then. I admire your dedication. It's important work and badly needed by these people. Bright Cloud must be relieved to have someone to help carry the load." Mark felt a rush of emotion with just the mention of Bright Cloud's name.

"As a missionary nurse, I never doubted my vocation. I've often wondered how I could fit into other people's lives and make a difference. Bright Cloud made it easy for me. She's an angel, if there are any on earth. She needs all the help she can get, she works so hard, yet, she never complains."

"I'm sure she doesn't," he replied.

"Dear Mark," said Michelle, linking her arm through his. "You can't hide your feelings! I can tell by the way you say her name what you think of her. I've known of her feelings for you for quite some time now. I've got to get back to the infirmary. Would you care to walk back with me? Duty calls!"

"It would be my pleasure, Michelle. I admit to caring more than I should, but it's not meant to be!" There was a resigned finality to his voice that sparked a retort from Michelle.

"I must confess to you. That situation is the main reason I've been looking for an opportunity to talk to you. I know what you're confronted with, and I say rubbish to it all!"

Mark was stunned by her frank statement. His heart warmed as she continued: "When two people find each other the way you and Bright Cloud have done, you must look upon it as a blessing from God. The trials and tribulations that go with it are only a test of your resolve. Don't be swayed by the advice of others. The most powerful force in life is love, and to deny it for such a frivolous reason as race or culture is absurd. Give this new-found joy between you and Bright Cloud a chance. You deserve that. You owe it to one another. I've never had such a wonderful friend as Bright Cloud. I'm worried for her, because she is denying something that is stronger than either of you. Love, once found, and then denied, will destroy her. She deserves better."

Mark was silent for a few seconds, not believing what he was hearing. Wispy cirrus clouds filtered rays of the moon, darkening the trail as they walked along the path together.

"I'm encouraged by your support, and of course I'm concerned about her. I must say, I think of little else!" Mark confessed.

"I hope I've not been an intruder into your life. It's so sad to see Bright Cloud as she is now. She deserves a chance for happiness and so do you, Mark. If I've gone too far forgive me. Here we are already."

"Goodnight, Michelle. Tell me, where did a young lady like you obtain so much wisdom?"

"It's not wisdom; it's just common sense. Goodnight, Mark." She gave him a light kiss on the cheek and briskly climbed the stairs without looking back.

Mark thought he heard the voice of Bright Cloud as the infirmary door closed. He looked toward the sound of her voice. Mark reluctantly turned back down the path toward the police barracks, thinking about the things Michelle told him. Halfway to the station he glanced over his shoulder to see the lights of the infirmary one last time. At that brief second, he saw Bright Cloud leave the building. He nervously watched her walk towards her cabin. She seemed tired and deliberate in her walk. It was not like her! Mark threw all caution to the wind and ran after her.

Bright Cloud heard the pounding steps behind her and stopped, thinking someone wanted help. Then she heard Mark call her name.

"Bright Cloud, don't be alarmed; it's me, Mark. I just walked Michelle to the door and heard you come out. May I walk you home?"

"Yes, Michelle said you spoke to her." She was not too sure of her words. "I have to return to Bright Star. She's being cared for by a friend."

They walked side by side in silence for most of the way to her cabin. Being this close to her gave Mark a sensation of wholeness. The subtle smell of bayberry came from her long shiny black hair, and he fought back his instinct to take her in his arms. As the lights from Running Deer's cabin came into view, she turned towards him and said, "I can find my way from here. Thank you, Mark."

"Where I come from, it's customary to see a young lady to the door and safe inside."

"Yes, I understand."

"Please, before you go, Bright Cloud, let me say one thing." Mark was determined to fight for their love. "If you really want me to get out of your life, then I promise to do as you wish, but please give me a better reason than you did earlier today. If I've offended you, I beg your forgiveness. I can complete my work here and be gone shortly, if that's what you think is for the best."

"I'm not sure what to do, Mark. My head tells me what I said is wise and probably best for everybody, but my heart disagrees."

A small soft hand reached for his in the evening darkness. The touching of the two hands was electrifying to each of them. Mark thought to himself, if two hands can bring such a feeling of joy, think what two hearts entwined would be like. He took her into his arms and buried his face in her long black hair. They clung together for several moments letting their strengths and love flow from one to the other. It was a moment of release for both of them. Tears came freely to Bright Cloud's eyes. This time they were tears of ecstasy. How could something so beautiful not be right?

"I wanted to die when you left the cabin today. I'm glad you came back, Mark, I don't ever want you to go away. Yet..." This time, it was Mark who touched her soft lips.

"Let's give it a chance. It's been such a short time," Mark pleaded.

"If it's God's will..."

"Come, I'll see you to the door. You must be exhausted after such a long day. I'll be going back to the center cabin tomorrow, so I may not have a chance to see you again. Think of what I've said, Bright Cloud. I've never said the words, 'I love you' to anybody else in my life. I can say it now with my heart. What we have found has got to be important. We're virtually strangers to each other, yet I feel that you have always been a part of my life."

"I feel that way too, but I'm afraid of the future."

"Enough, Bright Cloud, enough!"

She was silent as they faced each other in the soft light from the cabin window. One more embrace, one more step closer to heaven. Tonight would be remembered as one of the most important moments of their lives. A turning point to be cherished forever. With a final touch of her soft lips to his, Bright Cloud reluctantly released herself from their embrace and entered the cabin.

Chapter Twelve

Mark accepted Father Dumont's invitation to attend Mass. He had participated in all the services of the different religious denominations when he was in France. The chaplains of all the faiths represented in his command cared for the wounded men close to enemy lines without regard to their own safety. He admired them and found it easy to participate in their services.

Corporal Haynes gave Mark a missal to help follow the Latin liturgy. He took a seat at the rear of the church and watched Bright Cloud pass by on the center aisle to take a seat near the front. She was dressed in white with her coal black hair falling loose and full around her shoulders. A small white-laced hat with a thin veil covered her eyes. She walked with an air of regal dignity, and was as lovely as ever. Running Deer accompanied her with pride. The church was about two thirds full when Father Dumont started the Mass.

Mark had little trouble following the service with the missal. Running Deer and Bright Cloud went to the communion rail together to receive the sacrament. There was an angelic quality about her that blossomed even more upon her receipt of the sacred host. The source of much of her strength originated from the relationship she had with God. Mark was the first to leave the church after the Mass, trying to be as unobtrusive as possible. The rain had stopped; scattered clouds allowed the sun to shine through sporadically. He was reluctant to intrude on Bright Cloud and Running Deer on this day of devotion, so he started for the barracks. His decision not to disturb anybody was changed when the priest called him from the church steps. Running Deer and Bright Cloud were with him.

"Good morning, young man! I was pleased to see you this morning. Thank you for coming."

Running Deer scrutinized him closely and announced, "The council discussed much of your suggestions after you left last night. I would like to go over some of the things with you and Father Dumont."

"Anytime will be fine with me, Sir. My time is your time."

Bright Cloud had not said a word yet. Her eyes betrayed her feelings. It was evident for all to see what she felt for Mark!

"If you men can wait an hour, I can have dinner ready for us." She spoke with enthusiasm and received a unanimous agreement from everybody, leaving the small group with a light step towards the cabin.

"I'll be at your place in an hour, Running Deer. If you'll excuse me, Mark." Father Dumont was suddenly pulled towards a family of Cree communicants, leaving Mark and Running Deer alone.

"Before we get together, Running Deer, I'd like to get my notebook at the barracks," said Mark.

"Of course. I wanted to see the Inspector, also. You gave a very thorough presentation to the council last night. They're surprised at the extent of the details to be handled," said Running Deer.

"I'm sure you'll be able to take care of them. You're lucky to have the large paper company for a market. Without them, the project could never produce the benefits it's capable of sustaining for years to come. The tract would always be valuable for trapping, fishing and hunting, but of little value for commercial products from the trees themselves," commented Mark.

The Inspector met them at the door as they entered. "Good morning, gentlemen. You two are pleasing to God this morning, whereas I overslept and did not attend church. Therefore, I'll have to appease the good Father for the rest of the week!" Mark suspected that the statement was true; the priest would extract his payment in one way or another.

"We're going to have another meeting at the house with Father Dumont and Mark. You're welcome to come," announced Running Deer.

"I appreciate the offer, but I can't make it today. I have to leave the village shortly. What did you decide after I left last night? Did anyone volunteer more information about the whiskey runners?" The Inspector was interested in Running Deer's comments.

"I'm sorry to say there's nothing new to add to what we already know. I'm not sure they're all truthful about it. You expected that and so, I have a theory." Running Deer lowered his voice. Mark went to the barrack room to retrieve his notebooks from the pack and heard the two conversing in subdued tones. He intentionally lingered in the barracks until they had finished.

"I've got to get a patrol off today, so I won't be going with you, Mark. Ask Bright Cloud for a rain check on the dinner invitation."

"We'll all be thinking of you, Inspector!" replied Mark with a grin.

"I do believe," remarked Running Deer in mock surprise, "The Inspector will do anything for food. He and Father Dumont are very much alike in that respect."

Bright Cloud was not quite ready when Running Deer and Mark arrived at the cabin. The wood fire was cracking in the stove across from the fireplace and the smell of fresh risen bread filled the room. She was preparing moose stew with garden fresh vegetables from a small plot beside the cabin.

"Why don't you two go over whatever you have to do? I'll need a little longer to complete dinner," Bright Cloud announced.

Little Bright Star walked into the room from the bedroom and grabbed her grandfather's leg for protection against the stranger in the cabin. Her eyes never left Mark. She was a bashful four-year-old with big brown eyes. Her colorful attire made her look more like a miniature adult than a child. The hunting shirt was like the one Mark had seen on Bright Cloud at the cabin. The same colors of red and green and white in the same patterns across the front of the shirt. Soft doeskin pants complemented her colorful shirt. Her small feet were covered in darker colored hide moccasins full of red and blue beads that made a noise when she walked. She was not afraid of Mark, but she preferred to study him from a safe distance. Running Deer followed her every move reaching out with a reassuring hand touching her on the shoulder.

"She's a ray of sunshine in our lives. I wish Flying Eagle could see her now."

"Maybe he sees her more clearly than we do," Mark replied soberly.

"Yes, that's probably true."

Mark knelt down to Bright Star's level and called her name in a low voice holding out his arms to her. She was cautious at first, but his persistence removed some of her reluctance, especially since Running Deer was so close by. She watched as he pulled his watch from a pocket and held it to her ear so that she could hear the "tick tock" of the gears. Then, he showed her the second hand on the watch dial as a bribe to be able to coax her away from her grandfather and lift her to his lap.

"She's made a conquest," beamed Running Deer, pulling easily on his pipe.

Bright Cloud noticed from the far end of the kitchen with a smiling face. Little Star became so infatuated with the second hand of the watch that not much attention was paid to where she actually was. It took her just a short time to adjust to the new person in her home. She responded with the same trust and intuitive feeling that children seem to possess when they know they are safe. Soon the restless energy of youth manifested itself in the exploration of the shirt pockets where Mark had placed a few pencils and an ink pen hooked over the top of the pocket. She lifted the pen from the left pocket.

"Well, young lady, I don't think a fountain pen is good for you to play with, but a pencil might be fun."

"She can hold and use a pencil. She's a quick study like her father and her aunt," said Running Deer proudly.

Mark put her on the floor between him and Running Deer and produced a small notepad from his pack. Star quickly amused herself making marks on the pad with her new pencil.

"Were you able to settle things last night?" asked Mark of Running Deer.

"Yes, we agreed on a brand for the logs. One of the men will make up a supply of them for you before the Fall."

"That's great."

"We've also decided that the men will use teepees for the winter cutting operations the first year. We usually use them only in the summertime, because they're light and easy to erect. They can be comfortable enough for the men during winter. More permanent bunkhouses can be built as soon as we proceed each year. That way we can learn as we go along."

"That seems wise to me."

"We estimate that there will be about thirty men available for the first year's cutting operations. They will bring their own axes, wedges, and saws with them. Shelter and food will be provided by the council. I'm waiting for the Father to come because he understands the payments better than I do."

"You've made excellent progress. I hope to complete the plan sooner than I originally estimated," exclaimed Mark, pleased with the way things were going.

"We have one thing that puzzles us. We're hunters and trappers and do not have experience in high volume production of logs and pulpwood. Therefore, we will need some instruction and supervision of the work ahead. We have not selected any foreman, and were wondering if you would do this for us."

Mark had anticipated such a request. "I appreciate your offer, but I think the foreman should be one of their own so that communication can be as simple and harmonious as possible. Actually, the men could select him from their own ranks so that he truly represents all of them. I'll be busy marking out the cutting areas and the concentration yard locations for a while, but I'll always be available to help train them in the necessary skills to do the jobs. The foreman should be a person capable of maintaining cutting records of the individual men in the crew and checking that things are done the way they should be. I'll be glad to help him get started."

Father Dumont arrived in a somber state of mind. He had just received word of another casualty from the illegal whiskey trade. Some young men had been drinking when their merriment turned violent. One of the men was knocked into the river and drowned while the others stood around in a drunken stupor unable to assist him.

"Such evils being perpetrated on these people is an outrage that must be stopped! Now we have a young widow and two small fatherless children to contend with. It's difficult enough in this harsh land without the complications of cheap poisonous whiskey being sold by a few scoundrels for profit."

Mark had not seen the priest so upset. When he had finished, a silence filled the room, broken by Bright Cloud announcing that dinner was ready.

"I expect Running Deer has told you about the council's decisions and questions," continued Father Dumont. "I'll be making the agreement with the paper company because the Provincial rules are strict on such matters. Whereas I'm the administrator, all money matters have got to be approved by me."

"I understand how the system works, Father. What're they going to do about yarding the logs? The mill forester told me that they could provide a small crew to do that for us, if necessary. The pulpwood will have to be stacked for measurement in order to pay the individual men who cut it. The logs will have to be stamped with the brand. They will be scaled for the final measurement at the mill storage facility, after they go downstream."

"You make it all seem so simple, young man," commented Father Dumont.

"Father, it's just a matter of experience with what's going to take place. This forest enterprise should make quite a lot of money for the tribe. If no unnatural catastrophes take place on the land, it should be able to perpetuate the annual yield for an indefinite period of time. It's a stroke of luck to have markets available for a tract so isolated. Forestry as we know it cannot function without markets for its products."

"I'll go over the water rights with the company. I like the idea of the company doing the yarding the first year. We don't have enough animals of our own," admitted Father Dumont. Running Deer agreed with the Priest, motioning for them to sit at the table. "My daughter likes to feed us when things are hot. She gets angry at me if I'm late."

Father Dumont asked for God's blessing for everyone present. Moose stew was a staple of the North Woods. Bright Cloud had added fresh vegetables to it. The bread was still warm from the oven. Mark was hungry and ravenously ate the simple meal placed before him. Bright Cloud asked Father Dumont about the drowned victim. A sadness settled over the table as the indignation of the priest was matched by the concern of Bright Cloud and her father.

"I hope the Inspector has better luck than in the past," Father Dumont said, directing his words to Mark. "You should be extra careful and alert in the forest, young man. There are things that make me feel uneasy, and being extra vigilant in your forestry work may help to put an end to this unholy wave of evil that is descending upon us."

"I've been careful and alert in all of my work. The Inspector warned me that if I see or hear anything suspicious I should take whatever precautions are needed. I'm sorry to hear of an increase in whisky availability."

"It has an effect on all of the people," Running Deer added with a troubled look still on his face. "It's the worst influence to come from the white man. Sometimes I would like to see my people live as we did before the Hudson Bay Store became the source of all our needs. Back then the routine of life was simpler, following the caribou herds for our food, clothing and shelter. Now we do not move with the herd, and have lost many of our natural woodcraft skills. Our culture has been changed by a heavy dependence on trapping.

"At the same time, many good things have been given to us such as the enlightenment of the Church and the education that has been available to us in your schools. I will always be thankful for these things, but it's sad to see our old values and customs disappear the way they have. We've inherited some of the good things with the bad."

Running Deer would have continued all evening if Bright Cloud had not interceded. "We must not forget, Father, good and evil are a part of mankind, and neither the white man nor the red man can claim a monopoly on either characteristic."

"Well said, my child. The native populations have the opportunity to benefit from much that is good and noble in the western world. Sadly, it's true that people must learn the same mistakes all over again," commented Father Dumont.

Bright Cloud changed the subject by asking Mark if he had heard anymore from his friend Arlo.

"No, I haven't had word from anyone since Arlo's letter. He has probably been ordered to a new duty station by now. They're moved around quite frequently," replied Mark.

"Mark, I have not heard you talk much about your family in Maine." Father Dumont had a way of making conversation that eliminated the appearance of prying.

Mark was more than glad to reply. "I don't have anyone waiting for me at home in Maine, except a very dear aunt. My father died in the flu epidemic just before I returned from France. My mother died giving birth to me."

"I am sorry to hear that," commented the priest.

"I grew up in Maine near the coast with my father. He owned and operated a sawmill and lumber business. My father's sister, my Aunt Madeline, lives nearby. She was like a mother to me. She is my only living relative along with some cousins I haven't seen for years now. Of course I've got many friends and acquaintances in the town, but they've also been out of touch since the war years. I started my journey to

Canada two days after I arrived home from Europe. You know the rest."

After the meal, Bright Cloud busied herself with cleaning up the dishes and caring for Bright Star, while the three men completed the plans for the tribal forest operation. It was the first attempt at such an enterprise, and a lot of enthusiasm and pride went into the planning and implementing of the project. A large cloud of pipe smoke soon arose from the table, with all three men leisurely puffing on their pipes. Both Running Deer and Father Dumont urged and begged Mark to stay for the first winter operation. He agreed to do that; for he, too, had a stake in the success of the venture.

The tribal land would always hold a special place for him. It was at this outpost of civilization that he had found meaning for his own life, in the service of others. The biggest reward of all, he had fallen in love with Bright Cloud. For the present, he was content to let things take their natural course. There was much work to do before the winter descended with all its fury upon the northland; time was running out...

Mark planned to return to the central cabin the next day. The Inspector had a lightweight typewriter for him to use so that he could complete the written portion of the forest management plan. He would pack it along with a supply of paper to the cabin on his return.

Running Deer informed Mark that they had located several caches of dried and smoked fish for the worker's camp from the fish stocks of the Swift River and Lac Diamante. He was also prepared to replenish supplies at Mark's cabin very soon.

"It's a pleasant experience to work up here in the forest and not have to be concerned with foodstuff. I thank you once again for that," said Mark sincerely.

"Well," announced Father Dumont, "I don't mean to eat and run, but I have a number of things that need doing. Thank you Bright Cloud, and Running Deer for your hospitality. May God bless you both. As for you, my young American friend, I wish you Godspeed in your endeavors. If you have a need for anything else, you know where to find me."

"Thanks, Father," answered Mark, shaking the slender hand of the priest.

No sooner had Bright Cloud closed the door than Running Deer made an excuse to leave the cabin to talk to another council member. Mark and Bright Cloud were alone at last.

"I'm glad they've gone," said Bright Cloud. "I wanted to speak to you again before I return to the infirmary this evening. Michelle is there now, and I have to take care of Bright Star. I hope you're pleased with the way Father has handled the council."

"I certainly am. My work is much easier as a result of all the help from him and the council."

"I know you mean well, Mark, but believe me, I also know how some of your people feel about us. When I was in school I witnessed a few cruel and hurtful things that some people said and did to put me and others like me in our place. Oh, most were kind and good, that's true, but some were just hateful and wanted to strike out and hurt anybody different from them. I saw it often, and I think Flying Eagle did more than he ever talked about."

"I can't deny that, Bright Cloud. I've seen it myself towards others, but we can't let such a small group speak for all of us, especially for me. Flying Eagle may have had a difficult time with his command at first, I won't deny that either, but they soon learned to respect him because his character was strong enough to overcome the color of his skin. We have to judge people on that basis, or we're just plain wrong."

"Not everyone is as charitable as you are, Mark. One evening when I was at school, I went out with two friends of mine. They invited me to accompany them on what you call a 'blind date'. He turned out to be a charming young man until he found out that I was Indian. I was so excited and was looking forward to the performance of the Philadelphia Philharmonic Orchestra, that I accepted and tolerated his rude, insulting behavior. Throughout the evening he joked callously to his friends that he was going to be known as 'squaw man' after going out with me. I cannot tell you how deeply the pain and humiliation stung me!"

"I wish that I could have been there with you. He would not have gotten away with treating you in such a fashion without answering for it." The very thought of her being subjected to such brutish behavior struck a strong chord in him. "There are always some like him no matter where you go."

"I soon forgot him and his ungracious manners, but I never forgot the music," exclaimed Bright Cloud with her eyes aglow. "It was so beautiful, and so moving that I can still hear parts of it when I close my eyes."

"You liked the music then."

"Oh yes, it was one of the most thrilling experiences of my life. I had never heard such music before. The conductor was Stokowski, Leopold Stokowski. I kept the program as a souvenir. It was ironic. The evening was memorable to me for the beautiful music, and at the same time distasteful because of one person's conduct and prejudice. I've forgiven the boy for his manners, but I will never forget them either."

"I enjoy music, too," reflected Mark. "My father often played the piano at home. He loved all different kinds of music. You would've liked him. He was my best friend."

"If he was like you, I'm sure I would have liked him."

Sitting at the table beside her and listening to her talk brought as much contentment to Mark as any person had a right to expect. She was a delight to be with. She spoke her mind with honesty, conviction and passion.

"Did you enjoy the school in New York?"

"Yes, I was homesick at first, but there were so many new things to see and do that I eventually learned to enjoy it a lot. I made a lot of friends that I still write to. I was thrilled to come home here to do my share, but a part of me was saddened to have to leave school. There is much that is good to discover in the United States. There's a vibrancy of life there that is lacking here in Canada. I also saw that people took many things for granted that would be disastrous in the forest. Life is easier down there. People seem more concerned with making money than anything else. It can be a wonderful place to live and enjoy what it has to offer, but I think it could spoil you too."

Little Bright Star was entertaining herself with some playthings on the floor oblivious to everyone else in the room. Then, suddenly, she quickly left her toys on the floor and ran to Bright Cloud's side, asking her something Mark did not understand. "She wants to go play with one of her friends in the village. I had promised her that she could do that if she was good. We could take her over there, and while the day is still clear, we could climb to Lookout Rock. It would be fun."

"That sounds like a good idea. It'll give me a chance to work off the big meal you stuffed us with," Mark teased with a grin.

Bright Cloud made Star slip on a sweater for added warmth before they left the cabin. The three of them walked down the path towards the spring, then turned west following the trail as it meandered along the brook. Within a few minutes, a little boy came down the pathway to meet them. A small log cabin could be seen in the distance.

"You can play with your friend Lucien, but first, go tell his mother that you're here before we leave so that she'll know. Do you hear?" Her tone was firm while Star reached upwards with her arms to receive a hug. Mark patted her on the head and was rewarded with a quick squeeze around his legs before she ran towards the cabin to play with her friend. A moment later, the mother of the small boy waved to Bright Cloud from the door of the cabin.

"It looks to me as if the village is like a large family."

"Of course," she answered. "That's one of the things that makes this place so special. We depend on one another a great deal, unlike your towns where everybody seems too busy with their own affairs to hardly notice those around them."

The trail to the large bluff that dominated the northwestern portion of the village meandered beside the spring where crystal clear water cascaded over several small waterfalls. Half way up, the trees thinned out leaving stunted trees that looked to be very old. The view of the surrounding area was spectacular. To the north, Mark could see some of the forest tract he was so familiar with. Bright Cloud was quiet and pensive during most of the climb. He marveled at her ability for vigorous exercise. She was well conditioned.

The sun burst over them across the rocky ridge highlighting the forest surrounding Lac Diamante to the east. With a systematic randomness, the forest displayed the bright yellow flashes of deciduous trees along the moist waterways on the green mosaic of the spruce-fir forest. The beauty of the season was always tempered by the assurance that winter was not far away, and it had the power to detract from the enjoyment of the moment.

"It's a beautiful time of year. There's a touch of melancholia in the air. It's my favorite. I think it's because I enjoy the promise of solitude that comes with winter," said Mark.

"It's my favorite, too. Sometimes, I'm so busy with my work that I fail to appreciate the natural beauty that surrounds us. Let's continue. The top is worth the effort. We can rest there," she promised.

After the half way point, the pathway became steeper and veered south of the spring. Bright Cloud pointed out the rock outcrop above them that was known far and wide as Lookout Rock. Mark thought it resembled an elevated pulpit at a large church. The trail wended directly beneath it and entered the summit on a flat section of ledge to the north of the rock. Sparse deposits of smaller vegetation clung to cracks and fissures in the granite where moisture collected. It was relatively flat at the summit. The lookout point was a continuation of the large granite formation hanging over the wall twenty or thirty feet with the easterly edge a hundred feet or so above the sloping ridge. It could be dangerous if one was not careful, but the panorama was beyond description; it held Mark spellbound.

"On a clear day one can almost see Lac St. Jean to the south." Bright Cloud pointed out the village and the southeastern tip of Lac Diamante where it flowed into the Swift River. The view encompassed almost 200 degrees. The small trees below seemed to be little puff balls of green that you could almost touch if you reached out for them. The sprinkling of autumn colors of yellow and red accented the vista. Mark felt a powerful connection with the land.

The breeze blowing across the ridge from the west was cool and refreshing to the two hikers. They sat on a layer of rock about chair height silently enjoying the spectacle before them and the companionship of each other. Mark reached out to take her hand in his. She did not refuse.

"This is a beautiful spot. Do you come here often?" he asked.

"No, not as often as I'd like to. I've been here many times in my life, but today, I see it as if it was the first time."

Bright Cloud was serious and returned the gentle pressure from Mark's hand.

"Tell me Mark, what was your life like before the war?"

"Well, I was at school in New Hampshire studying forestry, after high school at Wells. Earlier in high school, I seriously thought of studying medicine, but money was too scarce for such a long period of time at school. I've never regretted my choice. During summer breaks I either worked to help my father or went to summer training camps

181

with the Army. I liked the military way of doing things, yet, I was content to start life as a civilian again."

"I mean did you have many girl friends?"

"Not many. I dated, of course. There was never anyone that I thought of as really special. There wasn't time for serious relationships with any girl while I was at college. I had what I believed were serious feelings toward a girl in high school, but it never went anywhere and faded away when I left for school. I haven't seen her since, and I understand she's married with a family now. I also thought that I was serious over a nurse in France but it turned out to be only an infatuation that soon evaporated. That's my history with girls. I was too shy and quiet to be a big party man. It was just not my way of spending time. How about you, Bright Cloud, is there anyone special in your life?"

She expected the question and was ready with the answer. "Not at all, Mark. There have been quite a few attempts over the years by several different young men who wanted to be more than friends, but nothing ever developed with any of them, because I didn't encourage it. Sometimes I think my life is not mine to give to anyone. The things I've told you about my feelings are true. I've never experienced love before; that's why I'm afraid for us, Mark."

"I feel the same, Bright Cloud. So where do we go from here?" Mark released her hand to place his arm around her shoulders pulling her closer to him.

"You have to realize that what's happening to us is not approved of by my father or by Father Dumont."

"That doesn't mean they're right and we're wrong!" answered Mark defensively.

"Life always seems to present such unsolvable problems. I don't know what to do next, except to go on with our lives and look for answers as we go along."

"You're always the realist, Bright Cloud. I can live with that because there's hope. I'll be here for the winter. The forest project means a lot to me and has given me more than you can ever imagine. When I came to Fort Lewis I had a tremendous need and desire to prove to myself that I could still make a contribution and be worthy of your brother's sacrifice. I frequently pictured myself as being unworthy. In the hospital, I even prayed for an end to it all. I don't ever want to go back to that state of mind again."

182

Bright Cloud turned to look at him. "Don't punish yourself with old memories. They should be forgotten. God has done his work and we must accept it. I think I loved you even before you came to Fort Lewis. Flying Eagle wrote often about you. His admiration and respect was sincere. He was a perceptive judge of character. Don't be so hard on yourself and stop judging your actions." Nestling her head against him, she gently kissed him on the cheek. She saw him as the compassionate caring person he was. Mark was unable to control the mist in his eyes that produced a tear he wanted desperately to hide. Bright Cloud wiped it away with her finger, and with that soft, melodious voice spoke softly in his ear. "No more tears, Mark, no more."

They locked in an embrace for a long time. Courage and the determination to make the future work for them flowed from one to the other. Two of God's children seeking refuge from the storms of life in each other's arms. The village and its problems were forgotten as they searched for and ultimately discovered each other.

They remained at the top of the bluff until dusk. It was a time when dreams and hopes were shared and examined. It was a time to discover each other and the more they revealed of themselves, the closer they drew together. Each had a need for the other.

The trip down the hill was much more rapid than the ascent. Descending from the fantasy world amongst the clouds, they entered the world of reality in the form of a young man hurrying to meet them near the bottom of the slope. He had been sent by Running Deer to find them. Bright Cloud was visibly shaken after a few words were exchanged in Cree between her and the messenger. She took off towards her father's cabin with long powerful strides, while Mark struggled to follow her. Unable to understand what was being said between her and the young Indian, he thought that something had gone wrong with her father. Bright Cloud was not only shocked and perplexed, she was beginning to exhibit a slow rage that propelled her ever faster toward Running Deer's cabin. As they approached the cabin, it was dark except for a single lamp on the table in the center of the room.

Mark and Bright Cloud bolted through the door, encountering Running Deer sitting before the fireplace with his dark eyes riveted towards the burning embers. Not a word was uttered until Bright

Cloud rushed into the bedroom to check on Bright Star. She was not there. Mark did not understand what was said, but he knew he had never seen such an angry outburst as he had just witnessed between Running Deer and Bright Cloud.

Running Deer completely ignored Mark and did not turn around to confront either of them. Even though Mark was not a part of the discussion, he impatiently shouted, "What's wrong? Why are you two hollering at each other?"

Bright Cloud could not hide the indignation and rage that consumed her. She grasped Mark's hand and ran from the cabin. On the way out he looked at Running Deer for some explanation, but he continued to stare at the embers.

Once she was outside, Bright Cloud paused to grasp her breath. "My father said Star had an accident while playing with her friend. She's with Michelle. It's not serious, but he still blamed me for being irresponsible and that I should not have left her alone to go off with you." She leaned against the cabin to catch her breath. "He has never done this to me before. Believe me, we've never had angry words like we just had. I've never seen him so unfair. He has made me feel ashamed for the first time in my life. I'm so sorry you had to see this, and I apologize for my outburst, and I apologize for him also." Tears streamed down her cheeks.

"Make no apologies for anyone, Bright Cloud, least of all for yourself. If I'm the cause of his displeasure, then he should tell me to my face and not take it out on you. This is not like him. I've meant no harm to him or to you."

"I know that and inside of himself he realizes that too. Come, let's see little Bright Star and try to make some sense out of this crazy mess." Bright Cloud felt as if she was waking up to a bad dream.

The infirmary was quiet. Bright Cloud called for Michelle as soon as she opened the door and was met by a very active Star who was happy to show the new bandage on her right hand. She had cut her hand and finger on an ax at the woodpile of her friend's house. She was immediately taken to Michelle at the infirmary. The messenger that came to find Bright Cloud and Mark had initially been sent to get Running Deer, who directed the young man to continue on his errand. By the time Running Deer got to the infirmary, Michelle had already bandaged the hand. However, she had not yet had a chance to clean up

Star's face, which was covered with blood from the bleeding cut. Running Deer had hastily jumped to conclusions and feared the worst. Michelle had more trouble settling him down than she did with Star.

"I heard you and Running Deer from here! He must still be angry. He's upset because he was powerless to prevent it. The cuts are not too deep. I sterilized them and the bandage is a badge of honor to little Star," said Michelle, shaking her head at the way things had turned out.

Star leaped into Bright Cloud's arms oblivious to the turmoil that was taking place in the small world around her.

"I should have been there for her!" Bright Cloud cried.

"Surely, you cannot blame yourself for an accident that kids are always having on their own. It's not your fault Running Deer is angry," Mark cried in their defense.

"Mark is right," Michelle agreed. "Your father needs to be more tolerant. It's not a big thing. Don't let him make more out of it than he already has. He's stubborn and, this time, he's just plain wrong."

Bright Cloud did not answer, wondering what was happening to her world. Nothing went smoothly. She always seemed to be floating between the dizzy heights of paradise and the painful depths of despair, and wondered how long she could stand it. Mark relieved her of Star and gently reminded her of her own words. "No more tears, remember?" He dried her moist cheeks with his clean handkerchief and playfully held it over her nose and said with a smile, "If you want, you can blow!"

She freed herself, took the handkerchief and did as he suggested. The spell had been broken.

"I'll walk you and Star to the cabin, then I'll tend to a few things tonight in preparation for my return to the center cabin first thing in the morning."

Bright Cloud and Mark thanked Michelle, and the three of them reluctantly headed down the trail together.

"It may be better for all concerned if I don't confront Running Deer tonight. What do you think?" Mark asked gravely.

"I think so, too. When things settle down, I'll talk to him and try to pound some sense into his head." He gave her hand a reassuring squeeze.

Thankfully, for everyone's sake, Running Deer didn't come to the door. Bright Cloud whispered in his ear, "Thank you for a beautiful day, Mark. I'll always remember today even though I'm sorry you had to witness such unpleasantness. I'll try to reason with him. Be careful in your work and have no doubts about me. When I'm with you I have a wonderful sense of fulfillment. I'll pray that God wants this for us as much as we want it for each other. I love you, Mark."

They kissed briefly in the shadow of the cabin.

"I love you too, Bright Cloud. I didn't know what was missing in my life until you became a part of it. I'll think of you often."

The cabin opened and swallowed Star and Bright Cloud from his sight.

Chapter Thirteen

Several weeks had passed since Mark and Bright Cloud last saw each other. The bright colors of autumn had faded. The landscape looked bleak and desolate as the days got colder. Preparations were being made by inhabitants all over the northern wilderness for the long winter ahead. You could feel it in the air. There was a sadness about the passing of summer and fall. It was like the death of an important part of life. The end of summer in the North Country signified a revised attitude towards the daily routines of living. It was deadly unless you were prepared for its ferocity.

Throughout this period of transition, Mark worked feverishly to complete his field work in preparation for the winter cutting operations. He delineated the areas to be harvested with openings of approximately five acres. Between the harvest zones mature trees were left in wide strips to provide adequate seed source for regeneration of a new crop of trees dispersed by the northwest prevailing winds. For the first few years the distance for the horses to yard the logs and pulpwood to the stream site would be less than half a mile. A buffer stretch of approximately one hundred feet was left along each bank of the rivers and streams where nothing was cut to insure the integrity of the stream and its banks from erosion and other disturbances. The logs could be concentrated as close to the edge of Swift River as the thickness of the ice allowed the horses and men to operate safely on them.

A young Indian worker showed up at center cabin one day to announce that he had been sent by Running Deer to be the wood crew's foreman. Mark took an instant liking to the man.

He said his name was James "Hawk" George and everyone in the village called him Sunny Jim because he always had a smile on his face and possessed an easy going disposition. He was of average height and weight similar to most Crees of the area. Long days and nights on his trap lines had conditioned him to the fullest extent. Mark did not see it as a requirement, but sometimes a woods foreman had to back up his orders with physical presence enough to make the orders stick. Mark did not doubt Sunny Jim's ability in that department. He spoke some French, which would help after the company teamsters started to yard the wood. Most of the company workers would be French-Canadian extraction.

In the rush of getting things organized, Mark had little time to think of himself. The last visit to the village remained strong in his memory. Running Deer had not been out in person to see what was taking place since his angry outburst. That in itself was out of character for him. Mark was nervous and anxious to have an opportunity to talk to him as soon as possible.

The ominous signs of winter began to settle over the North Country giving Mark a feeling of grave apprehension. All that he had worked for was about to meet its greatest challenge in the months ahead. His work to prepare a plan would be simply an exercise on paper, unless the men on the ground could implement its directives. Severe winter conditions could prohibit the harvesting. Mark, sitting at the table with a stack of papers in front of him, was unaware of the approach of the Inspector and Corporal Haynes, until a knock at the door broke his spell.

"Anyone home?" cried out the Inspector.

"Come in, you two are a welcome sight," Mark answered.

"We thought that we would pay a visit to the men today, then continue a patrol to the east and south for a few days. We wanted to be finished before heavy winter set in. These trips remind me more and more of my advancing age, so I made sure that Haynes got the heavier pack to carry." The two policemen were carrying small packs and removed them once inside the cabin.

"Youth does have its advantages, doesn't it, Haynes?" Mark commented with a wry grin. He was delighted to have the two visitors. "I'd be pleased to have you two as guests for the night. How about some coffee? I haven't heard from anyone on the Council for a while. You two can fill me in on the news from the village."

"Coffee would taste great, Mark," said Haynes with youthful exuberance. He was a young man of Irish ancestry. A large percentage of the RCMP were of English, Scotch, or Irish origin. They helped contribute to the relaxed competence of the force and were responsible for much of its favorable image in the eyes of its own people. Haynes spoke very little and was totally devoted to his superior. They acted more like father and son than commander and subordinate.

"What's new at the village? I haven't been back for a while." Mark hoped his excitement wasn't too obvious. What he really meant was how is Bright Cloud, and is there any change in the way Running Deer thinks?

"The normal routines at the village are being changed by the woods operation here. I see an excited involvement in the region that was not evident before you started this project. I've never seen people so enthused. Families are beginning to get used to the idea of husbands being away from home for longer periods of time." The Inspector paused for a moment sipping his coffee and watching Mark over the steaming rim of the cup. "You and Bright Cloud have the whole village buzzing. Running Deer is the only one still opposed to it. He can be stubborn when he chooses to be."

"He's made my position awkward to say the least. I don't dislike him for it, because I can understand his point of view. However, it's unfair to Bright Cloud who has to endure his tirades."

"I'm not going to be a part of it, Yank. I told you from the beginning what I think. I only hope you can salvage what is best for all concerned."

"Spoken like a true bureaucrat, Inspector," said Haynes with his good-natured air of whimsy. It brought smiles to everybody, but it left Mark unsettled.

"Don't be saddened, Yank. Things will get better and work out for the best. I saw Bright Cloud just before we left, and she asked me to watch out for you. To have such a lovely person concerned over your welfare is an accomplishment indeed. If I was a younger man, you would've had to compete with me for her favors. She's a rare person who stands up favorably to many of the accomplished ladies of the western world.

"I must tell you, Yank, one of the reasons Running Deer has acted so badly is that Bright Cloud represents a high point for all of the younger Cree children who use her as a role model every day. The whole village basks in her glow. She's a symbol of what a Cree can become if they are determined enough. If you remove her, then you remove a source of inspiration and hope for many. Don't be too harsh on Running Deer; he's not simply being a difficult father. It goes deeper than that."

"I never thought of it like that," Mark answered.

"I'm sure you haven't, but it's true. Now one of the reasons for our visit is to go through the camp area and talk with the men about whiskey. We really mean business, and we'll not tolerate any in the camp. Your foreman is a good choice and I know that he'll back us. We've arranged to have more paper delivered to you along with the typewriter that you requested. It should be arriving today some time."

"Ah, at last, I can complete the typing of the plan. The Bureau of Indian Affairs will be pleased. It will be completed by Christmas time," said Mark enthusiastically.

"Speaking of Christmas," the Inspector mentioned in a casual way. "The Hudson Bay Factor asked me to deliver this package to you. He said you ordered it a while ago."

The package was the size of a small box of chocolates. Mark blushed with the arrival of the purchase, hoping that it did not show to the wily policeman. He never mentioned what it contained and neither of the two policemen asked any questions, but the Inspector had a know-it-all look on his face after he mentioned the package.

"Thanks for bringing it out to me, Inspector."

"My pleasure, Yank, and I really mean that, too."

Preparing supper became a three way proposition among the men. After eating their fill of moose steaks and biscuits, they settled in for a good night's rest. Haynes was busy reading a book. Mark and the Inspector played a couple of games of cribbage. It was a tie-each won a game. The fellowship of the cabin was appreciated more than ever as the weather turned blustery. By morning, the first snow amounted to several inches. Mark had not yet seen the North Country under a blanket of snow, and he thought the landscape was beautiful in its new white coat.

The Inspector and Corporal Haynes left the cabin at first light anxious to complete their patrol before the snow got too high. They left Mark with a familiar warning of being careful in all that he did. They had barely traveled out of sight, when his thoughts turned to the package they left him from the Hudson Bay Store.

He knew what it was, and he was not disappointed by its delicate beauty and its plaintive melody. He had heard the song many times in the war. The package contained a fine porcelain music box that chimed the notes of the haunting "Lili Marleen" when the cover was lifted. The music filled the cabin with the melody that was as popular with the allied soldiers as it was with the German enemy. He had ordered it for Bright Cloud the last time he was in Fort Lewis.

As Mark listened to the familiar sounds coming from the music box, he saw a white envelope placed conspicuously on the middle shelf of the cupboard next to the door. He hurried to pick it up. His heart raced; it was a letter from Bright Cloud. The Inspector had brought it to him and left it in an obvious spot so that Mark could enjoy its contents in private. He made a mental note to thank the policeman for his thoughtfulness; it was typical of the man. Shaky hands ripped the letter open and hungry eyes devoured the contents.

Dear Mark,

The Inspector told me he was planning to stop by to see you, and that he would be glad to carry a letter. I was hoping to see you sooner, but I understand you are busier than ever now. I'm so proud of you! The whole village is talking of your progress with the logging operation.

We have had several cases of serious diseases at the infirmary and a doctor flew out from Quebec City to help us for a few days. We have things under control now.

Since our day together on the lookout, I have been filled with more happiness than I thought possible. My father is still unreasonable, but he has, at least, apologized for his words to me. Do not give up hope for us. I am pleased you had the wisdom to recognize what we have between us, and for your courage to want to see it through.

I am thankful for what you have given to me. I was lonely in my small world until you came to us. I can still picture you at the church talking about Flying Eagle. You were so handsome standing straight and serious in your uniform. Even then, I saw the little boy inside you. I can say in all truthfulness that I fell in love with you in those moments. Dear gentle Mark, don't ever stop loving me!

I pray for your safekeeping every night and send my love on the winds to watch over you.

Love,

Bright Cloud

Mark could have walked on air after reading the letter. A warm glow filled his heart. The weather turned sunny after the night's snowfall and in keeping with his buoyant mood, he decided to visit the logging camp to talk with Sunny Jim. By now, all of the crew had reported to the camp and work teams were already harvesting the designated trees. From the center cabin to the work site was less than an hour walk, Mark took his time along the way following the tracks of the mounted policemen due north until he crossed the river to the east. Two large spruce trees had been felled as a temporary bridge across the Swift River. One misstep could give a cold dunking into the roaring channel, so he proceeded with caution.

The crew members had set up living quarters with their more traditional summer teepees. Covered with caribou or moose hides, the shelters were comfortable. The small opening at the top did not draw all of the smoke away from the interior of the cone-shaped structures, and Mark found them smoky inside, but they could be easily moved in a matter of a few hours, so their portability made up for the other inconveniences.

The work was progressing satisfactorily within the designated cutting areas. The four foot long pulpwood sticks were piled neatly in rows ready for yarding and scaling. Mark measured the piles and numbered them to indicate to the yarders that the pile was ready for transportation to the concentration yard along the frozen river banks. The company yarding crews brought their own knocked down barns and forage for the horses, and slept and ate in their own bunkhouse.

Mark was impressed with the determination, cooperation and industrious nature of the Cree Indians he had at the forest site. They were making his plans come alive with a minimum of confusion. The workers came together as a unified whole like a well-trained company

192

in the military. He did not personally know many of the men at the camp, but after a few weeks of scaling their wood, he would know them on a first name basis. Collectively, they were a happy people that seemed to work well with each other. Mark did not interfere with the system set up by the tribal council and Sunny Jim. He did, however, praise good work when he saw it, and made himself available to anyone wishing to see him. He gave the project and the men the best that he was capable of.

It was important now for Mark to complete the final draft of the plan for the Bureau of Indian Affairs, so it could be copied for distribution to the interested parties. It was his understanding that once the plan was accepted, the lands would be deeded to the council at Fort Lewis. It would be a beginning for the tribe in its search for greater self-sufficiency.

Mark worked late into the evening on the plan, consuming several cups of coffee as he pored over the paper work. The snow was falling softly outside. The air was calm and getting colder by the hour. By the time he was ready to retire, the wind had increased in intensity. He was warned about this phenomenon of calm days turning evenings into raging tempests with total white-outs. In his snug bed Mark could have sworn he heard voices in the swirling wind, but he knew it was only his imagination. At times it would be a soft murmur barely audible to the ear. Then, it would increase in tempo to a crescendo of such energy that he feared the roof would be torn off the cabin. This night was his first winter storm in the North Woods, and his respect for the hardy native people grew as the storm relentlessly continued. His thoughts automatically went to Bright Cloud, and he prayed for her safety in the village.

The shrieks and howls of the wind beyond the cabin walls added to the feeling of isolation in the vast wilderness. Mark understood how a weak individual could be driven mad by the unyielding, screaming fury of the wind that was severing all ties to the world outside the cabin. He found it a fascinating experience and the snug, solid cabin became a welcome haven of security for body and soul.

Two weeks had passed since the Inspector dropped off the typewriter at Mark's cabin. The harvest operation was functioning smoothly after a few "start up" problems were taken care of by Mark and Sunny Jim. Several days of stormy weather confined Mark to the cabin, which he used to good advantage by completing the manuscript for the Forest Management Plan. He wrapped the gift for Bright Cloud as neatly as he could and placed it in the pack along with a lunch and the finished plan for the Bureau. Sunny Jim had given Mark a fine pair of narrow snowshoes for winter travel. They were comfortable on his feet, and was surprised at how fast he could get around with them.

His heart beat a little faster when the cabins of the settlement came into view. Smoke was coming from all the chimneys he could see, including Running Deer's. He had a strong desire to stop there first, but his better judgment held him to the intended visit with the Priest first.

Father Dumont was at the church, and he welcomed Mark with open arms. The two men talked for more than two hours as Mark reported the progress of the operation. Most of the time was spent going over the management plan so that the Priest had a better understanding of the growth studies and the projections. The plan itself was far-reaching in its scope. It was an inclusive document that served as a solid basis to legitimize the rightful ownership of the land for the tribe. The energetic Father Dumont was pleased with the plan.

"Your work has exceeded all of our expectations, Mark, and I'm proud to accept the plan for the council. They'll be pleased to see it in its completed form."

Mark reluctantly brought up a subject that weighed heavily on his mind. "Father, you must be aware of my feelings for Bright Cloud. I think she shares the same feelings for me, but Running Deer has made it very difficult. What advice do you have for such a situation?"

Father Dumont looked for a long time at Mark without saying a word; then, with honesty and fairness, answered his question. "If you're asking me as a friend, I would have to say that the two of you are probably right for each other. She deserves the best, and I believe you are worthy of her, Mark. If it was just the two of you, that would be one thing, but there are others to be considered, my son. I mean Running Deer and the infirmary and I mean Bright Star, also. As a friend, I would council patience and time to let things work themselves out. If you ask me as a Catholic priest, my son, I see it differently. First, there's a difference in faith...

"Mark, it's important for you to understand some things. I would never mention them to you except that you've asked me in confidence, and I owe you an honest answer. If this feeling between the two of you

194

continues, it could end in mixed marriage, which is saturated with danger for both of you and for any children that may result from the union. I have seen many white men take Indian wives, and some of them are leading happy productive lives. A lot of them, however, end up in ruins and that is reality in most instances. There are several reasons for this, but the most common is plain, ugly prejudice. Make no mistake about it, my son, even Bright Cloud will be viewed by some as unequal in our society.

"Sometimes the cruelty of others creates a burden to the relationship that causes it to break. The strain becomes even more difficult when children are involved. If I'm discouraging you, please don't personalize what I'm saying. As for Bright Cloud, I have seen how her eyes light up at the mention of your name. I see the same thing for you, my son. Such feelings must come from God, and who am I to stand in the way of two that are so blessed. In closing my long answer to your question, let me just say that I pray often for both of you. The path ahead of you will not be easy, so do not get discouraged. Our lovely angel of mercy is worth any sacrifice on your part. Be patient, God has a way of lighting the path to be taken, so let Him show you the way. I wish you good luck in the task ahead of you, my son."

Mark sat motionless before the Priest. He had just witnessed one example of the reason Father Dumont was such a legend in the North Woods.

Mark left the church feeling ten feet tall and headed straight for the infirmary with a light spring to his walk. The first person he saw was Michelle, who greeted him with a big hug and told him Bright Cloud was at her own personal cabin with two burned patients. "We use it when we're filled up as we are now. Go to her, Mark, I know she'll be surprised to see you. She's been working hard, and you'll be good for her."

Bright Cloud opened the cabin door with the intention of leaving when she saw Mark coming down the path towards her. She could not contain her joy. She ran to him knowing full well that some of the village dwellers would see them. "I'm so happy to see you, Mark, I was hoping you would come soon." They met on the pathway and embraced for a long time in silence. "Come inside, we don't want the whole village watching us any longer than they already have. You're looking well. The fresh air agrees with you, Mark."

"The most agreeable thing for me is to see you and be with you again, Bright Cloud. It's been a long time."

"I was looking for a chance to come out to the camp, but it has been worse than usual for us here. We had an outbreak of smallpox. Several people died from complications. I didn't go to the outlying cases, because we were afraid of spreading the disease. If you see any signs of it such as high fevers, keep the men isolated from the others as much as possible. I worry about you with these kinds of diseases around. Father Dumont and the Inspector are trying to get the new vaccination serum for us. It has not arrived yet, but we expect a shipment very soon."

"My Lord, I thought it was a disease of the past. You must be careful. I've read that it's very contagious."

"It is. Of course I'll be careful, but I'm here to take care of the sick, Mark," she answered firmly.

The small cabin that Michelle used was warm and clean reflecting her meticulous nature. "We have two small boys in the bedroom with bad burns. A spark from an old stove set their bed linen on fire while they were sleeping. They can't be moved, so we keep them in this cabin until some of their burned tissue has healed."

Mark held out the small package in his hand as an offering to Bright Cloud. She looked at it with sparkling eyes full of love.

"It's for you, and I hope you like it," said Mark.

"Oh, for me?" she asked excitedly.

"Yes, for you. Open it."

She was like a small child experiencing Christmas for the first time as she unwrapped the package exposing the porcelain box. Her eyes got bigger than ever when she opened the cover and the strains of the song "Lili Marleen" filled the small cabin. Touched by his thoughtfulness of the beautiful gift, she gently placed the chiming box on the table and grasped Mark in a strong embrace.

"You've made me so happy. Thank you, Mark. Flying Eagle wrote once to me that he had heard this song being played by the Germans not far from him in the trenches, and it made the men on both sides forget for a moment. It's the first time I've ever heard it. It's beautiful in a sad way, isn't it?"

Mark did not answer her. The feel of her in his arms like this made him realize again that his life could never be the same without her. She made the simple things important by giving meaning to his existence.

"Seeing you again like this makes me wonder why I stayed away for so long. I'm glad you like the music box."

"Of course I do, Mark. I've never been treated so special. I love you for that."

Mark thought it strange that Running Deer had not shown himself while Mark was present at the village. He could only assume that the one most responsible for his being involved on the forest tract, was openly avoiding him. It hurt Mark to think such things. It was the only obstacle in the path to greater happiness for him and Bright Cloud.

Mark said good-bye to Bright Cloud and Michelle in order to follow the trail back to the cabin before nightfall. When he left, Bright Cloud was at the open door of the infirmary waving good-bye, as usual. Pausing at the pathway to the cabin, Mark looked back, one last time, to see her framed in the doorway with the lights from the room behind her. She was like a vision from heaven, and he thanked God one more time for the rich gift of her love. The trail back to the center cabin was beginning to be difficult to follow. Physically and emotionally he was still flushed with the contentment he had found with Bright Cloud. He was a different person from the individual that first visited the village the previous summer.

The systematic crunch of his snowshoes was the only sound emanating from the blanketed earth. It was deathly still in the black forest. When Mark approached the cabin, he suddenly noticed a dim light showing through the window that opened to the west. As he approached the cabin, a thin sliver of light shone through the partly open door. He quickly removed his pack and snowshoes watching for movement within the lighted cabin. He heard things being thrown on the floor amidst loud guttural curses coming from the uninvited intruder. Mark crawled to the door with his pistol in his hand, kicked the door open and yelled "stop" to the lone Indian in the cabin.

The intruder had his back to Mark. He spotted the butt of a revolver on the man's waist. Mark did not want to fire unless he was threatened. His hand was steady holding the .45 in the middle of the man's back.

"Turn around and face me. I'm prepared to shoot if you don't obey me." The man was about medium height and weight wearing one of the familiar red and black plaid Hudson Bay coats of the region. The light was not good enough to see all of the intruder's face, until he turned around to squarely confront Mark. With more illumination from the single lamp shining on his face, Mark received the fright of his life. He was looking into the face of Flying Eagle! Mark was confused for a moment, which was all the stranger needed to act, knocking the gun free of Mark's grip. The gun went crashing to the floor out of sight as the intruder dashed for the safety of the door and disappeared into the night. Mark could not believe what he had seen with his own eyes; it could not possibly be Flying Eagle. He knew that for a certainty better than anyone else in the world, yet here was another human being that looked exactly like his wartime friend. The only difference Mark could detect between the stranger and Flying Eagle was the look in his eyes. The stranger had the look of a cunning and cruel person. Flying Eagle always had a gentle caring look about him. The look-alike was upsetting to Mark as he angrily recovered his pistol and replaced it in his arm holster. Who was this stranger, and what did he want in the cabin, anyway?

The damage to things in the cabin was minor. Mark must have surprised him just a few minutes after the intruder came through the door. The foodstuffs had been ransacked, so maybe he had only been looking for food. Mark had a theory that this person could be the one responsible for the uneasy feelings he'd had on several occasions since he came to the North Woods. Often he had felt the presence of another person watching him. Within a short time after the stranger had bolted out the door, Mark started the fire in the fireplace and threw a handful of coffee grounds in a boiling pot.

The stranger would not have stayed nearby, so Mark planned to pick up the trail at first light hoping to find some answers to his searching questions. In the meantime, he would take every precaution tonight, such as sleeping with his pistol under his pillow. He was angry at his culpability in allowing himself to be outmaneuvered by the stranger.

The wind increased with intensity that night. The wind and the incessant yipping of the foxes became his nightly companions. The incident with the stranger made sound sleep difficult for Mark. He was concerned that the swirling wind outside the cabin could be wiping out his steps. His final thoughts of the evening, however, were of the happy moments he had spent with Bright Cloud at the infirmary. The music box had pleased her. The happiness of the day was marred by the happenings at the cabin, and Mark could not escape the feeling that events of this evening would have an ominous influence on his relationship with Bright Cloud in the days ahead.

Snowfall outside the cabin in the morning was heavy enough to produce about six more inches of light fluff on top of any tracks the intruder may have left behind. Trying to pick up a track was out of the question.

Mark decided to head for the workers' campsite to see if anyone had seen something that could answer the questions he had running around in his head. He also wanted to speak to Sunny Jim about the incident last night. Most of the workers were already at the cutting area, so Mark went straight to the teepee Sunny shared with three other men. Snow had filled around the base of the structures making them warmer and more comfortable than ever. The entrance flap was open, and Sunny hollered to him as he entered.

"I still have coffee if you would like some," Sunny said in his usual relaxed manner. The interior was dark and took a little getting used to. The only light source was the fire in the center of the room.

"No thanks, Sunny, I ate before I came over here." Mark surveyed the interior of the teepee, then impatiently launched into the main reason he had come. As he told the story of his encounter with the Flying Eagle look-a-like, he noticed a slight grimace on Sunny's face.

"Who was this man, Sunny? Was I seeing things, or did I actually see a person like Flying Eagle? His facial expression was the same except for the eyes. They were like two dark glowing coals. They were also the eyes of a person who was surprised, but not afraid."

"You're lucky he just left when he disarmed you. I don't know of any such person in our camp. He could have been a lone hunter that was hungry," responded Sunny Jim.

Sunny's response to the incident was not convincing to Mark. He left to seek answers back at the village rather than waste his time at the logging camp. The snow was packed hard in places making it relatively easy snowshoeing until he hit the soft spots and sunk in so deep it very quickly became extremely strenuous work.

The towering spires of the "lob-stick" cenotaph was coming up on his left when he heard excited voices in the distance, apparently on the trail toward the village. Mark increased his pace and saw two figures shouting and waving to him. At first he could not make out who it was, but as the distance between them narrowed, he recognized Bright Cloud and Father Dumont. Mark's adrenaline jumped the instant he saw them. Something must have happened.

Bright Cloud was leading the elderly Priest. Both wore snowshoes and were following a track heading northward across the trail. She was the first to speak.

"Thank God it's you, Mark! Michelle has been kidnapped by three men going north on this trail! One of those men we have kept secret from you because he has shamed us all. He's my brother, Red Fox. He's an identical twin to Flying Eagle!"

Chapter Fourteen

It took Mark a few seconds to understand what Bright Cloud shouted to him. The look of terror in her eyes was enough to galvanize his desire to do something. Father Dumont was exhausted from the strain. Mark helped him to a nearby spruce tree for support.

"Thank you, the snow is difficult and I'm not as strong as I used to be."

"It's hard going for anyone, Father. I was on my way to the village. Last night I surprised someone in my cabin and got a good look at him. It was as if Flying Eagle had returned, but of course I know that's not possible."

Bright Cloud understood and saw the questioning glance, first at her and then to Father Dumont. She felt ashamed and regretted never telling him the full story.

"I'm so sorry we never told you about him, Mark. He's been responsible for so much heartache and pain to me and my father! He was the exact opposite of Flying Eagle. Red Fox always took whatever he wanted without a thought of how much it hurt us. He's been guilty of some whiskey trading in the area, too. Now he has committed the worst of all crimes — he has taken our Michelle! There are two other men with him. Sometimes trappers and sailors from James Bay will do anything, and pay any amount, to have female companionship for the long, isolated winter months to ease their lengthy exile. It has always been a sordid problem for some families, because the women are mistreated and discarded like trash when the spring ice break takes place. Now my own brother has become that kind of an animal! I'm so outraged and so ashamed!"

Bright Cloud was hysterical, and Mark tried to console her. He had been thinking about a plan of action while she spoke.

"We've got to formulate a plan, Bright Cloud. You've got to control yourself. Come take a moment next to me. I love you!" Mark gently kissed her on the forehead. She raised her lips to his and closed her misty eyes.

"I love you too, Mark."

Father Dumont witnessed the scene and beseeched his God to watch over this young couple. He saw the tenderness that passed between them and knew that this love was made in Heaven.

Mark questioned Father Dumont and Bright Cloud: "Where do you think they're going, and how much of a head start do they have?"

Father Dumont spoke first, and pointed north. "There's a cabin several miles from here due north towards James Bay. The trail seems to be heading in that direction. There are cabins about a day's travel apart all the way to the west and north. It's a miracle that I saw what was happening at the infirmary this morning before it got light; otherwise, we would not know. They're a few hours ahead of us."

"My father is trying to reach the Inspector, who is out on patrol to the south, away from the village. We picked up the trail as soon as it got light. The village is empty of men, and that is probably the reason they have chosen this time to do their evil thing." Bright Cloud was still in an agitated state, but at least she was thinking clearly.

"I wouldn't be surprised," interrupted Mark. "Father, you can't continue in the shape you're in. Why don't you return to the village and organize a group to follow our tracks as soon as possible? Bright Cloud and I will make a small detour back to my center camp for food and supplies, then we'll go cross country to intercept Red Fox's trail heading north. Are you okay to travel, Bright Cloud?" He looked her over carefully and saw that she was well-dressed for the long trail with a heavy fur parka and hood and mukluks in sturdy Hudson Bay boots.

"I'm fine, Mark. Nothing in the world could keep me from going with you! What you suggest about supplies is true, but I hate to lose the time. Will you be okay to go back to the village alone, Father?" Bright Cloud went to the elderly priest and placed her arm around his shoulders. She was concerned for him.

"Yes, but you cannot go against three men who may be armed. There's just the two of you. Stop at the logging camp and get more men."

"There isn't time, Father. If we do that, we'll lose most of today," replied Mark. "Our best tactic is swift pursuit and surprise. I'll get what weapons we may need at the cabin. Remember, we're depending on you to send help as soon as you can."

"I will, and may God be with you," replied the exhausted Priest.

The urgency of the task before Mark and Bright Cloud put an added spring in their steps back towards the cabin. There was much that Mark wanted to say to her, but held it for a later time. He sensed that she had the same feeling, too. At the cabin they both took off their snowshoes to pack a survival kit. Mark strapped a small camp ax to his knife belt and checked his automatic pistol for ammunition. He took another clip from a shelf beside the door. Reaching under the bed he retrieved a small nickel plated .32 caliber Smith and Wesson revolver, loaded it, and passed it to Bright Cloud.

"Take this and keep it with you at all times. It's small and light but it will stop anything you shoot at. Put it in one of your pockets so that you can easily find it in an emergency." She said nothing and placed the weapon in her parka pocket. The gravity of the situation was left unspoken, yet understood by both of them. One item he did not want to forget was the small silk service tent given to him by the Inspector. He grabbed a large handful of candy and stuffed it in his jacket packet. The last thing he took from the cabin was the short barreled .35 Remington autoloader carbine. Bright Cloud shuddered when he held it out to her.

"Do you know how to shoot this rifle if you have to?" Mark asked her.

"I can shoot very well, yes, we must hurry." Bright Cloud could have told Mark that she had been able to shoot from the time she was a small girl.

They adjusted their snowshoes for rapid travel and headed cross country. The weather was beginning to change. The sun was completely hidden behind heavy cumulous clouds and the wind was picking up in intensity out of the northwest. Visibility was decreasing by the hour; it was not a good sign. Mark calculated that they should be able to intercept the tracks of the kidnappers near the ridge.

Mark's concern for Michelle was uppermost in his mind, and he prayed that they would not be too late for her. The unknown was grim, and it was painful for him to contemplate the fact that he was leading Bright Cloud into a dangerous situation beyond his ability to control or guarantee her safety. Bright Cloud's face reflected her grave concern for Michelle. The dark thoughts only drove her forward with greater energy. The pace she set was grueling. Both of them were motivated by the possibility that they might already be too late to make a difference for Michelle who was in mortal danger.

They climbed a steep slope covered with banksiana pine where the light was beginning to cast dark shadows. The wind was increasing from the north and the landscape was looking more and more forbidding. Mark was anxious to cut across Red Fox's trail, but his main fear was that one of the men could double back on the trail and set up an ambush for them. He said nothing to Bright Cloud, but stayed alert to the possible danger. Just below the northern shoulder of the ridge, Bright Cloud noticed a thin line in the snow ahead of them and pointed it out to Mark.

A close examination of the tracks indicated that several snowshoers had preceded a toboggan that probably carried Michelle as a passenger. The kidnappers ahead of them must have been hoping for the bad weather to wipe out any evidence of the trail. Mark had a sobering feeling that they may get their wish. The sky looked more threatening than ever. The weight of the toboggan compacted the snow, but the trail was still not hard enough to remove their snowshoes and pursue on foot as Mark had hoped.

"How do you feel about continuing? We could wait here for help if you want. It could be dangerous for you, Bright Cloud." Mark was worried about her; she was going on nerves, and he saw a look on her face that frightened him — she was near the end of her endurance.

"Mark," Bright Cloud paused almost too tired to say anything more. "We've got to continue for Mike's sake. Oh, what must be going through her mind at this moment! We've no choice but to hurry. I'm okay, but I'm afraid for everything. I'm afraid for you too, Mark."

They embraced briefly to gain sustenance for the task ahead. Mark handed Bright cloud a candy bar, put his arm over her shoulder and said, "We don't know what's ahead for us, or anyone else, but I want you to know without any doubts, that you're the best thing that's ever happen to me. I'll always try to be worthy of your love and trust."

Fear of the unknown propelled them even faster beyond their exhaustion. They passed through the northern boundary of the tribal forest tract. The way before them was completely unfamiliar territory to Mark. He watched in all directions for some sign of life or trickery on the part of the three men ahead. The weather was rapidly turning against them. Winds whipped in swirling motions blinding them with snow. It was not snowing yet; it was just the loose flakes already on the ground that were being buffeted about. Mark figured it had to be mid-afternoon, yet the shadows were lengthening. He was concerned that they might not catch up before darkness overtook them.

"We may have to stop and prepare for the night." Mark had to holler to make himself heard above the roar of the wind. Bright Cloud shook her head in agreement.

They selected a sheltered spot on the trail near a thick stand of spruce. Before they had a chance to remove their snowshoes the wind suddenly increased to such a ferocity that it produced a total whiteout. They could not see anything beyond a couple of feet in front of them. Borea, the God of the north, was showing his wrath. There was nothing they could do except try to find shelter from the storm erupting around them. It was hard to stand against the fury of the wind. Snow was blowing in every direction. Worst of all, the temperature was beginning to drop. Mark knew that the tent would be useless in such winds.

Bright Cloud kneeled to remove her snowshoes. At the same time, she tugged on Mark's leg directing him to do the same. She took one of the snowshoes and, using it like a shovel, started to scoop out a trench the size of a grave. She hollered for him to cut branches from a nearby tree for the bottom of the hole and for the top. Mark quickly jumped to the task, for she seemed to know what she was doing. The trench was almost three feet deep when Mark returned, dragging a large bundle of tree branches behind him. They placed a layer of soft branches in the bottom.

The tent was placed on top of the branches at the bottom of the trench with the excess length and width folded along the walls of the pit. Bright Cloud covered the top of the trench opening with the four snowshoes and, finally, covered them with the remaining boughs Mark had cut. She turned two of the snowshoes outward from one another and dropped the pack through the opening. She motioned for Mark to crawl through the opening first. He carefully wiggled himself into the crevice under the fragile roof, placed the pack under his head and took the rifle Bright Cloud handed to him. She followed Mark into the shelter, gently closing the opening above their heads. Both of them wrapped the excess length from the tent over their heads and bodies to produce a cubicle of snow as snug and warm as the beds they had left behind.

"Our feet are facing toward the way we were traveling. I hope the tracks will not be covered. Poor Michelle." Bright Cloud cried, wearily. "I hope and pray that God is with her tonight." Bright Cloud was tense and discouraged with their failure to reach the cabin. Mark wrapped his arms around her. "I cannot believe Red Fox is doing this to all of us. He and Flying Eagle were so different, yet they came from the same seed and grew up with the same love as I did. Now you have to see him at his worst by kidnapping my dear friend Mike! God is not always just." Mark could feel the tenseness in her body. She buried her head in Mark's parka and softly wept.

They laid like two spoons pressed together while the storm raged out of control above them. Occasionally, some snow would fall through the roof, but the branches on top of the snowshoes soon collected some of the blowing snow, adding to the thickness of insulation above the cubicle. Mark felt the revolver in Bright Cloud's parka as he wrapped his arms around her for protection and warmth.

"I hope you don't have to use that tomorrow."

"If I have to, I will, Mark. This is a harsh land we live in, and justice must be fair and severe in order to protect its people. The three men ahead of us will be desperate, because they've crossed the line that decent men could never think of doing. Don't give a chance to anyone of them. Think only of Michelle," sighed Bright Cloud, nestling her head on his shoulder.

"You know, holding you here like this makes me almost forget what we came for. Your hair smells good." Mark was proud of her courage and that incredible spirit that met any challenge straight on. He said a silent prayer for her safety. "You must be hungry, I know that I am."

Mark reached for a candy bar in his jacket pocket and tore off the wrapper with his teeth while he groped for Bright Cloud's face in the inky blackness.

"I can feed myself, but you're doing a good job," she said, with a girlish giggle. He loved to hear her laugh at simple things. He wanted her happiness more than anything in the whole world.

"This reminds me of the trenches in France during the war. You must have done this before by the way you did it so quickly. I'm amazed how comfortable it is."

"My people have used this trick many times, and so have I. Storms in the winter are life threatening, like the one blowing up out there now, so it becomes a matter of survival to go under it." The storm continued unabated while they waited in their snow cocoon for the light of day to come. Bright Cloud brought them back to reality with a simple question for Mark.

"Are you afraid for tomorrow, Mark?"

"Of course I am, but fear is not so bad. It makes you think more about your situation and makes you more alert to the dangers ahead. I'm not afraid for me as much as I am for you and Michelle. I'm also afraid of how I should handle Red Fox. After all, he's your brother and I don't know what to expect from him. Will he listen to you when we eventually approach them?"

"No," responded Bright Cloud emphatically. "He's like a stranger to me and always has been. This contemptible act of his against our people, his family, and Michelle puts him beyond our family support or concern. He has freely chosen to be an enemy to us. The Inspector has been trying to arrest him for a long time for peddling whiskey. He has nothing to gain by listening to anything I would have to say. Consequently, we have to think only of Michelle's safety. I'm afraid too, Mark, for all the same reasons, and I wish that tomorrow would not have to come."

"I'll feel better about tomorrow if I could leave you behind to wait for help."

"No. I will not let you go on alone. I have got to do this, Mark. Michelle may need me."

He took the last chocolate bar from his pocket and shared it with her. The warmth of the shelter and the satisfaction of food in their stomachs relaxed their tense bodies. It had been a strenuous day and Bright Cloud found a warm solace in Mark's arms that she could not resist. Within a few minutes she was sound asleep.

A savage buffeting of the wind above awoke Mark to the blackness of the shelter. It took a moment for him to realize where he was. Bright Cloud was still sleeping with her head softly resting against his arm; she seemed so fragile and helpless. A smile brushed his face as he realized how she could be several different people at the same time! Exhaustion claimed both of them for the rest of the evening. It was early morning when Mark awoke a second time. The storm seemed to be slowing down. Bright Cloud also stirred and whispered that she was hungry again.

"I think the storm is slacking some. Maybe by daylight it will be okay to continue on, if we can pick up any sign of tracks," said Mark, feeling refreshed after a night's sleep.

"I expect Father Dumont and my father will have organized something by now. They should not be far behind us. I slept well in your arms. I knew when you were sleeping. Your breathing was regular and I could feel your heartbeat," said Bright Cloud, preparing herself for the new day. "You haven't said much, Mark. What do you think about what's ahead?"

"Our best chance is to continue as soon as we can, provided we can pick up a track. Hopefully, we'll find them at the cabin you mentioned. That would make it easier for us. They'll surely have a man watching the trail behind them, so it would be helpful if you can recognize the terrain as we approach the cabin. Maybe we can flank it and even our chances by separating some of the men from one another. That'll give us an element of surprise. They won't be as alert after this kind of storm. Even if we can't pick out their tracks, we should follow the path to the cabin and assume that they're there." There was a calm conviction in Mark's voice that gave Bright Cloud hope.

"I think I'll be able to tell when we're near the cabin. I fixed a man's arm when he fell off a cliff on the west side of the trail a year ago. I should be able to recall the location when we get closer."

"Good, we'll wait and make our plans as we go along. I can reach the pack if you want to eat something now. I can see some light above us."

"Let's open up a little to see how it is outside," suggested Bright Cloud. She was the first to stick her head out of the warm shelter. The weather was suitable for travel. They climbed out of the trench, glad to have a chance to stretch their cramped legs and arms.

"I'll cut some dry wood so that we can have a fire in the trench where it can't be seen at a distance. We really should have something warm to drink. It's cold out here." Mark disappeared in the thick spruce stand to collect dead branches for a fire.

The contrast between the shelter and the open forest was enough to chill both of them. The cold penetrated every pore of their bodies, and Bright Cloud warned Mark to be sure and pull his mouthpiece around his nose and mouth so that frost did not injure his lungs. Within minutes though, Mark had a cheerful fire going in the trench. Bright Cloud unpacked the two tin cups and a small tin pail with a wire handle to prepare some tea. First, she filled the pail full of snow, then slipped a long stick through the wire handle to suspend it above the crackling fire with both ends of the stick on each bank of the trench. She fed the fire with sticks Mark piled beside her and kept adding snow to the pail until there was enough water for the two of them. After the water started to boil, Bright Cloud threw in a fistful of dry tea leaves. The wonderful aroma of hot tea floated over the small campsite. Holding a warm cup of tea between their hands in the middle of desolation and blowing snow would make anybody thankful for small pleasures. It buoyed their spirits.

"I'm going to cut some bread for us. It may be a while before the opportunity comes again. There's enough for later and for Michelle, also." Mark cut thick slices of bread and placed them on a stick to toast on the fire.

"I learned to do this bread at the center cabin while I was alone. I like it. What do you think?" Mark looked into Bright Cloud's eyes to see how she was holding up. She didn't have the same look of exhaustion that she had last night, but she was preoccupied with their situation.

Bright Cloud sat on the edge of the trench when Mark handed her a piece of the toasted bread. Watching him, she thought, was like watching a little boy. He had a wholesome quality about him and an intensity of purpose that seemed to make everything around him new and wonderful. Bright Cloud liked that about him. She accepted the bread, took a bite and shook her head in agreement. "It's good, Mark. I'm hungry, too. Thank you. Did you bring that small jar of marmalade that was on the table?"

"Yes, here, try some. It'll hide the taste and go down easier." Mark teased her. Her eyes were bright and alert this morning. The faint smile that came across her face as he teased her could not completely hide the sadness and the strain this trip was having on her.

She opened the jar, finished swallowing what she was chewing and said. "Being with you here like this makes my heart want to sing. If it could only be under different circumstances. I know that we're facing a dangerous situation today, but my greatest fear is that something could happen to you and I would be lost forever."

He hugged her until he thought he was hurting her. She clung to him in return. They kissed one last time at the site of their snow cocoon.

"We've got to hurry. It's getting light enough to see the trail. I pray that God is with us today."

They left the camp behind and were pleasantly surprised to find that the old marks made by the travelers of the night before were still slightly visible. Mark checked the .32 revolver in Bright Cloud's pocket, one last time. She told him that she could shoot a pistol quite well. The small Remington autoloader carbine was an ideal weapon for the job ahead of them. It was ready to fire as soon as the safety was clicked off. The third weapon between the two of them was Mark's personal automatic pistol, which he checked again for proper operation. They were as well armed as any two people could be. The three men ahead of them were also armed, and possibly waiting for them.

After an hour of steady walking, the trail was still faintly visible. The men had stopped a few times to exchange places pulling the toboggan. The sun was still hiding behind threatening dark clouds.

"We're nearing the cabin, Mark," Bright Cloud announced, pointing to the ledges on their left. "It should be within a half mile of here. It's partially sheltered by large trees."

"We should get off the trail here," Mark whispered in her ear. "Be careful my love. They'll definitely have a guard that will be checking the trail between here and the cabin."

Every nerve in their bodies was alert for whatever emergency lay ahead. Mark strained his eyes to pick up a smoking chimney or anything unnatural looking. He methodically scanned the distance from where Bright Cloud pointed to the direction of the cabin. At last, he detected a slight movement on his left. Mark automatically reached out for Bright Cloud's arm, pulled her down to a crouch and pointed at the spot he saw something move off to their left. He motioned for her to take off the snowshoes and leave them behind. He removed his pack and snowshoes, and retrieved a box of ammunition for the rifle from the pack.

The cabin still wasn't in sight. They were in a small depression with a sliver of higher ground between the outpost guard and themselves. Bright Cloud drew a diagram in the snow pointing out the location of the cabin. There was a door and a window on the eastern side and no other windows in the cabin anywhere. To Mark, that meant that the cabin could be dark inside, except for a fire in the fireplace.

Mark knew that the lookout guard had to be dealt with first, hopefully without warning the occupants of the cabin. He whispered in Bright Cloud's ear what his plan was and passed the rifle to her with clear instructions on the safety switch. All she had to do was release the safety and pull the trigger as often as she needed. She shook her head in acknowledgment, and took the rifle with grim determination. Mark began a slow crawl in the snow towards the guard. The wind had picked up in intensity, which helped to muffle any sounds Mark might make. He was alert and his heart pounded so hard he felt sure the guard must hear it. As Mark expected, the man was watching the trail they had veered from. With the .45 in his hand in case he was detected, Mark hoped that he would not have to shoot him and alert the other two at the cabin. When he was less than fifty feet from the guard, his heart stopped! The Indian took a couple of steps sideways to pick up something on the ground. It was a dark bottle, probably whiskey to ward off the cold. The outpost guard continued to watch the trail area as he took a drink from the bottle, leaving his backside open so that Mark could creep closer toward him. Mark hoped he had drunk enough booze so that he would be unaware of what was about to happen to him. Slowly the distance shrunk to twenty feet, then Mark pulled himself to a crouch behind a large spruce tree between him and the sentinel.

Grasping his pistol firmly with both hands, Mark leaped forward with every ounce of strength at his command and hit the Indian with a swinging motion at the back of the head. The Indian never uttered a sound when the heavy barrel of the pistol crashed across his skull. He went down against the tree beside him with a thud. Mark was quickly on top of him checking for a weapon. He found an old .22 caliber pistol which he threw as far as he could in the snow. So far no sound had come from the cabin. Mark figured that they were still undetected and triumphantly crawled back to Bright Cloud.

"So far, so good. Now keep your eye on that guard. I hit him hard, but you never know how long he'll stay out. I'm going to enter the cabin through the door. When I first crash through it, they'll be stunned momentarily because they're not expecting it. Surprise is our best defense. There's a fire going, so it should be light enough for me to see who is inside. The guard up there was not Red Fox. I may have to shoot the first one I encounter. If so, maybe the other will surrender. I don't see any other way." Mark was deadly serious and outwardly calm for whatever was ahead of them. His main concern was still for Bright Cloud, but his body was steeled for the next move, wherever it came from. Bright Cloud saw a side of Mark that she had not seen before, and her heart beat with pride for his calm courage.

"I don't either, Mark," Bright Cloud whispered in his ear. "You know what's best, but don't take a chance for the sake of Red Fox. It's a cruel decision, but they set the rules and must suffer the consequences now. I'll be right behind you at the door, and no matter what happens inside, I will always love you."

Mark heard the words and said, "My precious Bright Cloud, I pray that God would take this responsibility away from us, but we're the only ones here and Michelle needs us. I love you, too."

Without another word Mark cautiously approached the cabin door with Bright Cloud holding the deadly Remington at the ready close behind him. A few yards from the door he stood up, took a deep breath and charged as fast as he could crashing his shoulder against the door. The door smashed open with a bang. Mark's momentum carried him into the cabin, where he rolled to the floor with his pistol still in both hands, and quickly surveyed the situation. He saw Red Fox lying on a blanket near the fireplace. On the rough lumber bed beside the fireplace was a figure which he assumed to be Michelle.

The thing that stopped Mark from rolling any further on the floor was a leg belonging to the third man of the group. Mark saw his hand move with a knife ready to lunge at him, and without hesitation, Mark fired twice at the figure. The noise of the shots echoed off the walls. Mark was on his feet in a flash, still watching the third man. He was a marksman with a pistol and knew that his shots had been true and deadly. The lead from the potent .45 lifted the third Indian into the air. By the time he crumpled to the floor he was dead.

212

Turning towards the fireplace and Red Fox, Mark saw a drama being played out that he was powerless to stop or effect in any way. Red Fox had leaped to his feet with astonishing agility before the limp body of his partner crumpled to the floor. He grabbed an ax beside him and was in the middle of a step towards Mark with the ax held high over his head when three shots in rapid succession stopped him in mid-air. Bright Cloud was lying on the door step with the .35 Remington auto loader at her shoulder. She saw Red Fox and hollered at him, but the sound of the pistol within the walls drowned out her voice. With firm courage and iron discipline, she instinctively protected the one she loved. Her aim was unerring and deadly. She squeezed the trigger three times with Red Fox in the sights! She had just taken the life of the stranger she had once called her brother! The magnitude of what she had done hit Mark before the noise cleared his ears. Red Fox landed at his feet with the ax clattering harmlessly against the wall of the cabin. The small figure on the bed stirred to see what was happening. Michelle saw Mark standing beside her, the shots continued to vibrate, and a look of relief came over her haggard face.

"I'm all right, Mark," Michelle cried out to him.

Mark heard Michelle, but he was more concerned with Bright Cloud at that moment. He knew how much courage and strength it took for her to pull the trigger. The reality of the deed struck Bright Cloud immediately after it was completed. She dropped the rifle, and walked away from the cabin in total shock. Mark called to her from the door but she didn't respond. She was only a few feet in front of the cabin door when a sharp crack exploded and echoed across the frozen landscape. In horror, Mark saw the Indian guard he thought had been subdued, standing with a Winchester carbine at his shoulder. Mark started to scream, but he was too late. He saw Bright Cloud double over from the impact of the blunt nose bullet and watched helplessly as she was propelled against a tree behind her. In disbelief and horror, Mark saw her limp body come to rest at the base of the tree with blood spouting from her mouth, staining the white snow red...

Mark still had the pistol in his hand and instinctively ran towards the shooter screaming as if to drown out what his own eyes had just witnessed. Before the Indian guard could lever another round into the carbine, Mark placed all the remaining shots in the pistol in his body. The man was dead long before his body hit the ground.

A short distance down the trail south of the cabin, a small group of men were running as fast as their snowshoes would allow towards the sound of gunfire. The Inspector was in the lead followed by Corporal Haynes and two Cree Indians armed with rifles. Bringing up the rear was Running Deer, frightened, exhausted, and nearly at the end of his ability to continue. The gunshots were painful for him to hear. He knew with certainty that death was waiting for them in one form or another at the old cabin.

Inspector Clough breathlessly came upon the scene trying to make some sense out of what he could see. There in the middle of the opening in front of the cabin he found Mark kneeling over the fallen Bright Cloud. Inspector Clough cried out in a painful cry, "Oh my God...no...not Bright Cloud!"

Mark was totally oblivious to the rescue party that surrounded him. All he saw was Bright Cloud's white complexion and red blood oozing from her mouth. He could not detect any breathing! The one person who had given meaning to his life lay cold and heavy in his arms. Mark was transformed to another dimension, yet he maintained enough rationality to understand the look of death. He had seen what death was like in France! The amount of blood from Bright Cloud's mouth indicated to Mark that she had been hit in the lungs and that his beloved Bright Cloud was dead. He had seen the same thing too many times before. Her cheeks were white and cold to his touch. Mark's despair and grief took control of his senses.

Running Deer took a little longer to arrive at the tragic tableau before him. When he saw the still figure of his beloved daughter in the arms of her lover, he became enraged. The cry that came from his lips started from the lowest depth of his soul and reached a crescendo that unnerved all who were present. He grasped Mark by the shoulders and roughly pushed him away from Bright Cloud. The Inspector grabbed Running Deer, for he feared the worst.

"You were not satisfied to come into my village and my home as a guest. You had to continue seeing her when I had absolutely forbidden it. You have done your deed, now go! Go so that I may never lay my eyes on you again. Go!"

"Running Deer, this is no time for…

"Not now, Inspector. I see only sadness for the rest of my life, and this stranger has been responsible."

Some of the men went into the cabin and helped Michelle to the door where she announced, "I'm unharmed, Inspector, but Red Fox is in here on the floor. Bright Cloud shot him to protect Mark."

Another shriek came from Running Deer running frantically to the cabin, collapsing at the inert form of his remaining son. He cried in agony. His tears fell on his wayward son's lifeless body.

Mark, unable to stay at the scene any longer, obeyed Running Deer's command. He retraced the steps he and Bright Cloud took to the cabin. Her snowshoes were as she had left them! His mind was a blank.

It was late in the afternoon by the time he arrived at the center cabin on the verge of total collapse. Mark was still in shock. Years later, he could not recall what he did after Bright Cloud was shot. Loss of his beloved Bright Cloud left him irrational and empty of feelings. Despair consumed him. The stinging remarks of Running Deer still echoed in his head. He had failed everybody, especially Bright Cloud. There was nothing left for him now in this barren northland. He decided to stay the night to rest, then continue in the morning for the southern part of Quebec. He owed the men of the logging camp an explanation, so he took out a pencil and paper to write a good-bye note. It helped him to pass the evening.

To Whom It May Concern:

I am writing this letter to let you know that I am leaving Canada. My work is not completed, but the tragedy of Bright Cloud's death while she was in my care makes it impossible for me to continue. Running Deer has demanded that I leave. I bear him no ill-will. His actions were motivated by love for his daughter and two sons. My heart and my prayers will always be with him. I ask for his forgiveness, because I have been a party to the death of all three of his children. I understand his pain and grief for he is a good man and I respect him. It is the saddest day of my life. I hope he can believe me when I tell him that no man could ever love and respect his daughter as completely as I do. I will always carry the pain of my own inability to protect her and prevent her death. Would that God took me instead!

I ask Father Dumont to pray for the comfort of Running Deer. I thank you, also, for your kindness to me, Father.

To my dear friend, Inspector Clough, I want you to know that I have valued your friendship above all else. You must know by now that I killed the Indian inside the cabin in self-defense. Bright Cloud shot her brother Red Fox. I also shot and killed the Indian guard outside the cabin after he fired at Bright Cloud, and I do not apologize for the way I did it. My intent was to prevent him from firing again.

The workers at the cutting camp have been top rate. My admiration for them continues to grow. Sunny Jim has done a great job and should be able to complete the winter's schedule without me. If you ever need to contact me in the future, I'll eventually be at my father's home in Wells, Maine.

With much respect,

Mark Leroux

Chapter Fifteen

Postscript

Salt spray from the surf pounding against the rocks was still cold in the early spring on the Maine coast. Mark found comfort in the swirl of the thrashing water. It matched his own turbulent soul. His days were filled with remorse and self-reproach. The image of Bright Cloud struck by the impact of the bullet, was indelibly etched in his brain. No person on earth was less deserving of such a fate. It was a test of his own faith and he was still questioning God's actions in that windswept land of snow.

When he left the center cabin he snowshoed out of the North Woods to Lac St. Jean, where he took a train that eventually carried him to Wells. It might have taken days or months, he did not remember. He was like a blind man wandering aimlessly in search of the familiar. By the time he got off the train at Wells, Mark was a gaunt shell of the man he had once been. He had lost so much weight that his clothes hung loosely on him like a scarecrow. When he showed up on his Aunt Maddie's doorstep, she did not recognize him until he spoke her name...she cried out in fear at the sight of her young nephew.

Mark was reluctant, at first, to talk about things, but within a few days after he was home, he was talking freely to his aunt about what had happened to Bright Cloud. It all seemed like a different world to him. He had gone north to Canada hoping to find direction and meaning in his life. He had found that and more, only to lose it in a clash of violence and tragedy so painful that he was afraid he was losing his mind. Upon his arrival, in Canada, Mark was fragile physically and emotionally, but the forest and Bright Cloud had worked miracles to condition him. The forest hardened his body, while the love of Bright Cloud brought an element of softness and clarity to his shell-shocked life. Bright Cloud had embellished his experience in the North Woods into a dream-like quality that would always be a part of him. He could still hear her soft angelic voice everywhere, and see her face in everything he did.

Under the watchful care of his Aunt Maddie, he began to gain his weight back and mended physically. She was so frightened for him. His depressed state had sunk so low that she manipulated her schedule so as to not leave him alone for any extended period of time.

One day he went to the Naval Yard in Kittery, to see if Arlo was still there. But Arlo had been transferred from the Marine Barracks to another duty station. He felt an undercurrent of nostalgia for the military while he was there, and he mentally made a note that it could be an option available to him if he wanted it again. Right now he did not care about anything. He was still filled with grief. There was nothing left in life to look forward to. He was a lost soul aimlessly filling up each day with no thought of tomorrow.

A month had passed since Mark returned to Maine. It seemed longer to him; time weighed heavily on his conscience. One day, Aunt Maddie asked him to not go very far because she had something for him to do around mid-day. She was a dear soul. Mark loved her for all the attentiveness she lavished upon him. He checked his watch. It was close to noon. Mark had been at the shore for three hours where he felt a close kinship with the restless sea. It was his favorite haunt. He walked up the pathway toward the house. Aunt Maddie was standing in the doorway of her house. She saw Mark coming up the path, and waved for him to come over. She patiently waited for him at the threshold to announce that he had company in the parlor. She was beaming with excitement as she led him inside to the cheerful sitting room where the sun shined through the windows. Suddenly, there, standing across the room, was Inspector Clough and Running Deer! Mark was stunned. The Inspector spoke first.

"Hello, Mark, your aunt has been a most gracious hostess to invite us here. I've been looking forward to seeing you again, ever since you left us in such a hurry. There are a lot of things that should be explained. I'm not quite sure where to start..."

"I can start by asking this young man to forgive me," interrupted Running Deer in a choked voice, extending his large hand. Mark eagerly stepped forward to take it in both of his.

"You've done nothing in need of forgiving, Running Deer, I understood and respected your position." Mark searched for words without success.

"Ah, but I have. I judged you and I was wrong in every way about you and Bright Cloud, and I'm sorry for all the misery I have caused you." Running Deer's eyes were moist.

Just the name of Bright Cloud on her father's lips gave Mark a shudder. Emotions ran high in the parlor while the Inspector hurried to explain what happened after Mark left the North Country.

"Michelle had not been mistreated. Evidently they were bringing her to a stranded whaling crew on the shore of James Bay. You saved her from a horrible fate, Mark, and we all thank you for that."

"But I was unable to…"

"I know what you want to say my friend, but hear me out; it's why we are here. You have been living under the most cruel misconception. You feel responsible for the death of Bright Cloud, when in reality, she didn't die."

Mark heard the words but was not sure he got them right! "Bright Cloud did not die?" He cried in disbelief!

"No, I tried to call you back from the cabin when you left so suddenly." The Inspector reached into his pocket and retrieved a small revolver. "This is the revolver you gave to Bright Cloud. God was with you on that day, Yank. The pistol saved her life! The bullet from the .30-.30 Winchester struck the gun in her pocket and deflected it away from her. The force of the shell made her fall back against the tree, which knocked her out. She bit her tongue as she fell. It bled a lot and you thought she had been hit in the lungs. The cold and the severe blow against the tree made it look as if she was dead. Michelle revived her just a few minutes after you left."

The room was still. Mark wasn't sure he understood all that the Inspector was telling him. Then, he heard Aunt Maddie's voice behind him.

"There's someone here that's anxious to see you, Mark."

He turned, and there standing in front of his aunt was Bright Cloud in a white dress with her black hair falling over her shoulders. She was an apparition from Heaven!

Two hearts cried aloud as they crossed the room to each other.

Other Historical Romance Novels
BY
Clifton LaBree

A Song for Lisa   A Historical Romance

This is the story of a young American woman captured by the Japanese in the Philippines, 1941. Like most prisoners, she was brutalized and sadistically treated with a cruel disregard for human life. Three years later, Lisa and her companions had reached the low point of starvation and abuse .....

Lake of Three Sorrows   A Historical Romance

A warm spiritually uplifting story of courage, commitment, and sacrifice. This is the story of Dale Cooper, a battle-weary American soldier who served in two world wars.

Flickering Flame *(Colonial Series Book One)*

A historical novel, about the Cullen family who settled in Portsmouth, New Hampshire, and their participation in events prior to the French and Indian War. Freedom and opportunity were on the march, but it extracted a heavy price. Frontier settlers were ruthlessly killed and butchered by rampaging Indians lead by French officers and Jesuit priests who frequently incited them to greater levels of inhumanity...

Raising the Torch *(Colonial Series Book Two)*

A continuation of the saga from Flickering Flame, Colonial Series book one, of the Cullen family in Colonial Portsmouth. This is a moving story of love and sacrifice when a small colony had the audacity to fight for independence from their motherland...

NON-Fiction Books

By

Clifton LaBree

NEW HAMPSHIRE'S GENERAL JOHN STARK,

LIVE FREE OR DIE: DEATH IS NOT THE GREATEST OF EVILS

Publisher - Fading Shadows Imprint

A fresh look at one of America's staunchest defenders of liberty and freedom. John Stark was a courageous New Hampshire citizen-soldier who fought in both, the French and Indian War, and the Revolutionary War. His pursuit of leadership excellence on the battlefield distinguished him as one of the most successful combat commanders of the war, and one of the least appreciated.

His selflessness, modest life style, and devotion to the cause of freedom are an inspiration that time has not diminished. He remains today the embodiment of the frugal, independent, and cantankerous New Hampshire Yankee.

GENTLE WARRIOR, GENERAL OLIVER PRINCE SMITH, USMC.

Published by - Kent State University Press. Kent, Ohio, 2001

The Story of one of the United States Marine Corps best General Officer. His flawless performance in Korea is a story that needed to be told.